PRAISE FOR THE
NATIONAL BESTSELLING
KEY WEST FOOD CRITIC MYSTERIES

"Food, fun, and felonies. What more could a reader ask for?" —*New York Times* bestselling author Lorna Barrett

"What fun! Lucy Burdette writes evocatively about Key West and food—a winning combination. I can't wait for the next entry in this charming series."
—*New York Times* bestselling author
Diane Mott Davidson

"[For] gourmets who enjoy a little mayhem with their munchies." —*Publishers Weekly*

"Sprightly and suspenseful, *Murder with Ganache* has a unique piquancy. Like a gourmet meal, it will leave you wanting more." —*Fort Myers Florida Weekly*

"A fine plot, a delightful heroine, a wealth of food—and all the charm and craziness of Key West."
—*Richmond Times-Dispatch*

"One crazy adventure ride. . . . Lucy Burdette does not disappoint." —MyShelf.com

"Burdette . . . [is] as skillful at spinning a yarn as her protagonist is at baking pastries. And unmasking killers." —The Florida Book Review

"Enough to satisfy both casual readers and cozy fans alike, though be forewarned: You'll be left craving more." —Examiner.com

"The characters remain as fresh as the breeze off the ocean, as does the plot." —The Mystery Reader

Other Key West Food Critic Mysteries
by Lucy Burdette

KILLER TAKEOUT

A Key West Food Critic Mystery

Lucy Burdette

AN OBSIDIAN MYSTERY

OBSIDIAN
Published by New American Library,
an imprint of Penguin Random House LLC
375 Hudson Street, New York, New York 10014

This book is an original publication of New American Library.

First Printing, April 2016

For more information about Penguin Random House, visit penguin.com.

ISBN 978-0-451-47483-4

Printed in the United States of America
10 9 8 7 6 5 4 3 2 1

This book is dedicated to the memory of my extraordinary,
indomitable mother-in-law, Dorothy Lindsay Brady

And for John, always

ACKNOWLEDGMENTS

Writing is a lonely job, so it means the world to have friends. My talented blog sisters, the Jungle Red Writers, Hallie Ephron, Hank Phillippi Ryan, Deborah Crombie, Rhys Bowen, Julia Spencer-Fleming, and Susan Elia MacNeal are always in the background, willing to lend moral and actual support whenever needed. Thanks also to wonderful writers Krista Davis and Daryl Wood Gerber, and the members of our Delicious Mysteries fan group and the Cake and Dagger Club. In fact, thank you to every reader and fan—I love writing for you!

Lots of folks made great suggestions about names in this book. Thanks to Celia Warren Fowler for the name of the truck, Beach Eats. Thanks to Denise Terry, Jane Fricker, Rhys Bowen, Jim Benn, Randy Thompson, Michelle Palmer, Scott Haas, Tammy Haussler Cantrell, Susan Soerens DeGraef, Kate Flora, and Katfish Karash for amazing suggestions for the name of Grant's new restaurant. They were so good that I figured out a way to use them all. Thanks for local details from Christy Haussler, and face-painting ideas from Jennifer Montgomery. I'm grateful for medical brainstorming about the murder from Dr. Molly Brady. Thanks to Linda Remer and Kathy and Vince Melendy, who gave donations to the Florida Keys SPCA and allowed their pets' names to be used in this book. Welcome, Dinkels and Jack, and welcome back, Schnootie!

I named the hurricane bearing down on the island in this book Margaret, in honor of Margaret Brady, my sister-in-law who died too young last summer. I hope that she would have taken this as a compliment to her energy and independence.

Thanks to my amazing Key West pals, especially Steve Torrence, Leigh Pujado, and Ron Augustine. Love you guys!

Angelo Pompano and Chris Falcone, I marvel at your steadfast friendship. Thank you.

Thanks to my persistent and optimistic agent, Paige Wheeler, to Sandy Harding (who is gone but not forgotten: her fingerprints are all over this series—for the good), to Katherine Pelz, who picked up the job of editing without missing a beat, to Danielle Dill and all the folks at Penguin Random House who ushered this book to life.

And thanks to my family, especially my talented writing sister, Susan Cerulean, and my darling husband, John Brady.

Lucy Burdette
October 27, 2015

1

Sometimes in life, all you need is a little hope, a lot of courage, and—oh yes— butter.

—Beth Harbison,
When in Doubt, Add Butter

Resident islanders couldn't remember a hotter Key West summer. Not only hot enough to fry an egg on the sidewalk, they agreed, but hot enough to crisp bacon too. So far, the advent of fall was bringing no relief. Today's temperature registered ninety-three degrees and climbing—fierce-hot for October, with the humidity dense like steam from my grandmother's kettle. And the local news anchor promised it would get hotter as the week continued, along with the party on Duval Street.

Me? I'd rather eat canned sardines from China than march down Key West's Duval Street wearing not much more than body paint. But one hundred thousand out-of-town revelers didn't agree. They were arriving on the island this week to do just that—or watch it happen—during Fantasy Fest, the celebration taking place during the ten days leading up to Halloween, including a slew of adult-themed costume parties culminating in a massive and rowdy parade.

Worst of all, the Weather Channel was tracking the path of a tropical storm in the eastern Caribbean. They had already begun to mutter semihysterical recommendations: Visitors should prepare to head up the Keys to the mainland and take refuge in a safer area. But based on the crowds I'd seen, no one was listening. These hordes weren't leaving until the event was over. Besides, with a four-hour drive to Miami on a good traffic day, getting all those people out would be like trying to squeeze ketchup back into a bottle. Might as well party.

Since no right-minded local resident would attempt to get near a restaurant this week, I had fewer food critic duties at my workplace, the style magazine *Key Zest*. I was looking forward to covering some of the tamer Fantasy Fest events for the magazine, including the zombie bike ride, the locals' parade, and a pet masquerade contest. And maybe the tutu party, if I could convince any of my pals to go with me. Since restaurants are my beat, I'd also promised my bosses an article on reliable takeout food. My personal mission statement goes like this: I refuse to accept or condone subpar tourist trap food. If you take the time to look, you can find pearls of deliciousness anywhere, maybe even find killer takeout.

If that didn't keep me busy enough, my own mother, Janet Snow, and Sam, her fiancé, were arriving for the week to visit with my dear friend Connie's new baby, and then get themselves hitched on the beach. The food for their reception had still not been nailed down.

And finally, in a weak moment, I'd allowed Miss Gloria, my geriatric houseboat-mate, to talk me into being trained as a Fantasy Fest parade ambassador. Our job would be to help patrol the sidewalks, which would be lined with costumed and tipsy revelers scrambling for the colored glass bead necklaces thrown off the floats.

"If we aren't going to go to the foam party, or the Adam and Eve bash, or the Tighty Whitey Party, we should at least attend the parade," Miss Gloria said.

I closed my eyes to ward off the image of my elderly friend at any of those events.

"And if we're working as ambassadors, we'll be stationed inside the crowd control barricades. We'll have the best seat in the house. Get it? *Seat.*" She broke into helpless giggles.

At the time, the idea seemed palatable. *Barely.*

I parked my scooter in front of the Custom House Museum and Miss Gloria and I forded through the early sunset crowds on the pier along the water. These were viewers seeking front row positions for Sunset and for the zany Sunset performers, who were already warming up in their prescribed spots. As we passed by, we waved at the cat man arranging his cages of trained house cats, and paused to watch Snorkel the potbellied pig practice his bowling. Ahead, a man dressed in a battered rice paddy coolie hat, a long-sleeved lavender shirt, and black pants was setting up a card table. Lorenzo, my tarot card–reading pal. His face glistened in the fierce rays of afternoon sun, and he had damp circles of a deeper purple under each arm.

"Hayley Snow and Miss Gloria—my two favorite ladies. Did you come for a reading?" he asked after we'd greeted one another. "I would have brought the cards to your houseboat. Anything to get away from this madness." He fanned his face with his hand.

"No, actually, we're headed for the Fantasy Fest parade ambassador training," said Miss Gloria.

Lorenzo's mouth fell open as he first looked at me—on the small side, but plump like a baby leg of lamb, as my father used to say. And then his gaze swept over Miss Gloria—a true runt, and scaring the far side of eighty years old besides. His dubious expression suggested that we were not the kind of volunteers that the organization had envisioned when they put out the call for people to help hold back the crazy crowds during the biggest parade on the island.

"Do you attend any of the Fantasy Fest events?" Miss Gloria asked him.

"No! I crawl as far away as I can. By Tuesday the brassieres are off, by Friday these people are totally naked. It's horrifying," he said, clasping his arms to his chest. "What I ought to do is get out of town. The closest most of these folks come to understanding tarot is Rocky and Bullwinkle asking the spirit rock to talk."

He began to chant and Miss Gloria joined him: "'Eenie meenie chili beanie, the spirits are about to speak.'"

"'Are they friendly?'" Miss Gloria asked, and they both cackled with laughter. "You're probably too young to have watched the show," she said to me.

"Stop it, I watched Rocky for hours on TV Land. We're going to be late," I said, smiling and tapping my watch. And to Lorenzo: "We'll see you soon, okay?"

By the time we located the Grand Cayman room in the Pier House Resort, the room was almost full and the meeting had started. A tall young woman with long brown hair was stationed at the podium. The only two seats left open were first-row, front and center. She waited while the two of us trooped up the aisle and sat down. She reintroduced herself—Stephanie—and then resumed talking.

"As I was saying," she said, waving for the chatter to die down in the crowd, "if you see unattended packages, alert an officer. Please don't announce that they are suspicious—we don't need a stampede on top of everything else. Public works employees will be emptying trash cans during the parade." She blew out a breath of air. "I don't need to tell you this I'm sure, but full nudity is not permitted in public."

"Oh drat," called a woman from the back, to a ripple of laughter. "Are bosoms okay?"

"Only if they are painted," said Stephanie, her face deadpan, but a bit of impatience in her voice. She went on to discuss the finer issues of crowd control and safety, parade pacing, and closing gaps between the floats.

Managing this event sounded like an awful lot to expect from a bunch of greenhorn volunteers whose only props would be official yellow T-shirts.

"Talk to the float drivers," she said. "Have fun and show a pleasant attitude. Talk to the bystanders in your section and get to know them a bit. We know you wouldn't volunteer if you weren't outgoing. Give your peeps beads. It makes them happy."

A woman behind us raised her hand. "Will we be issued rubber gloves?"

Stephanie made a face. "I don't understand why you'd possibly need them. You shouldn't be touching anything weird."

She pointed to someone at the back of the room, and Lieutenant Steve Torrence strode forward. I felt an instant wash of relief, seeing his familiar face. Over the course of the last two years, he'd become our trusted friend. The world felt manageable when he was nearby.

"I like the orange tie," Miss Gloria whispered. "Not so sure about the beard."

"Good morning, everyone! Or I should say afternoon?" said Torrence. He laughed and twirled a finger around his ear. "That underscores my first point: As our ambassadors, we need you to be oriented to place and time, as many of our visitors will not be. Try to watch your beverage intake and remain in your right mind. You can join the party once the parade is over."

He went on to describe what we should do if we saw a fire (dial 911, duh) or caught fire ourselves (drop and roll—good gravy!). "We'll have police officers stationed all along the parade route, and undercover cops too. Any questions about who they are, ask them to show a badge. If you feel unsafe at any time, please contact an officer for help. We thank you for your time and hope you have fun."

He gathered his phone and a pen that he'd set on the podium, then paused a moment. "One more thing—be aware that every year we have protesters come to Key West because they object to our parade. Key West wants this weekend to look like great fun—and to be fun. These people don't have the same thing in mind."

The radio clipped to his belt began to crackle, and then I heard the voice of my heartthrob, Detective Nathan Bransford, boom out: "Officer Torrence, report ASAP to The Bull and Whistle. Two of the Fantasy Fest Queen candidates have gotten into a mean hen fight."

2

Sympathy butters no parsnips.
—Mrs. Patmore, *Downton Abbey*

Leaving the scooter and Miss Gloria at the parking lot near the Custom House Museum, I sprinted the few blocks to The Bull and Whistle Bar—an open-air establishment featuring live entertainment and the clothing-optional Garden of Eden bar upstairs. (And for the record, no one I knew had darkened the door of that second-floor bar—including me.)

Although not everyone in the Key West Police Department would agree, I'm not a naturally nosy person. But I've come uncomfortably close to more than a normal person's share of murders, so I worry when I hear about violence. Especially when one of my friends or relatives might be involved—in this instance, Danielle Kamen, our sometimes dizzy but always lovable receptionist at *Key Zest*, who had been freshly crowned queen of this year's Fantasy Fest.

Danielle had been so happy to run for Fantasy Fest Queen, an honorary position that benefits the AIDS Help charity. The fact that she is shapely and blond and beautiful did not hurt her chances. But the contest is no beauty pageant: The winners for king and queen are chosen according to the money they raise during the eight weeks leading up to the festival. In the final tense moments at the Coronation Ball, the winners are determined according to their fund-raising total, including number of votes bought at the party.

Danielle had thrown herself into planning events and fund-raising with the same enthusiasm that Julia Child applied when whisking her sauces on television. She seemed to love the idea of wearing beautiful costumes, attending multiple parties, and donating a big wad of cash at the end. She had shown not one bit of the reticence that I would have felt about calling and e-mailing friends and acquaintances to ask for their support. And last night, her diligence had paid off when she went home with the coveted sash and crown.

A crowd had gathered outside The Bull and Whistle and the sultry afternoon heat baked the sidewalk; powerful odors of alcohol and sweat floated up from the cement like hot steam from a dirty griddle. The noise deafened me as I waded into the onlookers who shouted encouragement to the fighters. I wormed my way through the costumed bodies, hoping desperately that Danielle was not in the fight ring.

"Cat fight! Cat fight! Cat fight!" chanted one tipsy reveler.

"Carpetbagger, go back to where you came from!" shouted another.

Two women wearing sparkly rhinestone head-
dresses and toga costumes circled around each other.
The older, heavier woman lunged in to take hold of
Danielle's beautiful hair and began jerking her in
figure eights. Her body flopped like a freshly caught
tarpon.

"Somebody help," I yelled, trying to figure out
whether—and how—I could dart in and distract the
bigger woman so Danielle could get away.

"Ladies, stop right this minute," called Lieutenant
Torrence in a stern voice.

Danielle's glittering tiara flew off her head and
sailed into the crowd. The people standing in the vicin-
ity of where it landed scrambled for it as though it was
a home-run baseball. Danielle looked terrified, but also
stubborn and angry. A stocky woman police officer
waded into the fight, brandishing a warning nightstick.

"Knock it off ladies," she yelled. "I don't want to
have to use this thing." Neither the presence of the cops
nor the nightstick dampened the fury of Danielle's opponent.

Torrence pulled a whistle out of his pocket and blew
an eardrum-shattering shriek. The woman holding
Danielle startled, and loosened her grip just enough
that the cops could pull the two of them apart. Lights
flashed from the smartphones in the crowd, and one
of the *Key West Citizen*'s photographers muscled in to
snap photos. Danielle's beautiful hair hung in clumps
around her face, her royal purple sash choked her
neck, and the right shoulder of her dress was shredded, leaving glimpses of too much bare skin. This was

not the kind of publicity that Danielle craved for her campaign and her reign.

"What the hell is going on here?" asked the police-woman.

"This witch is an attention-grabbing cheat," shrieked the heavy woman, lunging at Danielle again like a mean dog on a short leash.

The crowd began to chant again. "Cat fight! Cat fight!"

The cop pulled the stocky woman's hands behind her back and snapped them into handcuffs. "You women are supposed to be representatives for chari-table giving and ambassadors for our city," she said. "This is ridiculous. We expect this from tourists, not from our locals."

Danielle began to sniffle, quickly escalating into weeping so hard she couldn't get any words out.

"Let's get these ladies out of here," Torrence said, taking my bedraggled friend by the elbow and leading her toward the cruiser with flashing lights waiting up the block toward Caroline Street. "We'll sort this out down at the station."

I trotted after them. "Does she need a lawyer?"

Torrence paused, looking at me over the top of his glasses. "We'll take care of her, Hayley. We need to get them out of here, away from the maniacs."

"I'll phone Wally to give me a ride home," Danielle called, flashing a tremulous smile. "I know you have company coming."

3

*Food and everything associated with it,
especially the quality of ingredients,
should be marked by generosity.*
— Patricia and Walter Wells, *We've
Always Had Paris . . . and Provence*

After wading into the crowd to wrest Danielle's crown
from a bystander, I trotted back to the Custom House
to recover my scooter and Miss Gloria, who was pacing by the giant Seward Johnson statue of a dancing
couple.

Miss Gloria's eyes widened as she saw what I was
carrying. "What in the world?"

"I'll tell you on the way home."

As we buzzed up Fleming and over the Palm Avenue bridge to our marina, I shouted over my shoulder
to explain what had happened. I felt terrible about
abandoning Danielle to the wolves, but my mother

and her fiancé, Sam, would be arriving at our houseboat at any moment.

I had purposely planned a dinner that would be
easy to produce after a busy day, but special enough
to welcome Mom back to the island. Food is a major
deal in my family—life-sustaining, of course. But it
also provides clues to the cook's inner life, like a psychologist's inkblot test. According to my mother, and
her mother before her, the menu that the hostess se-
lects always, always sends a message to the guests.

Tonight's meal was a delicate balancing act. Because
we were going to be out most of the day, I'd organized
the ingredients for a shrimp boil so we wouldn't have
to fuss much once the company arrived. The boiled
part of the dinner screamed "utilitarian," which my
mother would no doubt notice, even though no one
would argue with the quality of the ingredients. But
the strawberry sheet cake with cream cheese/whipped
cream/strawberry icing that waited in the fridge was
totally fit for a bride-to-be and would trumpet an enthusiastic welcome.

Once home, Miss Gloria worked on rinsing the let-
tuce and chopping radishes, tomatoes, and cucumbers
while I washed the purple, white, and red heirloom
baby potatoes and cut the black pepper sausages into
chunks. As I was whisking Dijon mustard, olive oil,
and balsamic vinegar into a salad dressing, the boat
rocked slightly and I heard my mother's voice out on
the deck.

"Yoo-hoo," she hollered. "The honeymooners are
here!"

They appeared at our screen door and Sam knocked before pulling the door open. "Not honeymooners yet," he said with a deep chuckle. "I still have the week to change my mind."

I rushed to greet them, kissed my mother's cheek, and then gave Sam a big hug and whispered into his ear: "Better not make any changes now, buddy; the rest of us could never live with her."

He blew a kiss at my mother. "I've made my bed and I plan to happily lie in it for the rest of our natural lives."

She grinned and fluffed her auburn curls, looking younger and lighter than I'd seen her in years. Then she turned to hug Miss Gloria and greet the two resident cats, Evinrude and Sparky. "You all look wonderful. Now, where's that new baby?"

Our friends and neighbors Connie and Ray, as if sensing my mother's force field, came down the finger from their boat, carrying their months-old daughter. Cheeks were kissed and greetings exchanged, and then my mother settled into a spot of shade on the deck, the baby nestled in the crook of her arm.

"So you're calling her Clare. After your mother, of course. It's lovely—she's lovely. Your mom would have been so thrilled."

Connie's mother had died of cancer during our freshman year at Rutgers—so all the transitions that a mother would have attended and cherished were tinged with a little sadness. The baby kicked her tiny little feet and cooed, and the bittersweet moment was broken.

I passed out flutes of sparkling prosecco and we

toasted everything—the baby, the upcoming nuptials, the idea of the strawberry cake. Then I returned to the kitchen and dropped the heirloom potatoes into the pot of bay leaf and Cajun seasoning–scented water boiling on the stove. Sausage and shrimp and lengths of corn on the cob followed the potatoes. When the timer went off, I drained the mixture in the sink and served the steaming bowl on the table outside on the deck. As the sun dipped behind the houseboats across the finger, with the help of a little breeze, the temperature dropped too. Lucky, because our tiny window air conditioner and tiny living area would be no match for a roomful of people. Miss Gloria brought out the tossed salad and a lovely sliced baguette stuffed with walnuts and Maytag blue cheese from the Old Town Bakery and lots of extra napkins.

We descended on the dinner, chattering about what to serve at Mom and Sam's small reception. Should it be the raspberry cake recipe I'd developed last winter for Valentine's Day? Or Eric's famous coconut? Or even those pale lime cupcakes I'd made for Connie and Ray?

"No chocolate?" Sam asked.

"For a wedding, darling?" my mother asked, her eyes wide.

He only grinned.

"Actually, we've been thinking seriously we should have the party upstairs at Louie's Backyard. It fits more people than you can manage here on your deck, and Chef Martha has wonderful menu suggestions," said Mom. "Maybe a buffet of chilled Key West pinks, and Chinese green beans, and smoked scallops, and a Caesar salad, and sake beets—"

"And frites," said Sam. "And fried artichokes and short ribs."

"Everything on the menu!" I laughed. "Whatever you guys want is fine with me," I told her. "It's supposed to be so hot all week, not cooking sounds appealing."

I was peeling my third enormous pink shrimp, ready to dunk it into the cocktail sauce we'd mixed with horseradish—almost but not quite too hot to bear—when my phone rang. Danielle.

"Hayley, can you pick me up at the police station? Wally seems to be out. I've called him six times over the last hour. He's not answering his phone." Her voice quavered and I feared she was crying. I felt instantly guilty that I'd forgotten about her, assuming she'd long since gone home. Poor thing had been at the police station now for hours.

"Of course. Are you hungry? We're just having dinner." I excused myself, leaving Miss Gloria to explain the fight between the women in front of the Duval Street bar. "She sounded awful," I called back over my shoulder. "Don't eat everything. I have a feeling she'll need some shoring up."

Sam hurried after me. "Let me drive you over."

Five minutes later, we arrived at the shell-pink police station across Roosevelt Boulevard. Danielle was huddled in a sad-looking lump on the tiled bench in front of the building. I leaped out of the car and ran over to hug her. Her makeup was smeared around her eyes, with runnels of black down her cheeks. Her lovely toga was stained with black streaks and pinned together, and the purple sash had been torn almost beyond repair. "I'm so glad you called," I said as I hugged her again.

Sam walked up behind me. "Let's get this young woman back to the boat and get her something to eat and drink." He put a comforting hand on her back and rubbed her the way a mother would pat a child.

My mother had found a good man this time. Not that my father isn't a good man, but he's not touchy-feely. And he sometimes overlooks the finer points of empathy. I hoped that my almost boyfriend, Nate Bransford, would grow into all that. If pressed, I'd explain his attributes this way: He is very good at sparks and flame, less accomplished at tending embers.

Mom was waiting at the end of the dock as we pulled in. She rushed to greet Danielle as soon as we parked, taking her hand and looping a strand of my friend's golden hair behind her ear. "Not one question to this girl until she's had a glass of wine," she warned us as we trooped back onto the boat. Within minutes, Danielle was settled in the chair with the best view, a glass of white wine in her hand. I set a small bowl of pre-peeled shrimp on the table beside her.

"Protein," said my mother. "You need protein and alcohol right now. And sugar later," she added.

Danielle mustered a smile.

"Tell us what in the world went on," I said. "And good gravy, what is that awful woman's problem?"

She took a dainty sip of her wine and set the glass on the table. "All the royal candidates had a meeting this afternoon to go over the timing for this week's events," she said. "And then we were asked to do a meet-and-greet along lower Duval Street."

"Danielle won the contest two nights ago," I said to the others. "She's the queen of Fantasy Fest for the entire year."

"That's wonderful, sweetie," said Mom. "How did the competition work?"

"It's basically a fund-raiser for AIDS Help," Danielle explained. "So the results were based strictly on how much money you raised. It didn't really have to do with talent."

"But Danielle was tireless," I said. "The coconut bowling party at Blue Heaven was a huge splash. And everyone loved the homemade brassiere party. It had a little zip of Key West without being raunchy or gauche.

"Women and men were absolutely fighting to bid," I told my mother and Sam. "The creativity was staggering. And it didn't hurt that the gals Danielle had modeling were young and pretty." I raised my eyebrows to indicate that those were not the only assets they had.

"Honestly, I don't know why she went after me. It's like the pressure was building for the last couple of weeks and suddenly she lost control and blew sky-high," said Danielle. One great big tear squeezed out of her right eye and ran down her cheek. "I can't really explain it."

"It sounds like you won fair and square," said Sam. "Your opponent was simply a bad sport."

Danielle adjusted her torn toga costume, her lower lip quivering a little.

"People have been so generous," said Danielle, tears glazing her eyes again. "I can't believe this dumb fight is how I'll be remembered. Guaranteed it's going to be on the front page of the *Citizen*. And that will reflect so poorly on the magazine. Wally and Palamina are going to have a fit."

"Pffft, don't worry about those two," my mother said, patting her knee. Evinrude took that as an invitation, jumped onto Mom's lap, and began to butt her hand with his head and rumble his signature purr. "With all the ruckus over Fantasy Fest, this will blow over in an instant."

"Worst of all," Danielle said, "I lost my crown in the fight. It was handmade by Neptune Designs and I'm sure it cost them plenty." Her voice wobbled. "How will I ever tell them it's gone?"

"Not to worry, I rescued that," I said, and ran into the houseboat to retrieve it from the galley counter. Danielle smiled her teary thanks.

My mother stroked the cat and continued to chat with Danielle about the upcoming activities of the royal week. I could see my friend relaxing by the minute under her cheerful nurturing. Then Mom dislodged the tiger cat from her lap and turned to Connie.

"Now that we have Danielle's problem solved, I suggest you hand over that baby and help Hayley serve the cake."

Connie grinned and deposited Clare into my mother's waiting arms. The baby smiled and tapped my mother's chin with one perfect little hand. "Oh my goodness," said my mother. "I've died and gone to grandmother heaven. What are you all doing tomorrow? I need more time with this child."

"Tomorrow is the zombie bike parade," I said. "Last

year they attracted ten thousand participants. We've been working on our costumes forever. Ray's going to paint Connie's face and his own, but he's got a lot on his plate, so I'm getting my makeup professionally done. The three of us are going as the zombie vaccination squad."

"We've got scrubs, and we'll wear face masks and stethoscopes around our necks, and carry giant fake syringes," Connie added. "And we've collected bandages and other medical stuff to put in our baskets. Ray's going to paint red spots on our arms and legs as if we'd come down with the measles."

"But what about the baby?" asked my mother.

"Oh, she's going with us," Ray said. "We figured with the vaccination theme, a baby would be the perfect touch. And we have a very comfortable carrier that I can wear while riding a bike."

"A baby? On a bike? At the zombie bike parade? A baby zombie? I don't think so," said my mother, hugging the child to her chest until she squawked in protest. "I'll babysit and that's settled."

Ray shrugged and smiled. "Okay."

Connie and I returned to the galley, where we cut generous slices of the cake frosted with cream cheese icing and bits of ripe strawberries throughout. Once we had served everyone and my mother had tasted and declared it unparalleled, she swiveled around to look at me. "And when are we going to get another look at his majesty?"

I felt my face flush red as one of the strawberries and I busied myself smoothing nonexistent crumbs off Miss Gloria's lace table topper. "By that I guess you mean Nathan? First of all, the department is crazy busy with Fantasy Fest—they don't have time for dinner parties." I stood up, brushed the hair out of my eyes, and looked at her dead-on.

"And second, to be honest, Mom, you scare him worse than any criminal."

4

The burger goes well with the cocktails, which are better than you'd expect from an establishment that might have hired Jimmy Buffett as its interior decorator.
—Jeff Gordinier, "A Showstopping Cheeseburger Does a Star Turn," *The New York Times*, July 8, 2015

Before the excitement of the zombie parade kicked off this afternoon, I had promised myself to get some work done on the takeout dining article. The idea that I'd pitched (and lord knows I should stick to it or risk the wrath of the big boss, Palamina) was to sample the carryout skills of various restaurants around town. Did their food stand up to the stress of getting packed in plastic or Styrofoam and shuttled across the island? Was the staff careful about packing the orders, and cheerful about it too?

I'd already hit the White Street Station, a food truck

at the corner of Truman and White Streets—with their heart-stopping but irresistible fried dishes and quirky motto "Location, Smocation." Today I planned to focus on small places with tables and chairs that also managed a brisk carryout business. My first stop would be Garbo's Grill, a food truck tucked into the back of an open-air patio that had served a variety of purposes over the past few years. A tiny kitchen behind the building that housed the Grunts Bar had served fish sandwiches and other locally sourced dishes for several years, until the customers seemed to overwhelm the kitchen's facilities.

Now Garbo's Grill was open Monday through Saturday. On Sundays, a man billing himself as Tennessee Steve slathered giant racks of ribs with mouthwatering, spicy red barbecue sauce accompanied by (my only complaint) small containers of luscious baked beans.

Although the Garbo's food truck was a new addition to the Grunts patio, its food made quite a splash when previously parked on Greene Street. Over the past couple of years, the chefs had crawled to the top of several online review sites and even made an appearance on the TV show *Diners, Drive-ins, and Dives*. More recently, they had been invited to compete with Bobby Flay at the South Beach Wine and Food Festival. How could it be that I'd never tried their mango dog or their mahi-mahi taco or their ginger habanero glazed shrimp? This needed to be remedied. Sam, my mother's fiancé, would be my happy apprentice. He announced last night before they left for their hotel that he'd take on the onerous duties of my first assistant, rather than choose wedding flower arrangements. Or even babysit.

Because there'd be two of us eating, I'd also planned to take a few dishes out from Paradise Pub, a local bar and restaurant that had recently promised extensive revitalization of their menu and dining room under new management. Some rumors had it that a report of cockroaches and illegal workers contributed to the necessity of this change. On the other hand, the chef and new owner, Grant Monsarrat, was extremely popular with the locals. A second stop for lunch would stress our stomach's capacities, but hey, a food critic's work is not always glamorous.

Once I had the tools of my trade in my backpack (pad, pen, phone, camera, plastic containers for unusually good leftovers) I buzzed over to the brand-new Mile Zero Marker resort on the harbor. Sam had insisted on splurging for the week leading up to their marriage, which I was certain stocked points in his already bursting account with my mother.

A text from him came in as I parked. Getting coffee next door.

I found him comfortably settled on the porch of the Coffee Plantation a block away from the Marker, watching the world go by while sipping a caffe latte. He waved when he saw me and trotted down the steps to the scooter.

"I'm afraid Danielle was right," he said, holding up the *Citizen* so I could see the headline and its accompanying photo of the two women fighting in front of The Bull and Whistle. "She made the front page. And it's not her best angle."

The photographer had managed to snap a photo of the two women tangled together, fierce-angry expressions on both faces. My stomach dropped—Danielle would be sick over the bad publicity.

"Anyway, I didn't eat any breakfast," he said, "so I'm starving. Absolutely ready for your excellent adventure."

He popped onto the back of my scooter, with no sign of the painful limp that had preceded his hip replacement last fall. I drove up bumpy Caroline Street to our first stop, Garbo's Grill. An eating buddy has become almost mandatory on my biweekly excursions. Having a second body allows me to sample more menu choices and avoid pointed comments about the accumulation of avoirdupois from my trainer at the gym.

We entered through the gate, filed into the open-air patio lined with palm trees, and walked back along the Grunts Bar to the food truck at the rear of the property. At the window, I ordered a glazed habanero ginger shrimp burrito, mahi-mahi fish tacos, and a mango hot dog that came wrapped in bacon.

"Don't eat everything," I warned Sam, "even if it's amazing. I learned the hard way that indigestion spoils a review. And besides, my mother will kill me if you can't fit into your wedding suit." We sat at a metal table near the truck and watched the chef bang around in the small kitchen space, frying and chopping. His wife took orders, delivered food, and fetched ingredients from a storage area steps away from the truck as he needed them.

"These folks are professionals," Sam said, as the scent of grilled meat warmed the air. He leaned back in his chair and tipped his face to the sun. "And this is heaven, pure and simple." Then he cleared his throat and quirked one eyebrow. "I should warn you, your mother's worried about your relationship."

I clapped both hands to my head. "What else is new in the universe? It's going fine. He's not as sweet as you, but who could be? And Wally was sweet like the icing on a grocery store cake, but that didn't amount to dried beans in the end."

"No sign of the detective's ex?" Sam asked.

I imagined he had to doggedly tick through my mother's questions. Unfortunately, this one bore right to the painful heart of past problems—I was sure my mother had planted it in Sam's mind. Detective Nathan Bransford and I had had one date the first year I moved to Key West, but any fire between us had been quickly extinguished by the arrival of his ex-wife. She'd wanted to give the relationship one last chance before they moved on, and he'd agreed that was the fair and honorable thing to do.

"Is this on the record or off?"

Sam grinned. "You know your mother well enough to understand that she'll worm it out of me no matter what I tell you."

"Nate has his strengths and his weaknesses," I said, covering my eyes with my hand and peeking through the fingers. "The strengths, well, I can't necessarily describe all of them in mixed company, if you get my drift." I knew my face was flushing and my freckles popping, tan against the pink. "He still hears from his ex, even though she finally left town, but he tells me there's nothing left between them. He just feels sorry for her. She's having trouble finding herself."

I made air quotes with my fingers as I said the last two words. I was sure my voice would convey exactly what I really thought about her neediness and his on-going urge to protect her from everything, even her own silliness.

The buzzer that we'd been given to notify us when our order was ready began to skid across the table, flashing red lights and vibrating. Saved by the bell. Not that I was permanently saved because Sam would have to report what I'd said to my mother and she would use these scanty facts to investigate further. Big sigh. It wasn't that she was nosy; she simply wanted the best for her only daughter.

Sam and I went over to the cart to collect our food, as three big plastic baskets would be too much for one person to juggle. I'd added the mango dog to our order at the last minute, thinking it would be more Sam's speed than mine. But the combination of the fragrant grilled all-beef hot dog, wrapped in crispy bacon and slathered with slices of bright yellow mango, red on-ion, and jalapeño pepper, and topped with some kind of pink sauce, looked irresistible. Once we took our seats again, I cut the sandwich in two pieces and we began to eat.

"Oh my god," said Sam, "this thing is amazing." He wiped a dab of Caribbean sauce off his lips with a paper napkin. "This is a takeout article, right? Aren't we supposed to be taking these off-site?"

I laughed. "I believe you'd fight me if I tried to take

that hot dog away from you." He laughed too, and then growled like a slavering beast.

I licked my fingers and took a slug of water to put out the jalapeño fire in my mouth and clear my palate for the next dish, the glazed shrimp burrito. A flock of browned and glistening shrimp with a slick of hot sauce had been tucked inside the skin of the burrito, nestled onto a bed of thinly sliced cabbage and carrot slaw. I skewered one shrimp with a white plastic fork and chewed.

"Oh my gosh," I said. "This is even better than that hot dog."

I cut the burrito in half and moved the larger piece into Sam's yellow basket. Five minutes later, the only thing remaining of the sandwich was the burrito skin that I'd abandoned to save room in my stomach. We moved on to taking a few dainty bites of the fish taco. I made notes on my iPhone about the spicy sauce, fresh fish, crunchy coleslaw, and then more notes on the incredible shiny glazing on those Key West pinks. I wondered, could I could wheedle the recipe out of the chef at some point?

"I hoped we could fit in the burger and the Korean short rib burrito as well," I said, "but I don't think that's in the cards."

"Not if we're going someplace else too," said Sam.

We gathered up our trash and bottles of water and headed out to the scooter. The second restaurant, Paradise Pub, was located closer to the harbor, a few blocks away from Edel Waugh's successful restaurant, the Bistro on the Bight, and the old standbys Turtle

Kraals and the Conch Republic. I parked the scooter in an alley near the restaurant and we went inside.

At first blush, the so-called refurbished decor was not so new—a combination of Dade County pine walls, nautical barstools, and old photographs of fishermen and their catches. The bar was made of wood layered with shiny lacquer and dinged with years of use.

After almost ten minutes, a waitress appeared behind the bar.

"Can I help you?" she asked in a frazzled voice.

"We called in a takeout order," I said. "A burger and a Key West Cobb salad and your fish sandwich?"

"I'll check on it," she said, and swished off to the kitchen.

Sam and I perched on the high stools in front of the bar and looked around the restaurant. The previous longtime owners had gone with a heavy Key West theme, including just about every icon that had anything to do with our island. Hemingway was there, but so was Jimmy Buffett, singing on a beach in shorts and bare feet. There were girls in bikinis sipping cocktails, and enormous dolphins kissing the adorable faces of tiny key deer. The dining chairs were upholstered in pink tropical fabric that had probably looked bright and pretty when they first arrived in the restaurant— shopworn now. Maybe the new owner hadn't yet begun the renovation. Down a ways at the bar, two men were drinking beer and watching the TV while downing enormous plates of curly fries and hamburgers glistening with grease and blood.

I checked my watch. One o'clock. In an hour I would

need to be getting my face painted. An hour after that, I'd be riding in the zombie bike parade. I drummed my fingers on the bar, willing the waitress to emerge from the kitchen.

"I wonder how your friend Danielle is doing this morning," Sam said. "She was so sad about her campaign yesterday."

"A couple of hours in the Key West police station will take the starch out of you," I said. "Chances are, she'll have perked up overnight. All of the candidates were exhausted from those parties. A good night's sleep will put things in perspective. And hopefully today they'll keep that nasty woman away from her."

The doors from the kitchen swung open, followed by a string of curses. This time a woman with a deep tan and a dark braid down her back and wearing pencil slim pants and high heels hurried out. She stuck out her hand and shook each of ours. "I'm Catfish Kohls. We're so very sorry. Chef Grant doesn't have any record of an order for takeout," she said, her voice quite definite. "The waitress claims she took the order and put the ticket in the queue." Her raised eyebrows showed us what she thought of that. "I swear I don't know what she's been smoking. But I promise we can turn it around fast if you'd like me to put it in now."

She pasted a pained smile on her face. "And how about a free drink for your trouble? Shot of tequila? Or a beer? The bartender's not in yet or I'd offer you a fancy drink."

I ran through the possibilities in my mind. Neither one of us was hungry, as the food had been too good at Garbo's Grill. We had not paced ourselves as we should have. And who ever really needed a shot of tequila, especially in the early afternoon with a long day ahead?

"We'll come another day," I said, "and we'll take a rain check on that drink too. Thanks anyway."

"We so appreciate your business. Please do come back," she said, scribbling a note on an order pad. "We're closing the lunch service early today, so things have gotten a little turned around." She ripped the sheet off and handed it to me. "Drinks on the house!" it read, decorated with a smiley face.

5

*With her barrel shape and red and white
dress, she looked like an oversized can of
Campbell's soup. (Chicken noodle maybe
or minestrone. I could tell I was getting
hungry.)*

—Roberta Isleib,
Preaching to the Corpse

After dropping Sam off at the Marker, I zipped up to
the houseboat, where I checked in with the cats, un-
loaded the dishwasher, put on my zombie costume,
and stuffed the accessories into my backpack. This
time on my pink Conch Cruiser bicycle, I headed down
island to the Truman Annex. I had a three p.m. appointment with Jennifer Montgomery, a woman from
Philadelphia who enhanced her living as an artist by
painting faces for parties and special events.

I locked the bike at a rack in back of the Shipyard
condominium complex, and found my way through a

warren of small apartments and tropical foliage to Jennifer's place. She looked exactly like her Facebook photo, with a mane of curly blond hair, a wide smile, and a lace top that showed off her tan. After a minute of small talk, she settled me in a chair in her kitchen next to a side table covered with paints and brushes.

"Are you looking for a beautiful zombie or a scary zombie?" she asked, a grin on her face.

"Scary zombie, definitely," I said. "Aren't zombies scary by definition?"

"But I like to keep my customers happy," she said with a laugh.

I closed my eyes and she sprayed my face with a base coat of white. It felt cool to the touch, and slightly heavy, like too much spray-on sunscreen. Or more like the time I accidentally sprayed my face with gold paint when my mother and I were decorating candy dishes for my eighth birthday party. As Jennifer worked, applying white, black, and red touches with her brushes, she told me about her history.

"I was going to work for one of the businesses on Duval Street. You'll see some of the painters working in little booths on the main drag. But the guy did not market my service as he promised, so I figured I could do it here in my apartment and not give half the money to him. I'm pretty good at screening out weirdos on the phone," she said, anticipating my next question. "And I've got a guy friend here"—she cocked her head at a well-muscled man who was drinking a beer in the living room—"in case one slips through."

When she was satisfied with her work, she stepped away and handed me a mirror.

"Oh my gosh," I said, sucking in a breath of air. "When you said scary, you meant scary." Over the white base, my nose was painted black, as were my eyelids. Droplets of red trickled down from the corners of my eyes, melding with shooting red and black fiery lines radiating from my lips that resembled the licking flames on a custom-painted hot rod.

"Do you paint people for Fantasy Fest, too?" I asked.

She nodded. "Some people would prefer not to have that done in public—though they don't seem to mind showing off the final product on the streets," she added with an impish grin. "Different strokes."

I thanked her again as her next customer arrived, a flustered woman with a wicked sunburn. How uncomfortable would she feel once the paint was applied to her raw skin?

I retrieved my bike and peddled over to the Atlantic side of the island, and then up the bike path toward Fort East Martello, next to the Key West airport. As I rode, more zombies on bikes filled in the empty spaces ahead and behind me. There were Santa zombies and retiree zombies and wicked witch zombies, and zombies of uncertain lineage heavy on dripping blood. I had to believe that my paint job ranked high in the ranks of realistic zombies. By the time I'd pedaled all the way to the fort, the crowd of zombies had mushroomed, their colorful cruiser bikes a strange contrast to their pasty, bloody faces.

I left my props—an enormous vaccination syringe, bottles of rubbing alcohol and hydrogen peroxide, and packages of gauze bandages—in the basket, locked my bike to the rack, and wandered into the party that throbbed on the grounds, looking for Connie and Ray. Zombies with giant brains made of pink Styrofoam peanuts attached to their helmets, zombies in bloody scrubs, and a pug zombie in a small, blood-spattered white coat all wandered by. I snapped photos of everything—I could sort out what would be useful for *Key Zest* later.

Across the courtyard, I recognized Danielle, who looked beautiful, even in full zombie garb—a white dress strung with streamers of black and gray. She was wearing a different crown with ZOMBIE QUEEN written on the front in rhinestone script. Her white and black makeup disguised any obvious consequences from yesterday's troubles. The local TV news station was interviewing her on camera, along with her newly elected king. The royal court was clustered behind them. She appeared to be enjoying her celebrity status—I decided not to try to approach her now. I'd give her a call tonight.

A rock band in tattered and bloodied shirts played in the roped-off street behind the fort, and long lines formed at the booths selling beer and soda. And a zombie waitress offered samples of spiked fruit punch in tiny paper cups. One of the bloodied Mrs. Santa zombies stumbled and fell, spilling her plastic cup of beer across the grass and dirt.

"Zombie down!" shouted two of her friends, and then dissolved in squeals of laughter. I felt the cell phone buzz in my pocket—a message from Connie that they were running late, settling the baby in with my mother.

I wished I had asked to use the bathroom at Jennifer's condo. Since it would be a long, slow truck down the island to Duval Street with ten thousand zombies wobbling on bikes, I went into the museum section of the fort. After using their facilities, I ducked down the cool redbrick hallway to pay homage to Robert the doll.

Robert, a life-size stuffed doll with a creepy face who was dressed in a sailor suit, had been enclosed in a big glass case. On the wall, letters were displayed from visitors who had not taken the proper precautions of asking his permission before taking his photo. Or worse still, made fun of his evil powers. He was famous for cursing tourists who didn't treat him with respect. He would make, I thought, an excellent feature for the Halloween/Fantasy Fest issue of *Key Zest*. If I asked for his blessing first. I felt a little silly talking aloud to a vintage doll, but the evidence was there on the wall: People who hadn't believed in Robert suffered with unexplained illness or loss of fortune or jobs. Many were now begging for release from his curse.

Another text message came in from Connie. We're here. A zoo!

I told Robert about my article. When he voiced no objection, I took a couple of quick pictures, thanked him for his cooperation, and went outside. Connie and Ray waited by the bike rack. It took them a moment to recognize me.

Ray made a frightened face and pretended to stagger away. "Hayley, you look horrifyingly, horrendously hideous," he said.

"Thanks. I think," I said, suddenly hoping that I wouldn't run into Bransford today. We were not approaching the event from the same point of view. To me, it was mostly fun with a little bit of work thrown in; that is, taking photos and a few notes to help write my article about the parade. To him, it would be all business: the scary business of keeping ten thousand tipsy people in zany costumes safe. And besides, our relationship was still in the early enough stage when a girl wants to be seen only at her prettiest. My zombie paint job would not qualify for "pretty."

Ray pulled out a small container of red paint from his backpack and added fake measles to my arms and legs. As he finished, a man dressed as a zombie prisoner wearing striped pajamas with dangling handcuffs and chains around his ankles called out through a megaphone.

"Zombies! Take your places. The unofficial parade is about to begin!"

The song "Monster Mash" began to pulse through the speakers. One of the four police cruisers idling by the curb flashed its blues and swung into the middle of the road to lead the procession. Danielle and the rest of the royal courtiers fell in behind the cops, a mob of unruly zombies crushing in after them.

After several minutes, a space opened up and we pushed our bikes into the queue. "How's Mom doing with the baby?" I hollered.

"So well we may never get that girl back," said Ray with a grin. "She looked awfully cute in her zombie onesie, but your mother was right—this is a lot of excitement for a baby."

We got onto our bikes and began to pedal. The crowd pressed in on either side. I dodged a wobbly elder zombie on a three-wheel bike to my left and three tricycles loaded with the Andrews Sisters zombies on my right. A radio in one of their baskets played a tinny version of "Boogie Woogie Bugle Boy." I snapped photos to the left and the right. Two very drunk zombie girls in black dresses whose hems fluttered dangerously close to their bike spokes approached from either side of me ringing their warning bells.

"Zombie on the left!" cried one.

"Zombie on the right!" said the other.

"Zombie down!" came another call from behind.

"These people are having too much fun. They have to learn to pace themselves over the week," I muttered to Connie. "I'm going on ahead, I think it's safer to ride single file." Not that I hadn't done my share of partying back in the day, but I'd learned my lesson. There was a good reason that one of the liquor stores in town was called Lost Weekend.

I spurted ahead of the others, staying to the right of the pack, concentrating on not getting run into the curb. I held my phone up to take a short video of the crowd following behind me.

"Zombie down!" echoed a call through the crowd.

This time, the "zombie down" did not sound like crying wolf. I stopped riding and spun around to see what was wrong. A zombie was splayed out on the pavement. The two tipsy girls swerved past, barely missing the figure in the road.

"Zombie down!" The shouts grew louder and more shrill as the costumed revelers passed their call up the slow-moving bicycle cavalcade to the front of the parade, like a twisted version of telephone.

As none of the zombies around me were stopping to help, I got off my bike, tucked my phone away, and crouched beside the person on the ground. It was impossible to tell who she was or what her color was normally like. Her face was painted mostly white, with patches of black and red almost the opposite of my pattern. She was dressed in a flowing white gown that made the most of her buxom figure, streaked with the requisite bloodstains and red glitter. Her headdress, which looked like a Cinderella tiara, zombie-style, had been knocked off her head in the fall and landed a foot away. I snatched up the tiara so it wouldn't get trampled and shouted over the noise around us.

"What happened? Are you okay?"

She babbled incoherently and clutched her stomach, writhing on the roadway.

"Who did you come with?"

More slurred babbling. I leaned in closer to her, trying to understand her words, and noticed a fruity odor on her breath. She'd probably had way too much of the grain alcohol fruit punch that I had fortunately passed up.

"Can you sit up, or should I call for help?"

She answered with a low groan. My gaze flicked over her body, her arms splayed out, her legs akimbo. So much fake blood had been painted on the costume that it was hard to tell if she was really in trouble. I took her hand, which was cool, bordering on icy. Her pulse was racing.

And then I noticed a froth of red in the corner of her mouth. Immediately woozy, I sat back on my haunches and tried to think. Whether or not this problem was alcohol-related, helping her was above my pay grade.

There was no point in calling out for assistance; no one would hear me over the din of the crowd and the pounding music. I sent a quick text message to both Lieutenant Torrence and Detective Bransford, hoping one of them could feel the vibration or hear the text, and was close enough to help. Then I waved down a few of the passing zombie riders.

"Please, can you ride over and grab some paramedics and the cops? This person appears to be in trouble and in need of medical attention."

I turned back to the downed woman and took her hand again. I opened one of my packets of zombie bandages and dabbed at the blood around her lips and the sweat beading on her forehead. "What's your name?"

Truly, it would have been hard to recognize my best friend in this costume. When she didn't answer except for another groan, I chattered nonsensically about the costumes I saw in the passing crowd. More zombies stopped pedaling and began gathering around to rubberneck.

"Any real medical people here?" I begged. "Doctors? Nurses? Even a shrink?"

But no one stepped forward.

Finally, I heard the comforting whoop of sirens.

6

*Most spices, along with coffee and choco-
late, had some bitterness in their flavor
profile. Even sugar, when it cooked too
long, turned bitter. But to me, spice was
for grief, because it lingered longest.*
—Judith Fertig,
The Cake Therapist

I did not so much see Detective Bransford as smell
him: the scent of the lime shaving cream he used, and
under that, the slightly musky deodorant that never
quite masked the smell of man.

And then, of course, I heard him.

"Everyone move away," he yelled, spreading his
arms to clear out the gawking zombies. "Give this
woman room to breathe."

I stood up and took a step back, just as Bransford
stepped closer.

"Did you see what happened here, miss?" he asked

brusquely, looking straight at me. "Are you traveling with this person?"

"Nathan, it's me. It's Hayley," I said.

"Good god," he said, with a grimace that said a lot more—like *What have you done to your face? Why are you here? And good god, woman, you in the middle of something again?* Then he seemed to reset himself, from personal to professional. "Okay, Hayley, did you see what happened to her?"

I shook my head. "I was riding my bike and, suddenly, there she was, behind me on the ground. People have been shouting 'Zombie down' all afternoon, so at first I thought it was just more drunken silliness. Like maybe she was pretending to be dead." My voice hitched. "There's a lot of that around here and it's still early in the week."

"Did you see anyone run away before or after she fell?" he asked. "Anyone with a weapon?"

I threw my arms up in a gesture of helplessness. "There are weapons everywhere. Swords, knives, syringes . . . You name it. And everyone's got blood dripping down their costumes, too. So I didn't realize at first that she was really hurt. My theory is she got drunk and bit her tongue when she fell."

"Do you know who she is?"

I shook my head, then risked another glance at her painted white face. Did anything about her look familiar? Hard to say in that makeup.

"Did you hear an unusual noise? Like a gunshot?"

"No." I shivered, thinking about the time last winter when I'd been shot. I hadn't even realized that I'd been hit. It had taken the pain and the blood and the actual hole left by the bullet to make me understand. Had the same thing happened to the downed zombie woman?

When a uniformed cop arrived to secure the scene, the detective beckoned me over to the sidewalk, away from the worst of the craziness. By this time, Connie and Ray must have realized that I was missing and circled back to join me.

"What happened? Are you okay?" they chorused.

"I am, but she's not." I pointed to the woman on the ground. "You've met Connie and Ray," I told Bransford. We four had had drinks once since he and I had gotten together, but as Connie's pregnancy progressed and the baby was born, their socializing was much reduced. And besides, the chemistry between them and my detective friend hadn't been instantly obvious. "We were riding together," I added.

"Did you see this woman fall?" he asked them, without acknowledging that they had a personal connection. Me. Once they shook their heads, he started back to the spot where the woman had fallen.

"Don't go anywhere," he called over his shoulder. "We'll certainly have more questions."

"What in the world is going on? Is she drunk?" Ray asked. "Why can't you leave?"

"She had blood coming out of her mouth," I said. "And her skin felt ice-cold. I have no idea. Maybe she was shot or stabbed or something and he thinks I might've seen something."

"Did you?" Ray asked.

"Oh my god, not that I know."

Ray rolled our bikes away and locked them up in a nearby rack under a palm tree while Connie and I squatted on the curb to wait for Bransford to return. Two burly firefighter/paramedics rushed over and knelt alongside the downed woman. Last year, the fire department was awarded the ambulance contract in town, which some residents objected to as another example of the good old boys' "Bubba" network. To me, it made sense to have local guys in the vans, guys trained in emergencies who know the people and the craziness of the place. I tried to judge from their actions how seriously she was hurt.

"Can you hear me, miss?" one asked. "Do you have any chest pain?"

"Are you experiencing any headache?" asked the other. "Squeeze my hand if you can hear me."

As far as I could tell, she wasn't responding. The first paramedic took out a small flashlight and shone it in her eyes. "Can you follow this, miss?"

No answers. They slipped an oxygen mask over her face, which magnified the zombie makeup. "We're going to take you to the hospital, get you some good help," the man said. I appreciated his reassuring voice. If she could hear him, I suspected she did too.

Another EMT truck rolled up on the far side of the street. Two more firefighter/paramedics climbed out and raced over with a rolling stretcher. The four men loaded her onto the stretcher, strapped her down, and wheeled her away to the waiting vehicle.

Meanwhile Bransford and the other police officers

had begun to shuffle the people nearest the downed woman off the road. Possible witnesses were herded off to a picnic table in the shade. The remainder of the zombie parade lurched forward; most of the participants seeming to have no awareness that one of the costumed zombies was seriously down.

"This is not turning out to be much of a fun outing for you," I said to Connie. "At least you're not paying top dollar for a babysitter."

"Not much fun for you either," she said, putting a friendly hand on my knee. "Do you remember seeing that woman earlier this afternoon?"

I tried to review the forty-five minutes when I had wandered through the gathering crowd, waiting for my two friends to appear and the parade to get started. "It's all a blur," I said with a deep sigh.

But then I remembered that I had taken a lot of photographs. I pulled my cell phone out of my pocket and began to scroll through the images. I'd caught zombies drinking, zombies posing, zombies playacting in the roles dictated by their costumes. When we got to my photos of Robert the doll, Connie refused to look.

"I asked his permission," I said.

"Even so," she said, waving a hand and smiling. "I don't dare risk any bad juju with Clare and all."

I nodded and continued to sort through the photos until I came to the frames of the Fantasy Fest royalty. "Doesn't Danielle look cute?" I asked, showing one photo to Connie. "Even with her face painted white and wearing rags, she looks adorable."

"None the worse for wear, considering what happened last night with the tussle on Duval Street," Connie said.

I enlarged one photo that I had taken of Danielle with her king and the other three Fantasy Fest candidates. "Oh my gosh," I said, my heart sinking like a sponge cake in a cool oven. "I think the injured woman was the one that she was fighting with yesterday. We are headed for trouble."

Several minutes later, the EMT van pulled away with its lights flashing and a short blast of siren. Bransford made his way back through the crowd to where we were sitting.

"How is she?" I asked.

"I'm not the doctor," he said, not meeting my eyes.

Which I interpreted to mean she was in terrible shape if not already dead. I turned my gaze to follow the truck's slow exit with lights flashing but no siren on now. No real urgency there. Or was I over-interpreting?

"I can see what you're thinking," Connie said. "Let's be optimistic until they give us the facts."

I looked back up at Bransford, dashed a tear from my eyelash. "I think I know who she is." I pulled out my phone and showed him the photo of Danielle with the royal court. "She and Danielle were in that altercation yesterday. But Danielle didn't have anything to do with this, I am sure of that," I insisted. "She was way ahead in the parade—way up at the beginning, right after the cops."

"We don't know what happened yet," he said, a grim look on his face. "It might be a heart attack or something similar, not a crime. Maybe she was only intoxicated. But if it wasn't . . ." His voice softened a little and he patted my back. "You girls should probably go on home. I'll talk to you later." And then he walked away, shouting "Watch where you're going!" at a couple of stray zombies who wandered in front of him, nearly cutting him off.

"I'd better text Danielle," I said. "Somebody needs to be on her side."

"I hope she doesn't have a side," Connie said.

7

But would this cake transmit the message that I cared a lot, but without any pressure, and that it was for Valentine's Day, but no declaration intended, nor anything expected in return? Would it send the message of love and care, without appearing needy, too sweet, or clichéd?

This, I realized, was a lot to ask of any cake.

—Lucy Burdette, *Fatal Reservations*

We waited another fifteen minutes as the end of the parade trickled by, hoping for good news. Bransford separated from the cluster of cops by the far cruiser and came back over. "You all can go," he said, ducking his chin at me. "I'll call you later with an update." He waved and wheeled away to his SUV.

Ray looked at me, his eyes full of sympathy. "I know this has been a shock," he said, folding me into a hug, "but there's nothing we can do for that woman, right? And maybe we can catch up with Danielle and make sure she's okay. I'd love to buzz through town and see the rest of the scene on Duval Street. I don't think Connie and I will be getting out much the rest of the week."

So we fell in with the last of the stragglers and began peddling along the Atlantic. I tried to keep my mind focused on the light that glimmered on the ocean, rather than catastrophizing about the injured woman. Surely Bransford would fill me in with the facts of what happened, once he knew them. Since our relationship has evolved over the past few months, he's been less prickly about police business. Though he still worries about my tendency to get involved in dangerous situations. And this episode wouldn't help my reputation, even though the zombie woman's fall had nothing to do with me. I stopped to help only because, well, because any reasonable person would have.

As we rolled along the water, getting closer to the downtown's main drag, we began to see people in lawn chairs along the parade route. Some of them wore their own scary painted faces or other Halloween costumes. Some had brought children dressed in tutus, some wore tutus themselves, and many were busy enjoying coolers of beer and other beverages.

The zombies staggered past Smathers Beach, circled the upscale Casa Marina resort, and brushed by the official parade-watching station at Salute! On The Beach, the restaurant where Connie and Ray had had their rehearsal dinner last year. Then we turned inland on Reynolds, and down on South to Duval. By now, the sidewalks were thronged with viewers, which pushed the bikes together closer in the center of the street. A sense of claustrophobia crept over me. I wanted to bolt, but the only photos I had taken for *Key Zest* were the ones I'd snapped at the fort and a few during the parade before the woman went down. Then I saw the drag queens posing outside the Aqua bar, dressed in their own drag version of zombie attire.

"I'm going to pull over and catch my breath," I hollered to Connie and Ray. "Take a few extra photos for the magazine."

"We're going to head back to the marina and pick up the baby," Ray said.

"See if Mom and Sam and Miss Gloria want to order some takeout?" I asked. "Tell them I'll be along in an hour or so?"

My friend Victoria, one of the performers at the Aqua, gave me a huge hug. "You look positively ghoulish girlfriend," she said.

Tonight she had her face painted pure white, like a geisha, and her hair was dyed red and gelled into peaks that shot away from her head like a fright wig. She wore a short white dress with plenty of cleavage, tall black heels, and black lipstick.

"And you are beautiful, even dressed as a zombie," I said. "How did the final TV show taping go?" Victoria, aka Randy Thompson, had been chosen two years earlier to appear on a new foodie television show—the taping for the second season had recently wrapped up. The original recipe that wowed the judges and launched his second career turned out to be his grandmother's recipe for cheese grits with shrimp, bacon, and scallions. Just the thought of it made my mouth water.

"A blast," Victoria/Randy said. "We'll have lunch soon and I'll dish."

"You don't look so hot," she added. "Is everything okay?"

I gave her a brief recap of the downed zombie incident. "I have to get back to work, but call me tomorrow," she said, patting my back.

I took a few more photos of the passing zombies, got back on my bike, and peddled slowly up the island to my home. I was feeling emotionally wrung out, and my thighs and calves were burning from the unaccustomed long bike ride. I couldn't wait for a glass of wine and a heaping plate of whatever food my mother had chosen.

But the SUV in the marina parking lot with the Key West police logo suggested the evening might go differently than I'd hoped. I was not looking forward to seeing what I saw on my houseboat: Detective Nathan Bransford settled in a lawn chair between my mother and Sam, Miss Gloria hovering close by. Bransford couldn't have looked more uncomfortable. Was this a social visit, a get-to-know-the-parents kind of deal? Surely he would have given me a heads-up about that.

Pausing for a second on the dock, I studied him to assess how much trouble he'd taken with his appearance. His hair looked as though he'd wet it down but not washed it, then run the rakes of a comb through. The blue shirt that picked up the green glints in his eyes was the same one that I'd seen on him earlier, and his jacket was rumpled.

No, the visit was not social.

Suddenly aware of the paint drying my face and the bloody shirt I was wearing and the red measles spots Ray had added to my arms and legs, I couldn't have felt more unattractive.

"Look who turned up," my mother warbled, tapping Bransford's wide shoulder with two pink-painted fingernails.

"We have been having such a nice chat," said Sam in his faux hearty voice, which made me suspect they had been struggling to keep a conversation running.

Bransford was not big on social niceties. When I'd dared mention a few weeks ago that he didn't try very hard in social situations involving my friends or people he didn't know, he told me it came of seeing too much of the dark side of humanity. Small talk was meaningless in the face of all that darkness. And I told him that appearing to listen with genuine interest goes a long way to smooth the rough patches in life. And that even in the heart of my home state, New Jersey, known more for gangsters and raunchy reality show stars than etiquette, we understand that friendly chit-chat oils the most difficult interactions.

"You look a little bedraggled," my mother said as I came aboard. "Did you have fun? The baby was so sweet and delicious."

"You ate the baby?" I said and forced a laugh.

Mom grinned, patting the seat beside her, inviting me to sit. "I'm going to watch her again tomorrow, right after we have our premarital counseling with Lieutenant Torrence."

Torrence works as a part-time pastor in his time off

from the police department, and my mother had insisted that, given how helpful he'd been to our family, she'd allow him and only him to consecrate their marriage.

"I'm glad," I said, mustering a big smile and hoping Bransford wasn't taking this grandmotherly enthusiasm as a personal message. He was about as far from being ready to have kids as I was—triple light-years. "Did you tell them what went on today?" I asked the detective.

"I was waiting for you." He set down his mug of coffee and stood up. "Would you like to talk privately?"

"It's fine for them to hear whatever you have to say," I said. "They'll hear it anyway."

"Everyone sit down, sit down," said Sam, gesturing at the chairs on our little deck. "Can I get you something? More coffee? A beer? A leftover piece of that killer strawberry cake?"

I was dying for a glass of wine but this didn't seem the time for it.

"That woman didn't make it," Bransford said, his eyes boring in on me.

I felt myself droop. I so hoped for everyone's sake, especially her, that she would be fine. Overheated, maybe, or too much to drink. Or even a tiny heart problem, something that a short stay in hospital or a pacemaker might fix.

"What woman?" Mom asked, reaching for my hand. Her gaze searched Bransford's face, then pinged back to mine. "A friend of yours?"

"The parade had just started when a zombie behind

me collapsed. I stopped to help. She had a little froth of blood in the corner of her mouth and her hands were so very cold." I pressed my lips together, determined not to fall apart.

"What in the world happened?" asked my mother.

"We won't know for sure until the medical examiner gets a look at her," Bransford said. "But at first pass the possibilities include a heart attack and some type of poison. The symptoms can be quite similar."

"Oh, honey, that's terrible," my mother murmured.

Honey me or honey him?

"Who was it?" Sam asked.

Bransford said her name and my heart sank, even though I'd already guessed the truth after looking at my photos. Caryn Druckman.

"She was Danielle's rival in the royal court," I said. "If you don't mind, Sam, I think I would like that glass of wine." Sam leaped up to fetch it.

"Do you remember seeing someone with a sort of zebra design on their face about the time she fell off the bike?" Bransford asked me.

"Oh geez, not really. I was focused on not getting run over. Lots of those people had started their party early. Or maybe they weren't used to riding bikes. Anyway, there was a lot of swerving and wobbling." I put my head in my hands and squeezed, trying to remember more details.

"Tell me you don't think Danielle was involved," I said finally, looking up to meet his gaze.

"Interesting that you should bring that up right away," Bransford said.

"What does that mean exactly? She's a friend, a dear friend. Of course I'm concerned about her."

"A darling girl, really," Miss Gloria added.

"My bet's on a heart attack," said my mother. "People don't take care of themselves these days. Besides, Danielle wouldn't poison someone. No way."

Bransford managed a pained smile. "None of Hayley's friends are capable of murder—she tells me that every time we have an incident."

"Not funny," I said, and took the glass of white wine from Sam's steady hands, my own fingers shaking. "Where do things stand with Danielle?"

"She's a person of interest, along with half the town," Bransford replied. "We don't even know for sure whether Ms. Druckman died of natural causes, but it's important to gather the data before this place explodes later in the week. We'll talk tomorrow when the dust settles— you've had a long day. I'd appreciate it if you think of anything you might have seen pertaining to the situation, you call me right away?"

Just then, a deliveryman carrying sacks of food clattered up the finger. "Snow?" he asked.

"Never in Key West," Sam joked, pulling out his wallet. "Stay and have a bite with us?" he asked the detective.

Bransford shook his head. "Still on duty. Crazy week."

"Obviously," said my mother. "We hope to see you again, under different circumstances."

The detective stood, for a moment seeming to consider whether to hug me, but then he hopped the small gap between the houseboat and the dock and started away.

"He's a tough nut," my mother said, watching him go. "I hope he'll make you happy." Her voice told me she wasn't sure this was possible. She began to open the bags of food and then bustled into the kitchen to get plates and forks and napkins.

"We decided to order from the Café," said Miss Gloria.

"Mmmm, good choice." As I sat down to spoon spicy noodles with stir-fried vegetables onto my plate, I realized I should call Danielle and invite her over. She answered on the first ring, sounding small and weak. "We're just having a bite on the boat," I said. "Would you like to come over?"

"I suppose you've heard about the woman who died," she said. "And that I'm implicated?"

"Not implicated," I said, keeping my voice light and positive, "but a person of interest. All that means is that they'll continue talking to you because you had some kind of connection with her recently. Come on over and we'll give you moral support and extra calories."

"Thank you, Hayley, so much. I really appreciate that. But I'm already in my pajamas. I'm going to watch *Dirty Dancing* again—that movie always cheers me up. I'll see you at the staff meeting in the morning? I'd love to chat afterward and hear what Bransford told you."

"Just because we're dating doesn't mean he'll tell me any secrets. He's not big on pillow talk," I said, laughing. And then turned Twizzler red realizing that the older generation was listening in. The best thing to do would be to ignore it. "I'll see you tomorrow at eight thirty; get some rest," I told Danielle.

After dinner, my mother and Sam helped clean up and set off for their hotel. I retired to my little bedroom with my laptop and Evinrude the cat. He was acting a little clingy, walking back and forth over my legs and then swatting at my fingers when I opened up the computer. I suspected this was related to the amount of attention that Connie's baby was getting. Most of the cooing and fussing that had gone to him and Miss Gloria's Sparky in the past was now being diverted to the infant.

"It's not that we love you less," I explained to him while stroking his fur from head to tail, "but a baby is something special."

He started to purr. Then he licked his paw and began grooming the dark M on his forehead. I fired up my laptop and scrolled over to Facebook. Many of my friends had posted photos from the zombie parade. And there were photos on the official Web site for the event too. For forty-five minutes I searched through all of them, trying to find pictures of the people who might have been riding near me when the parade took off from East Martello. I also looked for the painted faces resembling the pattern of zebra stripes that Bransford had mentioned. Who knew if it actually meant anything, but it was the only clue he'd given me. I made a short list of people to chat with. Jennifer the face painter would be able to help me with painting style, I hoped. Second, I'd call Victoria/Randy in the morning and see if she could have lunch soon. She often had the pulse of the underbelly of Key West. And she'd performed several times onstage during the coronation festivities—she would have been backstage, privy to any conflicts emerging. She would have had the best view in the house. And maybe an inside track into what was going on behind the scenes.

And third, I needed to talk more to Danielle about the competition for Fantasy Fest Queen over the past week. Of course, I knew the highlights because I'd helped with several of her fund-raising events. But maybe she'd think of details that might clarify who wanted that woman dead.

8

Mrs. Morse said, "Well, there's nothing you can do about it so why don't I cut you a nice piece of chocolate cake?" She could fix almost anything with a piece of cake— or pie.

—Anita Diamant, *The Boston Girl*

I woke early the next morning, fed the cats, and started a pot of coffee. With a steaming cup in hand, I headed out to the deck, where the water of the bight was quiet—no waves, no birds, no sounds but the distant motor of a fishing boat. Even wacky Schnootie the schnauzer next door was still sleeping. The morning already felt hot, the air heavy with moisture, and so still that Mrs. Renhart's prized collection of wind chimes didn't stir. A bank of clouds diffused the peach of the rising sun off to my right.

I was relieved to have a little time to myself before the chaos of another day at Fantasy Fest crashed in around me. And also a little space from our visitors. I love my mother's company, but she has all the subtlety of a steak dinner. Which is to say, what you see is what you get—no subterfuge. Absolutely everything is on the table. With a second cup of coffee in hand, I spent fifteen minutes noodling the opening paragraph about my takeout article.

> *When people hear that I'm a food critic, they some-times think "snob." They imagine that what other folks enjoy, I'd find unpalatable. And they imagine that my days are full of foie gras and caviar-encrusted sushi. But if you object to flabby, greasy French fries, you can count on me to object to them too. And then tell you about them!*

When I had drafted the section about the lunch Sam and I had eaten at Garbo's Grill, I began a lighthearted piece about the zombie parade. Given the tragedy that had occurred yesterday, I was not convinced that it would be smart for *Key Zest* to run this, but I'd be ready in case Wally and Palamina insisted it should go.

I also made some notes about questions to ask Danielle. With any luck at all, the case of the dead woman in the parade would've been resolved overnight. But a heavy feeling in my chest suggested that it wouldn't be sorted out so easily. Surely the police would've already inquired, but I wanted to ask Danielle more about the competition for queen. What had actually happened with the voting the night of the coronation? Had she sensed any serious rancor with the dead woman? Or any of the other candidates? Who were her supporters? How had people reacted when the results were announced? And what had actually provoked the attack in front of The Bull and Whistle?

Danielle was born and raised on the island, leaving only to attend four years of college in Gainesville, which gave her the distinction of the label "saltwater conch." And conchs have a powerful reputation for sticking with their own. Did she have a friend or relative who would go so far as to actually destroy a perceived enemy? And why would this woman be considered an enemy of Danielle when my friend had already won the crown? I sighed. This seemed utterly ridiculous. For all we knew, the death had absolutely nothing to do with Fantasy Fest or Danielle.

I gobbled a bowl of granola, savoring the chewy dried cherries along with the crunch of nuts and oats drenched in milk and a splash of maple syrup. Then I dressed in my coolest linen shorts and a tangerine-colored swing top and burnt orange sneakers and drove down the island to *Key Zest*.

As was her custom on Monday mornings, Danielle had brought in a selection of doughnuts from the Glazed Donuts shop on Eaton Street. Though we all protested about not needing the calories from fat and sugar, the plate was always empty by the close of the workday. Danielle greeted me with her usual wide smile, but her face looked pale and pinched.

"Any news?" she whispered.

I shook my head. "You?"

"Didn't sleep a wink," she said.

I folded her into a quick hug. "We'll figure it out." Then I went down the hallway to deposit my backpack in my office nook and retrieve my notes for the meeting.

My phone buzzed and Lieutenant Torrence's name came up on the screen. I accepted the call. "Mom and Sam are so looking forward to meeting with you," I said, fingers crossed that was what he wanted to discuss.

"Me too. But this is a heads-up," he said. "We are going to do a press conference later on this afternoon. I left a message for your friend Danielle but figured you would be seeing her, too, and would want to know. We're putting out an urgent appeal to anyone who might have seen what happened during the parade yesterday."

"Won't that cause a panic?" I asked. "Make it look like the police don't quite know what they're doing?" Knowing that it would cause Danielle to panic anyway.

"We can't fool around with this, Hayley," he said. "The stakes are too high. There are too many damn people squeezed into this town and the chances of information getting lost are, well—" He sighed. "And it's only going to get worse as the week goes on. And some of our esteemed visitors have left their manners on the mainland, assuming they had any to begin with."

"What about the tiger stripes that Bransford mentioned?" I asked.

"Dead end," said Torrence, his voice final and dismissive. "Anyway, it was zebra."

"But I have a friend who paints faces—"

"We've had to move on," Torrence said. "I'm not asking for your help this time; I just wanted to keep you posted. And Bransford says you should please stay out of trouble. And for once, he and I agree about something." I heard a clicking noise that sounded as if he was grinding his teeth. "On another note, I've made a date with your mother and Sam to meet at the Fort Zach beach this evening at five to work on the wedding planning. It's the only time I'm free before Sunday. Can you make it?"

"Sure," I said. "See you there. Let me know if anything breaks on the zombie case, okay?"

Torrence gave a noncommittal grunt and hung up. Everyone was a little crabby this week with all the hordes descending on the island for Fantasy Fest. It wasn't quite like spring break, when thousands of college kids who'd been pent up over the winter appeared with their cases of beer and lids of pot and board shorts and bikinis. That could usually be managed with extra staff and a lot of vigilance. Those kids were younger and some even underage, and our cops had success with doling out community service for the ones who colored outside the lines. Fantasy Fest wasn't even like New Year's Eve—while intense, that party lasted less than twenty-four hours. This was a full week of crazy parties, and people who arrived in our town prepared to behave in ways they never, never, never would at home.

Wally whistled from down the hall, and I gathered my stuff together to join the staff in his office. I had thought at one time that Wally and I would end up a couple, but it wasn't in the cards. In fact, just about everyone on the island and in my family noticed the lack of chemistry between us before I did. His whistle pierced the air a second time and I had to chuckle: Our once-promising romance was reduced to him whistling for me like a pet dog. I hustled down the hall and took the last seat.

"Morning, everyone," said Palamina, the magazine's co-owner. In honor of Fantasy Fest week, she'd changed her hair color to platinum blond with a metallic blue streak beginning from her right temple. And she was wearing sparkly gold leggings and a boxy patchwork top made out of shirts from past years' festivals. Only Palamina could piece together a quilt out of ugly jersey T-shirts and come up with something that resembled the cutting edge of fashion.

"Let's hear what everyone's got for the Thursday issue," Wally said.

"The takeout article is going well," I said. "Though I'm sorry to say we were slowed down by Garbo's Grill."

"No good?" asked Palamina. She tapped her lower lip with a pink pen. "With all the great press they've gotten recently, that would surprise me."

"Too good," I said, grinning. "We couldn't do the Paradise Pub justice. Which worked out okay, since they lost our order. The chef was so mad—based on the cuss words we heard, I thought he might have the head of the waitress right back in the kitchen. We decided not to wait—I'll go another day."

"He has a French name, doesn't he?" Wally asked. "But the food is pubbish. I went once last year and was not that impressed."

"I'm always hopeful," I said. "Lots of the locals love the place and the chef will be the new owner, so he can make lots of menu changes if he likes. But meanwhile, I'm working on a piece on the zombie parade—mostly fun photos."

Wally rubbed a hand over his sandy hair until it stuck out like a hedgehog's. "Didn't someone die in the zombie parade?"

Danielle blanched.

"Yes, a woman did," I said. "Maybe a heart attack." If the bosses didn't know yet how close we'd been to the action, I wasn't going to be the one to tell them. "But just in case, the police are holding a press conference about the incident this afternoon. Hoping to smoke out some leads in case it was foul play. In case they have some helpful witnesses, and before they drink so much their memories are wiped clean."

"I'll cover that," said Palamina, slapping her pen on the desk. "What else?"

Danielle stammered something about creativity and costumes, which Palamina dismissed as too vague to use. "Come back to us when you have your angle worked out," she said, ignoring the stricken look on my friend's face.

"I'll help you narrow it down," I said, patting Danielle's knee. "What about trends in body and face painting, though?" I asked. "I have a body paint artist to interview. And we could do some man-on-the-street bits about how they choose their look and what's behind the effort."

"And while you're at it, find out why anyone wants to prance down the busiest street in town with no clothes on?" Wally asked. "It's not like the old days when you could do that and suffer no consequences.

The way social media works, people are sharing sights with the world that should remain in the darkness of their bedroom."

"Go for it," Palamina said to me. "And don't be a prude," she added to Wally, softening the words with a grin. "Let's all check back in here this afternoon? Say in a couple of hours, after the press conference? This week is churning like a riptide, and I don't want *Key Zest* to be gawking on the sidelines while everyone on the island reads the news in someone else's magazine."

When the meeting was over, I motioned to Danielle to follow me down the hall to my office. "Let's think things through," I said as she perched on the folding chair I keep behind the door for my occasional visitors.

She glanced around the tiny room. The slanted wall sloping into my desk was papered with some of my favorite articles from *Key Zest* along with other local publications. I'd included photos of iguanas and gravestones from the cemetery, tropical flowers, and wonderful meals. On my desk, I had a photo of our houseboat at dusk, Miss Gloria and my mother standing in front of it, each holding a cat. It made me smile every time I saw it.

Danielle heaved a sigh. "Your place is so cute—it shines with your personality. I still haven't gotten used to the changes she made out there." She hooked her thumb toward the main office space, now decorated in the world according to Palamina—textured burlap, Asian-style arcing fish, and photos that looked as though they'd been mass-produced for tropical hotel chains.

"Thanks, but she was right to update the office. It's more businesslike for the front of the house where people get their first impression of our magazine," I said, not wanting to foment ill will toward the boss. "Good for when advertisers stop by, or sources. I would hesitate to bring someone back here. It's like a little window into my brain—scary." I laughed but she didn't.

"Did you see that Palamina had the article about the fight between me and Druckman right there in her folder?" Danielle's face puckered and I thought she was going to break into pieces.

I leaned forward and took one of her hands. "Forget Palamina. Let's think about what the cops might want to know. It's better to be prepared than have them surprise you with questions. I found that out the hard way." I laughed again, desperate to lighten the mood. "Can you think of any of your supporters who might have played a prank on Caryn Druckman? I know you weren't involved," I reassured her. "But I also know how these things go. Someone close to you might have realized how hard you worked and got worried that this other candidate would win in the final moments. Suppose they felt protective and went too far. Anything like that?"

Danielle burst into tears.

I bit my lip and paused for a moment. "Okay, let's back up a bit. Tell me about who worked on your campaign. Who might have had a lot invested in you becoming queen of Fantasy Fest this year?"

Daniel grabbed a tissue from the box on my desk

and dabbed around her eyes, carefully so as not to disturb her mascara and sparkly eye shadow. She sniffed. "My family, of course. My mother was very active in recruiting people to attend the parties. She got a lot of our conch neighbors and friends to come to things, so it wasn't just the same group of snowbirds and wealthy folks that come out for all the galas. She won the title of queen of Fantasy Fest back when I was a little girl. So you can imagine how excited she was when I decided to run." Her eyes widened and grew shiny with tears again. "She did not pressure me one bit, honest. It did not mean that much to her—she isn't like one of those beauty pageant mothers or anything. She would never have hurt that woman."

"Of course it wasn't your mom," I said. "Who else worked on the campaign?"

"Her sister," Danielle said. "Her twin. We three are having lunch today at Louie's Backyard. Maybe you could come along and talk to both of them at once."

Torrence had told me to stay out of things. Easy for him to say. But not so easy for me to do when my friend was an obvious suspect and in such terrible distress. The least I could do was chat with her relatives over a fish taco. A girl had to eat anyway.

"Absolutely," I said. "How about the other royalty candidates? Did they get along with Druckman?"

"Nobody was feuding with her or anything," Danielle said, and I nodded my encouragement. "Seymour Fox ran for king and won. He works at the Green Parrot. Maybe he's a part owner too. I can't think of any problems with him. And John-Bryan Hopkins was the guy running against him. He's an outsider too, like Caryn was. He's a food blogger and a social media king. As far as I could tell, he was having a ball."

"Anyone else?"

"Kitty Palmer," she said. "She teaches tennis. I can't see that this is getting us anywhere." She slumped into her chair, a pout on her face.

"Better for me to ask the questions than the KWPD, though, right? We'll talk more at lunch."

9

It's a lucky carrot that ends up in Ms. Kong's kitchen; rarely is the vegetable lavished with so much attention.

—Pete Wells,
"Cooking as They Go Along,"
The New York Times, March 25, 2015

At eleven forty-five, I knocked off my work and rode over to Louie's, on the Atlantic side of the island. Though the food in this restaurant is good, the real draw is its outside deck and bar perched directly on the ocean. Sitting at a table, listening to the water slosh onto Dog Beach and gazing at the sailboats and Jet Skis on the horizon, you could have a plate of sawdust in front of you and feel perfectly satisfied. Visitors go nuts for it, but the locals love it too. This would be exactly the kind of place that would feel special for a regular lunch date between sisters.

A hostess met me at the front desk and delivered me to the table where Danielle was sitting with two other women. Danielle's mom, Mary, looked exactly as I imagined Danielle would look in twenty-five or thirty years: She wore her gray-blond hair in a swooping chignon. Her dark tan suggested happy hours on a boat or beside the pool, and a blousy sundress skimmed the extra fifteen pounds that she'd probably been trying to shed for years. Her twin sister had the same rounded cheeks and Roman nose, though her hair was short and she wore sparkly reading glasses dangling from a chain around her neck. Even with makeup, she looked a bit older than Danielle's mom.

Danielle made the introductions and they greeted me warmly. "I'm Marion," said the twin with glasses and spiky hair. She put her arm around her sister and grinned. "Our mother was into *M* names, as you can see, and without a lot of creativity. We think she was so stunned when two of us showed up that she split the difference."

The waitress arrived and we all ordered fish tacos and iced tea.

"Thank you for helping Danielle," said Mary, her face settling into worried lines. "We couldn't be more distressed about what's happened this week. My daughter worked so hard in this contest, and to think that anyone imagined she would hurt someone or cheat . . . It breaks my heart." Two big fat tears began to zigzag down her cheeks.

"It doesn't mean they think the worst of her. They have to look at everything," I said, patting the back of her hand. "Of course, we know Danielle did nothing wrong, but the police have to investigate all the possibilities, even if they're unlikely."

"The stakes are too high when someone dies," Marion agreed, nodding soberly. "The cops can't just stand around at Smathers Beach looking at girls in bikinis and chewing the fat."

I cringed. Torrence and Bransford would despise that description, even if it seemed she was joking.

The waitress approached with a tray of iced tea in tall glasses and set them on our table along with a bowl of lemon wedges and another with miniature packages of brown sugar and fake sugar. I doctored mine with a double dose of lemon and sugar and then asked: "Tell me more about the contest over the past month or so. Was everyone getting along, or were there problems between some of the contestants?"

The sisters exchanged glances, which made me wonder whether I'd be getting the whole story with all three Kamens at the same table.

"Honestly, between us, that woman was a pain right from the beginning," said Marion, sliding her glasses up the bridge of her nose.

"You mean Caryn Druckman." They nodded in unison. "A pain in what way?" I asked as I reached for a breadstick and began to slather it with butter.

"I don't think it's right to speak ill of the dead," said Mary. "And I wouldn't talk about this except that Danielle was so close to the situation. And we're scared to death that she's going to be blamed for something that she didn't do." She bit her lip, waiting for me to nod before she continued. "This Caryn was supercompetitive. I mean, she would have given anything to win. For gosh sakes, it was supposed to be all about raising money for charity, but she behaved like she was running for Miss America." She looked at her sister. "Am I being too harsh?"

"That's what it reminded me of too," Marion said, then glanced at Danielle. "It reminded me of when you ran for the prom queen during your senior year. Remember that awful girl who was in your court? She was certain she was going to be the winner. When she lost, she became vicious. She posted nasty things on Danielle's locker and spread awful rumors. And the funny thing was, she was a gorgeous woman."

"More glamorous than Danielle," Mary added. She reached over to touch her daughter's hair. "Though certainly not as pretty."

"For heaven sake's, Mother," said Danielle, her face and neck now pinked with embarrassment, "that was years ago."

"Not that long ago," said Mary. "And besides, the feeling is the same. People saw through her fancy facade and voted for the girl who was kind. That's the sort of thing you're after, isn't it, Hayley?"

I nodded vigorously. "Go ahead and tell me more about it. Because if the high school girl was intense in the same way that Caryn was, it might help us understand what happened to her. Who she was underneath the surface and why she might've died. Was Caryn born and raised in Key West?"

"No," said Danielle's mom. "And maybe that was part of the issue. It's annoying when people think that this is their island when they've barely arrived. Worse yet, if they act that way too. Never mind that the rest of us hardly make it off the rock once we land." The twins laughed.

"We're not total hicks; we did go to college in Gainesville," said Marion. "But you get the idea—we belong here in a way these newcomers never will."

I cringed a little, because I could probably be accused of the same thing. Shortly after I'd moved down, Key West seeped into my system like a sweet poison, and now I couldn't imagine living anywhere else. And I probably bragged about how lucky I was to be on this island more than I should. "Say more about it," I said. "How long has Caryn been around?"

"Maybe she came ten years ago or so?" Marion asked, glancing at her sister for confirmation.

"Probably closer to seven. Like the other people who can afford it and have a place where they can escape, she would leave for the hot summer months and go somewhere on Long Island," said Mary. "A mini mansion, if you believe the stories."

"And most annoying," said Marion, slapping her palm on the table, "she had this huge social media campaign—Twitter, Facebook, Instagram, you name it—with all the Key West news that she felt was worth printing. And when the news wasn't about her, it was about the 'high-society' people, not the rest of us schlumps slaving away in the trenches."

"If I read one more Facebook post ending with *love and sundrenched kisses from your friend Caryn*, I thought I might puke."

"Stop it. You'll make Hayley think we're awful people," said Danielle.

Mary laughed. "I forgot, we're not speaking ill of the dead."

"They're really not usually this bitchy," Danielle whispered to me. "But sometimes they get this twin energy going, and then you'd better get out of the way. It's like feeding chum to the sharks."

I grinned. "So Caryn thought she was going to win the Fantasy Fest contest, like that girl in your high school thought she'd win prom queen."

Mary nodded. "And like I said, the high school girl may have been prettier, but she wasn't nice to people the way Danielle is. And with this woman Caryn, it was similar. She had access to the people with the most money and she should have blown us out of the water with all those connections and the social media to spread her gospel. But in the end Danielle's earnestness and humility won out."

Danielle shook her head with a chagrined smile. "It's nice to have them on my side, but embarrassing too."

I grinned. "It's sweet; you should run with it. There was one other queen candidate too, right?"

"Yes, Kitty Palmer. I got the feeling she was pushed into running, because she ran a halfhearted campaign."

"She was busy though too," said Danielle. "She teaches at Bayview and she has to cram in as many lessons as she can while people are in town."

The twins spent a few minutes describing how they would have increased attendance at Kitty's parties had they been in charge.

"If you don't mind," I said to Danielle, "tell us again

exactly what happened on Duval Street in front of The Bull and Whistle. How did the fight get started? What seemed to really set Caryn off? You told me it was a mini meet and greet along that section of Duval?"

Danielle wrapped her hair around her hand and pinned it away from her neck with a pink barrette. "At first it wasn't a problem because she was snubbing me, as if I wasn't there at all. Not that easy, when I was the so-called queen and she was in the court." She flashed a lopsided smile that didn't reach her eyes. "But that didn't bother me because it only made her look small. Of course, people on the streets were a little tipsy, if not completely drunk. And some of them started hollering out 'hail to the queen' and 'long live the queen' and 'locals rule, visitors go home'—silly stuff like that."

Danielle heaved a big sigh and sank lower in her chair. Her neck was flushing a deep pink that spread like a stain up to her cheeks. "And then Caryn just boiled over, that's all I can say. Her face got purple. And she made this little huffing sound. And it looked like she was going to blow. Even the other royal court members noticed it. That John-Bryan who ran for king and lost tried to take her arm and chat with her and calm her down. He reminded her that they were off duty for the next year, while Seymour and I would have a million events to attend. And the fact that local people had won this year was probably a good thing for the island."

"Was your king involved?" I asked. "What is he like?"

"Seymour seems like a nice guy," Danielle said.

"I don't know him super well. We campaigned as individuals, not as a couple."

"Was he trying to help contain Caryn too?"

"No," she said. "He kept his distance. I think he was afraid of her."

"So what finally pushed her over the edge?" I hated to keep hammering at her about this, but the picture was still fuzzy. "Was it something you said?"

The waitress arrived with our tacos, giving us all a breather from the difficult conversation. And based on the tightness of her expression, I thought Danielle needed a chance to collect herself. I doused my sandwich with a squeeze of lemon and a few shakes of hot sauce and took a big bite. The fish was fresh and the cabbage crunchy against the soft shell. I tipped my face to the dappled sunlight and closed my eyes and chewed, thinking again how lucky I'd been to land on this island. And reminding myself not to brag about it in the future to those who weren't as lucky.

After she'd nibbled at her fish, Danielle put her fork on her plate and turned to me. "The real tipping point was when this woman came up to me and began gushing about what a great queen I was and how they chose the best woman for the job and how wonderful it was to have a local person serving in this position rather than some social-climbing scab and so on. And suddenly Caryn just flew at me and tried to claw my face." Danielle stopped and began to cry.

"That bitch," said Danielle's mother. "If she wasn't already dead I would kill her myself."

"Shhhh," said her sister. "It's not a good idea to joke about something like that."

"It wasn't a joke," said Danielle's mother.

"Anyway I saw what happened after that," I said. "Or at least the end of it when she had a grip on your hair and the cops were called."

"I tried to get away from her," Danielle said. She patted the tears from her cheeks with her napkin and inhaled a big breath. "I figured sooner or later she'd pull herself together and act like a normal grown-up person, not a teenager or a thug. I figured she would come to her senses if I could just duck out of her range and let some other people calm her down. But it didn't work."

"Did you know the woman who was congratulating you? And did Caryn know her?"

"I saw her at a few of the events, always with a glass of wine in her hand, three sheets to the wind." Danielle shrugged. "I have no idea whether those two were friends. It seems unlikely." The twins nodded their agreement.

I wiped my lips with my white napkin, feeling as though we weren't getting to the bottom of anything. "So the third candidate, Kitty, wasn't all that enthusiastic about setting up the parties?"

"Or maybe she didn't realize how much work it would be," Danielle said. "But she obviously wasn't that invested. So when Caryn was overbearing, she would just roll her eyes and back away. I can't imagine her caring enough to kill someone, I guess I'm saying. Not in this context anyway."

"One more question," I said, gazing at each of the women in turn. "And this may make you feel uncomfortable but I feel like it needs to be asked. Do you think it's possible that someone actually had it in for you, Danielle, and not Caryn at all? Of course it will depend on what the medical examiner says about how she died."

"I sure hope that's not true," said Marion, taking her sister's hand.

"The only person I've ever known to hate Danielle enough to harm her is dead," said her mom. "And if anyone else gets anywhere near her . . ." She fisted her hands in front of her chest and glared. Like a mother bear—I would not have dared mess with her cub.

The waitress came around again and we reluctantly waved off the key lime pie. "I've got this, Hayley," Danielle said, reaching for the check. "You've done so much for me already."

I thanked them all for the lunch, said good-bye, and headed outside to my scooter, wondering if anything was clearer than it had been. Now I knew that the dead woman was highly competitive, and not nice in the way she went about trying to win. Not that either of those things was big news. Nor did they really explain why she might have been a target for murder.

I had enjoyed watching the interaction between Danielle's mother and her twin sister. I grew up an only child, and after age ten, an only child of a single mother. I had always longed for a sibling. Though friends over the years assured me that brothers and sisters could be overrated, I loved the idea of someone aside from my parents who would have known me since birth. Someone who shared my history intimately. Sometimes it was not easy to be my mother's only child. All the love and hopes and dreams she harbored were pinned on me, not distributed—and diluted—among a group of other children.

Yesterday, after the call to pick up Danielle at the police station, I had wondered briefly why she didn't phone her own family. She tried Wally, I knew that. But her next call was to me, not to her flesh and blood.

Now that I'd met the twins and asked myself the question, the answer emerged. Danielle's mother and her aunt were very invested in the Fantasy Fest contest and Danielle's reign. My family's reaction to the fight was *Oh you poor thing, how can we help?* followed by offers of food and drink.

Her family would have been focused on how to hunt down and punish the perpetrator.

10

*But I wouldn't have tucked into a big,
steaming plate of offal even if threatened
by a gang of knife-wielding butchers.*
                                    —Ann Mah,
                  Mastering the Art of French Eating

As I inserted the key in my scooter's ignition, wondering whether I'd work better at the office than home, I received a text from Lieutenant Torrence. The press conference had been moved up to two p.m. on the steps of old City Hall on the far side of town.

Which gave me a sinking feeling, because what was the rush? And why in the world weren't they meeting inside the building instead of on the steps? Why not a small gathering inside the police department? This new arrangement gave me a sense that they were grandstanding or, even worse, communicating a feeling of panicked urgency that I hoped didn't exist. Even if Palamina planned to write this news up for our next magazine issue, I wanted to be there to hear it all for myself.

So I strapped on my helmet and drove across the island. A good-sized mob of people had already gathered on the steps of the old brick building that has served as the temporary location for city commission and other meetings, while the renovated City Hall in the former Glynn Archer school building was being polished on White Street. Is it only in Key West that projects are accomplished more slowly and suck down more money than anyone ever anticipated? Probably not, but I'd never paid that much attention to local politics back in New Jersey. But this town mattered—it felt like my home.

Without the sweet ocean breeze that we'd enjoyed at Louie's Backyard, the sidewalks around old City Hall were hot as the griddle top in a busy breakfast kitchen. I sniffed the air and wrinkled my nose, and amended my observation: a griddle top that hadn't been cleaned in days. Or weeks. Lieutenant Torrence and the police chief were stationed at the top of the steps, surrounded by several officers in uniform. A microphone had been set up in front of them, with wires snaking back into the building. The crowd seemed to comprise of reporters, townspeople, and tourists who'd stumbled onto the scene from Duval Street only one block south.

The microphone crackled and the police chief began. "Good afternoon, ladies and gentlemen," he said. "Thank you for coming. We will keep this brief and let you get back to your business. We wish to alert you to two items of public interest. Number one, we would like to ask for your assistance. You may have heard about the unfortunate incident that occurred during the zombie bike parade yesterday. Mrs. Caryn Druckman, a well-loved part-time resident of our island, fell ill and was taken to the hospital after collapsing on the street. We are seeking information from anyone who may have attended the event and seen something unusual prior to the launch of the parade. Anyone who might have noticed her interacting in an unusual fashion or ingesting something unusual should please come forward and report this to our office."

A ripple of conversation shuddered through the people listening. "What do you mean by unusual? Other than a mass of zombies on bikes," shouted out a reporter.

"Spot-on," said the chief with a mirthless laugh. "We don't see zombies every day. I meant anything threatening or conflictual." He glanced at Torrence, who stood beside him with hands folded over his stomach. They both nodded.

"And what about ingesting? What do you mean by that? Are you saying she was poisoned?"

There was another exchange of worried glances between Torrence and the chief. "If you saw her eating before the parade kicked off, or noticed anything unusual in her demeanor or behavior, please let us know," Torrence said. "That's as much as we can say right now."

"In another matter," said the chief, "we would like to request that all of you remain aware of the possibility of worsening weather conditions. We hate to rain on your parade, but our first priority is always your safety. As you may know, there is a tropical depression hovering off to the east of Cuba in the Atlantic Ocean. Some forecasters predict this is coming our way."

He swiped the back of his wrist over his forehead and tried to smile over the grumbling that had started up in the crowd.

"We should know more in the next twenty-four hours. Of course, many of you have been looking forward to this week all year, and we appreciate that it would be disappointing to have to leave the island earlier than you had planned." He raised his voice to be heard over the noise.

"But again, you will understand that our first concern must be public safety. We hope as fervently as you do that the forecasters are wrong. But please stay tuned to the local weather station or to our official city Web site, where we will post updates on the track of the storm. If winds increase and the storm takes a path such that a hurricane watch or a warning is issued for this area, we will greatly appreciate your cooperation. In those cases, a mandatory evacuation order will be put in place. Again, you will be notified by radio, Web site, and newspaper."

"No f-ing way!" cried a group of rowdy men standing behind me, and their derisive hoots were taken up by the folks farther back. They spilled off the sidewalk onto Greene Street chanting "Hell no, we won't go." Which seemed more than a little silly in comparison to the seriousness of the times when that phrase had first emerged.

"That's all for now," said the chief—he was shouting

now. "If I can hear them over this racket, I'm happy to take your questions."

Several hands waved furiously and the chief called on a frizzy-haired woman in the front row whom I recognized as a frequent presence at city commission meetings. Her byline often appeared on the front page of the *Key West Citizen*. "It sounds like Mrs. Druckman died and that you believe Mrs. Druckman may have been murdered. If this is true, are there any leads in the case? And from what did she die?"

"Thank you for that question," said the chief. "We always appreciate your attention to detail. Our thoughts and prayers are with Mrs. Druckman's family and we will notify you when we know more." A tight smile flickered over his face. I was sure he did *not* always appreciate her attention to detail. Particularly when it cast a shadowy light on the police department.

"But was she murdered?" the reporter pressed.

"She died shortly after reaching the hospital. We're investigating all possibilities," said the chief. "Nothing is ruled out. That's all I have to say. Except that, again, if—I repeat *if*—her death did not occur of natural causes, our investigation will confirm that and we will proceed to find the party responsible. As of now, the toxicology reports are not back from the medical examiner's office."

So it was looking like murder. I felt a little sick to my stomach thinking of Danielle's unhappy interactions with the dead woman. My impression of the dislike between the two women had only increased over the course of the lunch. I knew from my past experience with two bosses at *Key Zest* how toxic those feelings could become. And I wished I hadn't witnessed the intensity of Danielle's mother and her aunt—their fierce desire for Danielle to win the crown. Surely none of them had anything to do with the murder. But their rancor toward the dead woman made them look bad. And sound bad too. Gasoline on the fire of police suspicions.

The chief continued. "Because we have these concerns, we are taking the unusual step of asking eyewitnesses to make themselves known." He glanced over the crowd, making eye contact with a smattering of the spectators. "Many of you are guests in Key West and possibly not accustomed to working in partnership with the police." He tried a wide smile that I'm sure he meant to be friendly. Instead it reminded me of a barracuda circling his prey. "Let me assure potential witnesses that there will be no negative consequences for speaking up."

"No negative consequences," Torrence repeated, and then ran off several phone numbers for witnesses to use in reporting tips.

I waited for the crowd to disperse, then sped back over to Jennifer the face painter's apartment in the Truman Annex. The plan: do some research for the new bit I'd promised Palamina and pursue the question of the zebra-style face paint. Torrence had dismissed this as a dead end, but I simply didn't believe him. As I climbed the back stairs to the second floor, a woman emerged from Jennifer's place. She wore a short, sleeveless crop top over skin that had been painted

with swirls of blue flowers. The beak of a humming-
bird emerged from her cleavage. She flashed a friendly
smile.

"Here for a paint job?" she asked.

"Not exactly," I said. "Jennifer did my zombie face
yesterday, but today I have a few questions for her. I'm
doing a story for our local magazine *Key Zest* on personality in relation to body painting. Your meadow is
beautiful, by the way." I gestured at her chest and the
tendrils of flowers that snaked up to her neck and over
her shoulders, partway down her arms.

"A story on what?" the woman asked.

"I'm thinking about how personality is expressed
in the scenes that folks choose for their body paint. Do
you have any thoughts about that connection?"

"I wasn't really thinking that deeply when I asked
for the flowers," the woman said with a laugh. "Bodies
to me are beautiful. And so if I was going to show mine
to the world, I wanted it to be painted in a cheerful way."

She pulled up her shirt so I couldn't avoid seeing
the whole palette. "Gorgeous," I said, then hurried
inside, hoping I hadn't come across either as a prude
or a voyeur. Unfortunately, my eyes had probably been
popping. We didn't have naked people running
around in public in New Jersey, painted or unpainted,
and I still wasn't used to it.

Jennifer was washing her hands at the kitchen sink.
"Come on in, Hayley; I have a minute before my next
customer arrives."

"I saw your latest canvas." I grinned. "Can they
shower with that stuff on? How long does it last?"

"If she wanted to peak for the parade on Saturday,

she got painted too early," Jennifer said. "But there are so many parties earlier in the week, and lots of my customers attend those. Sponge baths are what I recommend to make sure the paint lasts."

This picture of naked painted people sponging their armpits flashed to my mind and I hid my eyes with my hands. Good gravy. On this point I was beginning to agree with Wally and Lorenzo: This week was too much.

Jennifer laughed. "But you said you had more questions?"

I explained quickly about the press conference and the dead woman, and my concern that my friend would be fingered if it did turn out to be foul play, which was the way I thought things were leaning. "I have two questions," I said. "First, I wondered if this paint job was familiar. Maybe you did it yourself or you could point me to someone who might have?"

I pulled out my phone and scrolled quickly through the photos of the zombie bike ride. I chose an earlier photo of the zombie down, aka Caryn Druckman, and expanded the photo to highlight the painting on her face with its elegant red glitter paisley near the outer corners of her eyes. "You can see that it looks kind of the opposite of what you did for me. She has more white, and then you'll notice the red glitter."

Jennifer took the phone and studied the photo, then finally shook her head. "It's not one of mine although it's pretty. And I do like glitter but not clumped like this one."

She clicked over one frame, which turned out to be

the video I'd taken holding the phone up over my head as I pedaled the bike before Caryn Druckman had collapsed. We watched her bike begin to wobble and slow until she finally fell off and clunked heavily to the ground.

"Wow!" Jennifer cocked her head and looked up at me. "This is the lady who died? Spooky to have this right on your phone. What in the world happened?"

"Something bad," I said, gulping, deciding not to go into the details of the poison idea. What was the point of spreading rumors? "The police are looking into it." I grabbed the phone back, not wanting to show her the next shot of the woman splayed out on the ground, almost dead; it was too creepy. And besides, the photo I'd taken was out of focus, the button pretty much pressed by error. I swiped backward until I reached the photos from the warm-up party. "You can see better here the different approaches to painting."

Then Jennifer scrolled through some of my zombie photos, commenting as she swiped about the creative costumes, the paint jobs, and the sheer number of people in the crowd. "It's not that we all have distinctive styles like famous painters do," she said. "I don't pretend to say I'm a Renoir or a Van Gogh or anything." She laughed and tossed her blond hair over her shoulder. "But I like to imagine that I understand what look my customers are going for. And I try to think about their costumes and match the painting to those. I like to use bold colors and glitters and pay a lot of attention to detail." She swiped through more pictures.

"Wait!" I said. "Go back one frame." I recovered the

phone from her and studied the photo that I had noticed as it flashed by. Danielle and the rest of the royal court had posed in front of the live zombie band and the Beach Eats food truck. The cups of punch were being served—maybe painkillers? And one of the servers had her face painted—I thought it was a her—in hallucinogenic zebra stripes. I was sure Torrence had mentioned stripes.

"Do you recognize this person?" I asked Jennifer.

"Not really," she said. She took the phone back from me and enlarged the view. "But I'd swear the art was done by Christy Haussler." She pointed at the screen. "Do you see the sharpness of the lines when the color changes? That's not always easy to do on skin. If a person has a tendency to an oily complexion especially, the paint tends to blur. But Christy uses a base coat like I do—it's expensive but if you care about your art, you feel it's worth it. And her paintings have an Asian flair."

"Where does she work?" I asked. "Do you suppose she would tell me who this person is? Or is there some kind of code of face painting privacy ethics?"

Jennifer grinned. "You saw the customer who was here right before you stopped by. This is very personal work and if I talked about my clients that might be the end of my bookings. But on the other hand, if I text Christy first, she might talk to you. In this case it's important because it could be related to the murder, right?"

"Right," I said. "Maybe. I sure would appreciate it if your friend was willing to chat."

Jennifer pulled out her own phone and sent a quick

text message. Meanwhile the next customer had knocked at Jennifer's kitchen door and I went down the short hall to let her in. I heard the zip of a return text as I led her to the kitchen. Jennifer jotted a name and number on the slip of paper and handed it to me.

"Good luck," she said with a wink. "And if you change your mind about getting painted for Fantasy Fest, I'll squeeze you in."

When Snorkel the pig flew instead of bowled, that's when I'd parade down Duval Street wearing body paint only.

11

"Rabbit," said Pooh to himself. "I like talking to Rabbit. He talks about sensible things. He doesn't use long, difficult words, like Owl. He uses short, easy words, like 'What about lunch?' and 'Help yourself, Pooh.' I suppose really I ought to go and see Rabbit."

—A. A. Milne,
The House at Pooh Corner

Once I had left Jennifer's apartment, I took the phone out of my pocket and looked at the mini video again. I had taken the film as a lark after seeing other parade participants capturing the moment with their smartphones. What were the chances that rather than capturing the zany joy of the occasion, instead I recorded the seconds leading up to a woman's death?

My breath caught in my throat, its rhythm growing fast and shallow. I mentally pinched myself: She hadn't died right on the spot. She'd been transferred to the hospital, where I was certain they applied all the medical assistance available. Rather than call the cops now with my video, I determined I could show it to Torrence before meeting my mother and company at Fort Zachary Taylor beach for the wedding rehearsal.

Meanwhile, I had just time to pop over to the office and check in, as Palamina had requested. I hoped this meeting would end up being short and pro forma—extra time sitting on the sand gazing at the horizon and listening to the salt water slosh on rocks could only help my state of mind.

Wally and Palamina had already gathered in their shared office by the time I arrived, but there was no sign of Danielle.

"Sorry to be a little late," I said. "The traffic out there is unbelievable."

"I'm finding it easier to walk than drive. Is Danielle coming?" Palamina asked, frowning and glancing around the small space as if she might be hiding.

"I'm sure she's caught up in traffic too," I said, though I wasn't sure. And I didn't know why I should suddenly suffer a surge of guilt. Palamina had turned out to be more judgmental than I had expected when I first met her. She got the job done with the magazine, but we all ended up keyed up higher and tighter than we ever had when Wally led the charge. "I'll send her a quick text."

"I saw you across the street at the press conference," Palamina added as I typed an SOS to Danielle. "I couldn't catch your attention in that mob scene. It sounds like they have another murder on their hands.

Any word from your friends at the KWPD?" They both stared at me expectantly.

"I don't know anything more than you do at this point," I said. Certainly not that I'd share.

"What did you think about the weather bit?" Palamina asked. "I have to admit, the idea of a hurricane has got me spooked. When do you think we should evacuate?"

"I've heard horror stories either way, stay or go," I said. "The year Wilma hit, people kept evacuating—"

"Eight storms that year, including Katrina," she said. "I just don't think I could bear the suspense."

Wally and I exchanged glances. Her New York anxiety was showing through.

"I'm inclined to clear out the minute they tell us to," she said. "Why would I think I'm a better judge of meteorological events than the scientists? And it's not like *Key Zest* is known for covering meteorological news. No one relies on us for the details of the weather."

"I'm inclined to go too," Wally said. "Mostly for my mother's peace of mind. And that way, if the storm veers up the East Coast in her direction, I can help her out. What about you?"

I shrugged. "Mom and Sam are in town getting married on Sunday, remember? So we'll wait a bit, hope for the best." I flashed a loopy smile. "Like the rest of the nutcases on this island."

"Keep us posted, then," said Palamina, glancing at her iPhone watch. "I think we should get started. It doesn't look like Danielle's coming. I hope she's not flaking out on us completely," she added, making me want to warn her she'd develop a permanent furrow between her eyebrows if she kept frowning. Though I was worried too. Why hadn't Danielle shown up or at least answered my text?

I told them a little about how the face-painting article was shaping up, and we discussed how and whether Palamina should write up the press conference. Then I excused myself, headed out to the soupy heat of the end of the day, and began to drive to the beach at the end of the island.

Reaching the spot where Southard Street dumps into the harbor, I passed the parking lot across from the Eco-Discovery Center on the right, and the police horse barracks and training ring on the left. Lately, the sustainability coordinator of the town was particularly proud of the compost material available there, and encouraged all residents to take advantage of it. But horse manure in flowerpots on a houseboat? Probably a no-go in the eyes of the Tarpon Pier Neighborhood Association.

Finally, I puttered by what always looked to me like abandoned military barracks. Key West had hosted an enormous military presence during the Cold War, and remnants of those scary days still remained. Within minutes, I was at the entrance to the state park, paying my fee and accepting congratulations from a friendly ranger.

"Most people don't take the time to enjoy nature this week," she said. "Though I suppose they're enjoying a different kind of nature." She winked and handed me a receipt that would grant me entrance into the park until eight p.m. this evening. "Be careful of rip currents if you're going to swim," she added. "That low pressure out east of us is doing weird things to our ocean. The swells are a lot bigger than we're used to."

Then I drove into the park grounds, past the parking lot that led to the snack shack and all the way to the end of the spit. Instead of palm trees, tall pines shaded the thin stretch of land between the pavement and the beach. These were not native plantings, and like many subjects in Key West, their presence was controversial. To me, it seemed a no-brainer. The trees provide a shady respite on an island that has gotten built up and crowded with commerce and humanity. Maybe native plantings would have been better for the environment, but right now anything green and quiet felt soothing.

I left my scooter by the bicycle rack and trudged over to the rock pile at the far end of the property. In the distance, I could see the top-heavy, rectangular shape of a cruise ship chugging from the harbor out through the channel. I often wondered—even worried a little—about the impression of Key West that cruising visitors left with. How many people who spend most of an excursion day drinking and perusing the weird and tacky shops on Duval Street could be left with a positive memory of the city?

I paused for a minute to jot down notes in my iPhone for a possible *Key Zest* article: decent eats within striking distance of the cruise ship dock. I crab-walked out ten yards onto the rocks, already feeling my blood pressure sinking and the stress wrinkles on my forehead relaxing. Not far from where I perched, a large pelican soared above the sea and suddenly plunged into the water, emerging moments later with his pouch wiggling.

With a big sigh, I forced myself to focus on Danielle's problem, the case of her dead rival. As far as I could see, the main reason that would point the cops in her direction was a lack of other suspects. And quite possibly, with the antics of Fantasy Fest stretching their patrols to the max, the police department would not have a lot of time to explore other leads.

Nathan Bransford despised it when I made statements like this. He'd told me more than once that my low opinion of the department's capability would be the death of our relationship. And that what I read as incompetence or disinterest was in fact a normal and necessary secrecy, a veil between the police department and the public (including or even especially me) that prevented the public both from getting hurt and from falsely accusing innocent people. I took a deep breath and cleared my brain again.

Once I'd spent enough time gazing at the water and keeping my mind focused on absolutely nothing, I began to feel as though my pulse rate was back to normal. I scrambled across the rocks in search of my mother and Sam. They drove up to the bike rack in their rental car as I emerged from the beach path. Mom opened her door and tumbled out, her face lined with concern.

"Will it be all right for the ceremony? Do you think we are trying to act younger than we are? Are we going to look silly out here?"

Behind her, Sam rolled his eyes but smiled fondly. "They say when the bride is having doubts about the venue, it's really about the marriage," he said.

My mother spun around and kissed him on the lips. "Point taken. I'm acting ridiculous."

"Besides, it's gorgeous," I said. "I think it's the most beautiful spot on the island. And that's saying something."

Torrence roared up in his SUV cruiser and sprang out. "Sorry I'm late. It's crazy out there." He whirled a finger around his ear and shook his head. "I can't believe people pay to come here at this time of year. I would pay to get away."

We started through the path under the pines, the air now scented with roasting hot dogs from a grill off to the left. A mother herded three small boys with energy like fireworks to the nearby picnic table and divided the hot dogs among their paper plates. With the fish taco receding several hours in my stomach's memory, my mouth watered. We stopped at the edge of the pines and looked out at the beach, where choppy waves slapped against the breakwater. A funny/sad expression crossed my mother's face.

"Are you okay?" I asked.

"Flashback," she said, gripping my arm so hard that I almost yelped. "You were with me the first time I did this too." She patted her belly. "But my father walked me down the aisle that time."

Mom had turned up pregnant during her senior year of college. Back in those days no one expected or condoned pregnancy out of wedlock, but she still claims it was the best thing that ever happened to her.

It gave her the gift of motherhood, the chance to raise a nearly perfect daughter. No pressure there, right?

"Your grandpa had such a scowl on his face," she said. "He actually threatened your father, right at the altar in hearing distance of the minister. *You'd better take care of her—better than you have so far.*" She reached over to cup my cheek. "And I wouldn't change a thing. Even if I did desperately want the white dress that I couldn't fit into at five months pregnant. We'll do that at your wedding." She smiled a smile so full of love and yearning that it made my own heart ache.

"We've got years, if not decades, to plan that," I said. I made a let's-get-on-with-it face at Torrence.

Then he talked us through the ceremony, how I would walk my mother to the point on the beach where the breakwater burst out of the ocean. There, Sam and Torrence would be waiting. "I'll welcome your family and friends and then Hayley will read the psalm you've chosen and Gloria will say the prayer."

"Oh, I forgot to tell you!" Mom gripped his wrist first, then grabbed Sam "Remember the trumpet player from Connie and Ray's wedding? As a special gift, they've arranged for him to pipe us in down the aisle."

"I think you're mixing your metaphors, darling," said Sam with a rumbling laugh. "Piping in is for captains coming aboard a new ship. I doubt you want to start the marriage off with that particular image in everyone's minds."

Torrence directed Sam to stand near him facing toward the pines, away from the ocean. Then I took my mother's hand, which felt slick with perspiration, and we started across the beach toward the men. The tears that had seemed to shimmer in her eyes most of the afternoon threatened to spill over. Torrence smiled with reassurance.

"Then we'll do the vows, and you both have rings, right?"

My mother nodded. Another sore point with my father, who insisted that a wedding ring would interfere with his tennis serve. (His tennis serve! As if he was a USTA international player, or a virtuoso pianist, or, for that matter, a construction worker who could realistically have caught the ring on his saw. Not a run-of-the-mill businessman whose biggest physical danger in life was a computer freeze.)

Once we reviewed the sequence to my mother's satisfaction, she and Sam stayed to watch the seagulls and pelicans on the rocks before their dinner reservation at Latitudes. I walked back to the parking lot with the lieutenant.

"You guys must be pretty darn sure that woman was poisoned to share all that insider information with the universe," I said, hoping to bait him into telling more than they had at the press conference.

He looked surprised. "What did we say, other than all possibilities are being investigated?"

"But you intimated that it wasn't natural causes, right?"

"Yup."

I heaved a sigh and tried to figure out how to wiggle my way into his confidence. He made his vacation pocket money conducting weddings. I'd start with some chitchat there.

"Any more nuptial ceremonies this week?" I asked.

"I don't know anyone crazy enough to get married during this particular week of the year," he said. "The weather's terrible and the crowds are too. There was the one couple who wanted me to officiate in body paint only so the guests wouldn't feel uncomfortable."

I giggled. "Let me guess. You were busy that night."

He cracked a smile and I dove for the opening.

"Seriously, the press conference sounded awfully grim," I said.

"Death is grim, Hayley," he said. "And why do I get a distinctly bad feeling that you're not staying out of this as we've asked you to?"

I pursed my lips, measuring the likelihood that he'd share something with me if I told him what I knew. Some of it. I pulled the phone from my pocket. "I accidentally got a video of Caryn Druckman before she fell off her bike," I said.

"Accidentally?" He took the phone and hit the PLAY button.

12

He spoke blasphemies other chefs recognized as hard-won truths. "Any chef who says he does it for love is a liar," Mr. White said. "At the end of the day it's all about money. I never thought I would ever think like that, but I do now. I don't enjoy it. I don't enjoy having to kill myself six days a week to pay the bank." Can you blame him, or any other chef, for wanting to live like his customers?

—Dwight Garner,
"A Bad Boy's Manifesto,"
The New York Times, April 8, 2015

As I puttered up to the parking lot in front of Tarpon Pier, feeling the breath of relief and gratitude that always greets me when I realize I'm at home, I heard a huge ruckus on the dock. The racket radiated from Schnootie the schnauzer, whose barking echoed hysterically from the Renharts' houseboat. As I strode up the finger, I spotted Miss Gloria on the Renharts' deck. This never happens because Mr. Renhart abhors socializing. Over the incessant yapping of the schnauzer came the shrieking and growling of what sounded like hyenas. A lot of them.

I was pretty sure I recognized Evinrude's angry cat voice among the yowls.

I broke into a trot, arriving just as Miss Gloria dove into a cartoon maelstrom of spinning legs and feet and fur and emerged with my tiger cat.

And that break in the action gave enough space for Miss Gloria's black cat Sparky to rush back into the fray. So much was happening that I wasn't certain who was fighting—or how many of them. But when Schnootie lunged into the whirling fur, I saw my chance and snatched Sparky out. Her chest heaving, Mrs. Renhart wrestled down two other long-haired cats, one pure black and one furry gray with a white face and neck and striking green eyes.

"Oh my gosh," she said, her voice squeaky with exertion. "What a way to meet the new neighbors. And I so hoped my new kitties could be friends with yours." She looked utterly bedraggled and forlorn, the two big cats clutched under her arms.

"These belong to you? Let us put our guys away," I said, gritting my teeth as I smiled. "Then we can have a proper introduction."

Miss Gloria and I carried our squirming, growling felines back to the dock and locked them in our houseboat. "What in the world was she thinking?" I muttered.

"I think she's mostly lonely," said Miss Gloria. "She sees how our animals get along so nicely and she wanted to copy us." She shrugged and grinned, the skin around her eyes crinkling with laughter. "Take it as a compliment."

"You're right as usual," I said, and gave her a quick hug. Another way I felt lucky in my life—this amazing and unlikely roommate. When I first met her, I sized her up as a frail but quirky old lady, a relic living out her last shaky legs on Houseboat Row. I couldn't have been more wrong.

We started back to the Renharts' houseboat, where our neighbor had—thank goodness—put Schnootie away in their cabin. Her new cats had retreated under the deck chairs. And Mrs. R was laying out a gallon jug of inexpensive white wine and a plate of Oreo cookies.

"I'm so sorry about all that; I just wasn't thinking." She poured the wine into three plastic glasses and passed them to us. In the background, Schnootie yelped and slammed her weight repeatedly against the screen door—a one-dog percussion section.

"It was our cats' fault as much as anything," said Miss Gloria, and thunked her glass against each of ours in a plastic toast. "They love a good fracas. Now tell us the story of these new kitties. Are you fostering?" She wiggled her fingers at the black cat who approached her cautiously and sniffed.

I scratched the big gray cat behind his ears. He closed his eyes for a moment as if to enjoy the rub, then darted under Mrs. Renhart's chair. I took a sip of my wine and a bite of the cookie, neither of which fit into my calories-for-today plan. But our neighbor had never invited us over before, and she seemed desperate to keep us there for a bit. "Red velvet Oreo? Delicious," I said as I knelt down on the deck and ran my hand over the big black cat's back. "Who is this beauty?"

"That's Dinkels," said Mrs. Renhart, breaking into a huge smile. "She's almost fifteen. Can you imagine sending a fifteen-year-old cat to the animal shelter? The workers said she seems to think she's a dog."

"She's got gorgeous eyes," I said. "And a powerful presence."

"And beautiful fur," said Miss Gloria dutifully. "And who is this other handsome fella?" She leaned down to peer at the gray cat.

"That's Jack," said Mrs. R. "They think he's even older than Dinkels, but he's sweet and dignified." Her eyes teared up and she ran her fingers through one cat's fur and then the other's.

"I don't know what came over me. I was sitting here yesterday, thinking about how happy I was to have Schnootie in my life, and how I should give back what she's given me by adopting more animals. And the next thing I know, I'm running a home for elderly felines." She hooted with laughter and took a slug of wine. "Mr. Renhart, as you can imagine, is not amused."

We laughed along with her, probably howling a little louder than was polite.

"Cheers," said Mrs. Renhart. "I hope you enjoy the snacks. Even though I'm not nearly the foodie that you are."

I avoided glancing at Miss Gloria, afraid we'd burst into giggles and hurt her feelings. Drinking a gallon jug of sharp chardonnay while eating Oreos? Definitely not the foodie way, though hungry as I was, it wasn't a bad combination.

"What was your day like?" she asked me. "Your job sounds so glamorous."

"Well," I said, "seems like it's been very busy though I can't say what I accomplished." I scratched my head and took another tiny sip of wine. "I had lunch at Louie's Backyard with my friend Danielle and her mother and aunt. That was fun—not really business. Though I'm sure I'll use it for deep background someday. Then I went to the police press conference about the murder. Or death, I suppose is the right thing to call it until they tell us something else for sure. They are asking folks to come forward with any information about the bike ride. And they're starting to get very worried about the weather."

"Oh, they are not the only ones," said Mrs. Renhart. "Mr. R is threatening to have our boat towed away tomorrow, or the next day for sure. He thinks if he can get it positioned in Miami or Fort Myers, we'll have a better chance of riding out the storm."

"I don't know about that," said Miss Gloria. "First of all, the weather people are wrong about half the time. And what if you move it right into the path of the storm?"

"I know, but once he's got something in his head, there's no deflecting him." Mrs. Renhart sighed and patted her lap. Both of the new furry, elderly cats jumped up and began to butt her arms.

"That is so darling," said Miss Gloria. "You have a

knack for picking out pets." She glanced out on the horizon where a mountain range of clouds had settled in, tinged pink and gold by the sun. "Gordon and I finally decided the best thing to do when a storm threatens is tie her up good, hunker down with friends until it passes, and hope we get lucky." A sweet smile ghosted over her lips. "We always did, right up until the day he died. We always got lucky, I mean."

I reached for her hand and squeezed and we sat quietly for a moment, flooded with sadness about the loss of her husband. No matter how old and sick he'd been and how many great years they'd shared and how much time had passed, she missed him fiercely.

"What *did* the cops say about that woman's death in the zombie parade?" asked Mrs. Renhart.

"They don't seem to know much. Or as usual, they aren't saying much other than if anyone saw something fishy that she was eating or drinking or doing, they should come forward."

Miss Gloria asked: "What do you know about her?"

"Nothing," I admitted. "Except for what Danielle told me about how she conducted herself during the competition. And obviously that's one-sided."

"That poor Caryn Druckman was the one who died, right?" asked Mrs. Renhart. "I'm on her Instagram feed and I liked her page on Facebook too. She posts lots and lots of pictures of herself in fancy clothes at parties all around town. I don't know what they wear in Long Island in the winter, but in my opinion she packed the wrong outfits for Key West. Who wears sequins at the beach?"

I looked at her with new respect. Why had I assumed she didn't know what social media was?

"Supposing I go get my iPad. I can show you," she said. She handed off a cat to each of us and hurried into the cabin. While she was away, I poured the rest of my marginal chardonnay over the side of the boat. Not compelling enough to waste the calories and the brain cells on. Though I should have done the same with the cookie. But who could resist a red velvet Oreo? The gray cat, Jack, purred as I rubbed his head and then began to knead my thigh with his claws. Miss Gloria was having the same effect on Dinkels.

Within minutes, Mrs. Renhart returned with her iPad and swiped through several pages. "Here's her Instagram feed," she said. "You and she had one thing in common, anyway: an obsession with food." She grinned and showed us the screen, filled with squares of fuzzy food pictures. Most looked like restaurant meals, rather than home cooked.

"May I see?" I asked and reached for the device. Caryn Druckman had posted more than four hundred photographs. I recognized the cooked grouper sushi rolls and banana chicken from Seven Fish, steak and chocolate lava cake from Michaels, more fish from Pisces, and the beautiful island backdrop of Latitudes, the only restaurant on secluded Sunset Key just off Mallory Square pier where my mother and Sam were headed tonight.

"It's almost like she was an aspiring food critic," Miss Gloria exclaimed.

"Or she just loved to eat," I said. But then I began to look more closely at what she'd written about the photographs. She used all the major foodie hashtags. And she noticed and commented on details about how the places were set, and how hot the food was served, and the unusual ingredients in sauces and the side dishes—things that an ordinary diner might not pick up. She was demanding about restaurant food in the way professional chef Edel Waugh was, over at Bistro on the Bight. And her writing wasn't half bad. She could easily have performed my job.

"I wonder where she got her money?" Mrs. Renhart asked. "It's probably not fair to assume that she didn't work for it, but . . . I saw her in church a good bit and never heard a whit about a job."

And besides, the sheer volume of the photos she'd posted on Instagram suggested that most of her energy was caught up in food and the social scene of Key West's wealthiest galaxy.

A text buzzed in on my phone and I pulled it out of my pocket. I was surprised to see a message from Danielle's aunt Marion.

I thought of a few other things, call when you can? And she left her phone number.

"We should be toddling along anyway," said Miss Gloria to Mrs. Renhart. "Before I get light-headed and fall over the gunwale. Thank you so much for the cocktails, and congratulations on the new cats."

13

Everything tastes the same if you cook it long enough.

—Jessica Soffer,
Tomorrow There Will Be Apricots

Our two cats were waiting inside the screen door; they sniffed suspiciously at the strange odors we were bearing from Mrs. Renhart's felines. Evinrude made a noise like a dog growling, a gurgling way back in his throat. "We're going to have to keep an eye on these two," I said to Miss Gloria. "I'm afraid they could hurt those old guys."

I went into the galley to forage in the refrigerator, and came out with a bowl of leftover shrimp, a jar of capers, a couple of sticks of celery, two scallions, and mayonnaise. "Shrimp salad and biscuits with sliced tomatoes?" I asked Miss Gloria.

"Sounds like a miracle to me," she answered.

"We've got a couple of ripe ones on the back deck." She perched on the banquette and watched me begin to assemble the salad. "Here we've lived next to Mrs. Renhart for two years and hardly said boo to her. There's more to her than I might have imagined."

"Unfortunately, her husband is like an invisible shield, repelling visitors," I said with a chuckle, picturing us slamming into a wall of Lexan as we tried to climb aboard their craft. Not that I'd honestly tried that hard—and shame on me for that weakness.

Once I'd finished shelling and cleaning the shrimp, I began to dice the celery. Miss Gloria went out to her minigarden on the back deck, returning with a few sprigs of fresh dill, along with two big tomatoes and some basil.

While I mixed the salad and sliced tomatoes, Miss Gloria popped two of our favorite frozen leek biscuits into the microwave and then the toaster oven. My theory on baking: Make more than you imagine you can eat—you will never regret it when you find an unexpected treat preserved in your freezer.

When the food was ready, we settled onto the sofa in front of the TV, our plates on fold-up tables. While we watched the news, I told her about my mother's wedding anxieties, Danielle's no-show at the *Key Zest* meeting, and finding the video of Caryn Druckman falling off her bike.

She wiped her mouth with a napkin and set her fork on her plate. "Can I see it?" she asked.

I found the right frame, handed her the phone, and clicked on the play arrow. We both watched the disaster unspool in herky-jerky time, right up to the point where I'd realized something was wrong, quit filming, and lurched off my bike to help her.

"I didn't see anyone approaching with a syringe or any other weapon," Miss Gloria said. "You didn't hear gunshots or anything like that just before she fell?"

"The cops asked that," I said, shaking my head. "If someone got to her, I think it had to be earlier."

I punched through the previous photos, pausing again at the one containing the woman with the zebra face painting. Was her shape or dress familiar? The zombie costume made that impossible to tell. In the background, I noticed for the second time the Beach Eats truck, which had never crossed my radar and might fit in well with my takeout article. I zoomed in to see who was working the kitchen. A slender man in a chef's toque with a blond ponytail and a neat beard was loading some kind of food onto little plates.

A text flashed onto my screen. Thanks for being there today and always. Love Mom.

"Hot date tonight?" Miss Gloria asked.

"Not me," I said, and placed the phone on the TV tray, feeling a tiny bit blue. "Nathan's just too busy this week. So I'm thinking of buzzing over to Duval Street to see what's happening downtown." I explained how Jennifer Montgomery had told me about the face painter who had done the work on both Caryn Druckman and possibly the zebra-faced zombie I spotted near the Beach Eats food truck. "And I'm hoping to catch Victoria at the Aqua before her performance tonight," I said. "The Aquanettes had a lot of stage time during the coronation festivities. And I have a feeling

Victoria might have seen something important—she's super perceptive about stuff going on around her."

"You need that at a drag bar," said Miss Gloria with an impish grin.

As we ate, savoring the crunch of the shrimp and celery with the hint of vinegary capers against the sunny taste of Miss Gloria's tomatoes, we surfed over to the Weather Channel on TV to watch the latest update. The tropical depression that forecasters had worried about for the last several days was still hanging heavy east of Cuba. The longer it stalled, the more organized its internal rotation grew, said the hurricane specialist. Which spelled more concern for Florida, especially our fragile Keys, tossed across the ocean like a string of antique pearls. Even so, the projections for the path of the storm were all over the place. He demonstrated this with a screen of different-colored lines that looked like the crayon doodles of a three-year-old.

Miss Gloria's oldest son called as we finished clearing the supper dishes.

"Are you thinking of evacuating?" I heard him ask her in a booming voice.

I tiptoed away to get ready to go out. She could handle that question without me—living on a houseboat in her eighties, she practically had a graduate degree in managing offspring anxiety.

I parked my scooter near the intersection of Duval and Truman, thinking I would walk a few blocks west to the Aqua bar, chat with Victoria, look for Christy the face painter, and then scoot home. Rather than cooling off, the temperature seemed to have risen ten degrees since the sun went down, and the sidewalks were thick with folks who were ready to party. Some dressed for success, and some definitely not. The biggest party happened next Saturday, the day of the parade, but lots of people start the partying early and keep the machine fed all week.

Not even a block along my route, two men began yelling at each other, and a circle of party people gathered around to watch the show. Early for Duval Street, but I supposed all bets were off this week. One of the men was dressed like a local, jean shorts to the knees and a faded Paradise Pub T-shirt. The other man appeared to have almost nothing on other than body paint and a G-string in the shape of a fuzzy tropical bird.

"Maybe you didn't get the memo about Fantasy Fest," the local man said to the other. I had the feeling he would have grabbed him by the collar if there had been a collar to grab.

"Leave me alone, man," said the visitor, pushing the other man away.

"Fantasy Fest is a costume event. Did you see anywhere that you were invited to come naked and show us every butt-ugly bit of you? Who do you think wants to look at that?" He pointed at the parrot and spat on the sidewalk.

The bird man threw a big plastic cup of beer in the first man's face. The man with clothes lunged at him and they began to wrestle, tumbling from the sidewalk, off the curb and into the street. Other bystanders crowded closer, hooting and cheering. I heard the whoop whoop of a police siren and slithered through a small space in the crowd to get as far away as I could. What if that stuffed bird got dislodged in the struggle—ugh! So not my scene. I would come back in the light of day to talk with Jennifer's face-painting friend, when the craziest people would be sleeping the night off in their rented hotel rooms.

Minutes later, puffing for air, I bolted toward the Aqua bar. As I stood in the doorway, catching my breath, I saw Victoria sitting down for a break at the far side of the room. I headed over and took the seat across from her.

"People seem unusually crabby out there tonight," I said, hitching my thumb over my shoulder toward the street.

"It's so darn hot," she said, shrugging her elegant but wide shoulders. She adjusted her tube top and patted her forehead with a white hanky. "And besides, it's a mood. Key West is like all us other divas." She grinned. "Moody. I've seen her like this before. It will pass. Have you noticed the rants on Facebook? Everyone in Key West who's lived here more than five years is yearning for the old days when people really cared about service and food and kindness." She made air quotes with her fingers as she said those last words.

"I hope murder isn't part of that mood. Buy you a drink?" She nodded and I walked over to the U-shaped bar and ordered two bottles of beer.

"Is this a social visit only?" she asked as I set the drinks on the table.

"You know me too well." I laughed. "Tell me what it was like at the coronation party," I said. "I mean from the insider perspective. From where I sat in the audience, it went as smooth as silk, no troubles at all. I'm trying to understand whether there was some reason related to the voting or the contest that Caryn Druckman might have been murdered. The police aren't coming right out and saying that's what happened, but I think all signs are pointing in that direction."

Victoria took a dainty sip of her beer and closed her eyes to think. "Druckman was definitely a diva in the worst sense," she said. "She had us rearranging dance numbers like crazy. She had opinions about the blocking of the transitions, the key the songs were sung in, even the words."

"But did you see her arguing with anyone? Was anyone frustrated with her?"

Now Victoria burst out laughing. "The dead diva, god rest her soul, was a genuine pain in the patootie. Everyone was frustrated with her, everyone." She sat back in the chair, blinked her eyelashes—enviously longer than mine—and rubbed her chin. "But was there anyone in particular?"

I nodded, waiting.

"Your friend Danielle was nervous—she obviously hadn't performed a lot onstage, the way Druckman and the male candidates had. Wasn't that John-Bryan a stunner? He had the moves, baby. If only I was single." She sighed and sipped the beer. "But I digress. Your friend Danielle had two ladies with her—they looked a lot alike—who were buzzing around and pushing back."

"That would have been her mother and her aunt. Twins. So what happened? What do you mean by pushing back?"

"So Druckman pulled Danielle aside and told her she'd better stay at the back of the stage unless she was actually singing a number, because she danced like she had two left feet."

"She said that to her right during the show? That was mean."

Victoria nodded, applying a new coat of lipstick where the beer bottle had smeared the perfect red bow of her lips. "Danielle, of course, started to cry. That's when one of the twins came barreling up and lit into Druckman. Telling her she was a bully and not all that light on her feet besides. And maybe if she'd lay off the cheeseburgers and French fries, she'd look like she belonged in front of an audience. I didn't hear the rest because I was due onstage, but the MC separated them."

"Wow," I said. "And we in the crowd had no idea the real drama was backstage."

Just then the manager for the Aqua announced Victoria's next set. She blew me a kiss and sashayed off to sing.

14

*"Where did you source your ingredients
from?" one of them asked. "Are they local?"*

*"Yeah," Pat said, "they're from the
store about a mile from my house."*
—J. Ryan Stradal,
Kitchens of the Great Midwest

I woke the next morning feeling a little heavy and
gloomy. I wanted to write this off as an artifact of the
weird weather and the Fantasy Fest crowds, but I had
to admit that it felt more like loneliness. I loved seeing
my mother so crazy for Sam, and him even madder
for her. But seeing them so happy made me realize that
my slown-burning, slown-budding relationship with
Bransford had suddenly screeched to a halt. I had two
choices: mope like a dope or do something about it.

So I leaped out of bed, slugged down a cup of coffee,
and fed the cats. It was early enough that maybe I

could meet up with the detective at the dog park and entice him to breakfast at Harpoon Harry's. Not letting myself obsess about dressing for success—whatever that meant in this context—I pulled on khaki shorts and a *Key Zest* T-shirt and started across the island. The air didn't appear to have cooled off overnight, and if anything, the humidity felt higher. Almost like taking a shower on my scooter.

I toyed with trying to convince myself that the point of the trip to the dog park was to see Ziggy Stardust, Bransford's mini Doberman pinscher mix. But the truth was, I missed Bransford himself. In a yearning, schoolgirl kind of way, all mixed up with hopes and fears about my future, both short-term and long.

I parked at Higgs Beach, across the street from the large half-grass, half-sand park, fenced in by chain links. Every hour of the day, passersby could find a cluster of dog people sitting on white plastic chairs in the shade and watching their furbabies frolic. Bransford liked to get here early, both because of his work schedule and because he wasn't quite as sociable as some of the other fathers. Understatement of the week, or even the month.

From that distance, I saw a cluster of dogs chasing balls and wrestling. Then a small blur of black and brown emerged from the pack and bolted after a German shepherd. That was Ziggy, all right. He did not consider himself to be a candidate for the small-dog section. Just as Bransford himself was not a candidate for chitchat with regular people.

I scanned both the big-dog and the small-dog sections of the park, but saw no sign of the detective.

Surely he wouldn't have dropped the dog off alone? I stepped inside the gate and whistled for Ziggy. He did an about-face, bolted across the well-trodden lawn, and threw himself into my arms, leaving no question that a dog gives a more obvious welcome than a cat. Even my own Evinrude.

Ziggy licked my face and then scrambled to get back down and resume his chase. Still there was no Bransford. A young woman with glossy black hair, large sunglasses, and short shorts approached me. "I take it you and Ziggy are pals."

Did I know her? I scrolled through the possibilities. Bartender? Waitress? Shopkeeper? Police department? Nothing rang a bell. "Yes, Ziggy and I are friends. And you must be related—you have the same beautiful hair."

She let loose a peal of laughter. "Neighbors. Dog sitter. Which is yours?" She gestured at the pack of dogs frolicking.

"Oh, I don't own a dog," I said. "I'm a cat person really. But don't tell Ziggy."

She pursed her poofy pink lips. "You bring a cat to the dog park?"

"No, no, I was riding by and thought I'd say hello to Nathan Bransford if he was here."

"I'll tell him you were looking for him."

"Not really looking for him," I said, adding what I hoped was a casual grin.

"He's hard to keep track of. Popular guy." She grinned back, and then winked. "He texted me last night to say he wouldn't be home until lunchtime to-day and could I take the dog—"

"Wait." Her brows crinkled in worried lines. "But you're not—" She got more and more flustered as the seconds that felt like minutes ticked by. "I mean, I thought when . . ." She clapped her hand over her mouth. "I never do know when to shut up. And it's not any of my business anyway."

"Don't worry about it," I said, adding a pained smile. Ziggy caromed by, close on the tail of the big shepherd.

"It's just, well, maybe it had nothing to do with Carolyn."

She looked as though she was going to break into tears. And I didn't feel that solid either. I'd assumed he was busy with work, not his ex. The thought of her resurfacing made me queasy. More than queasy; I felt as if the floorboards had rotted out from under me and I was plunging down.

The young woman continued to yammer, her face flushing with distress. "I'm sure you know she's been in town a couple of times over the past few weeks. Dropped in, you know, kind of by surprise? Oh, this is so awkward. And I know perfectly well what she looks like." Her eyes raked me from top to bottom. She cupped her hands by her chest, the universal sign for expansive cleavage. Something I did not share with his ex.

"And she's got the biggest brown eyes and that dark hair . . ." Her hands made sweeping wavy motions that mimicked the way the former Mrs. Bransford's gorgeous tresses cascaded off her shoulders. "She doesn't look a bit like you."

There was no graceful way to back out of this, so I

just waved and trotted across the street back to my scooter. I would not think about Bransford's ex coming to Key West, several times if that young woman was a credible witness. And possibly out all night with her . . . I slapped myself on the thigh. I needed to get to work, do something useful, write some sparkling words, and help Danielle. Quit dwelling on a man I apparently didn't know well enough to trust and certainly couldn't control.

But then the alarm on my iPhone began to beep, reminding me that I had an exercise training appointment with Leigh at the WeBeFit gym. No one would ever accuse me of being one of the gym rats who loved to exercise, but in my line of work it had become a necessary evil. I couldn't eat what I wanted to eat, as often as I wanted to eat it, without expending some calories in the other direction. I hired Leigh to keep me motivated, because I stunk at doing it by myself. I'd learned a few tricks too, like if I distracted Leigh with interesting conversation, she tended to go a little easier on me. Maybe even forget how high she was counting and cut the repetitions off early. Today I thought I had an excellent topic.

I powered into WeBeFit, trying to look as though I belonged in this gym community, which already bristled with energy and testosterone. The few other female exercisers in spandex and leggings looked fit and satisfied, not bedraggled like me, like someone who'd been out on Duval most of the night. Leigh was waiting at the front desk, a tall blond dancer, known for being tough but mostly fair with her clients.

She looked me up and down. "You're going to work

out in that?" she asked with a quizzical lift of her brows.

I mumbled something about being frazzled by Fantasy Fest and not getting to the Laundromat.

"You forgot your appointment, didn't you?"

I made a face and shrugged. "I'll get by in this, maybe even start a new trend in workout clothes."

"Mmm, doubtful." She directed me to begin by doing the bank robber shoulder stretches that she knew I hadn't had time to run through before the session. Sitting in the hallway with my back pressed against the wall, I raised and lowered my arms as if in a stickup, and she stood over me like the robber with a gun.

"You need a sense of humor about your laggard clients," I said once I'd finished.

"I know," Leigh said, "but can you imagine the weight I carry with ten to twelve clients a day who don't really want to be here? The worst are the ones who try to trick me out of their workouts." She raised an eyebrow. "I know you'd never do that, Hayley."

Then she waved me over to a horizontal bar and indicated that I should start a set of push-ups. She'd moved the bar several inches lower than our previous session. So far my distraction technique wasn't working perfectly.

"So what are you frazzled over?" she asked when I'd finished.

I explained the news about Mrs. Druckman's death, which she'd already heard, and the apparent lack of suspects aside from Danielle. "Say, have you eaten at the Beach Eats truck?" I asked. I slid my phone out of the back pocket and showed her the photo from the zombie parade. "Do you know this guy?"

"That looks a lot like Grant Monsarrat. He's good friends with the owner and was probably moonlighting for the event. He's usually the chef at Paradise Pub. I think I heard he's buying the place."

"The staff were crabby buggers when I was at the pub the other day," I said. "They lost my order and I finally gave up on it. In fact, everybody's crabby on this island, including me." I described the fight I'd witnessed the night before on Duval Street.

"You have to remember that the locals sometimes behave like eighth graders," she said, adding a grin. "And I'm including myself in there. Sometimes we're not so crazy about the outsiders swarming the island. And you might remember from junior high school, when a clique gets threatened, they can lash out."

"Are you saying Caryn Druckman was killed because she wasn't a local?"

"I'm not suggesting she was murdered by a local, but I'm saying feelings run high when it comes to this subject," Leigh said. "People waltz in here thinking they can shove a new business down people's throats and keep it afloat with tourist money. And locals get mad about that. And there's some legitimate reasoning behind this too, because who's here to order food or sit at the bar in the steamy off-season when no tourist would set foot on the island? The locals are, that's who." She started me on a series of squats and biceps curls that kept me breathless.

"I get what you're saying," I said, once I'd struggled

back to a standing position. My biceps quivered like the mint jelly my grandmother used to serve with a leg of lamb. "I try to be sensitive to that when I'm writing reviews. I hope I don't come off as a know-it-all insider."

She grinned. "Most of the time, you're okay."

We slogged through the rest of my workout without much conversation.

"See you next time," Leigh said, "unless the hurricane gets us first." She turned to greet her next victim, and I went to the ladies' room to gather my stuff and wash my face.

When I finally dragged myself out of the gym, feeling every muscle throb but unreasonably proud of my effort, I checked my phone. Nothing from Bransford—big surprise. Not a word from Danielle, either, which worried me. It wasn't like her not to show up at work yesterday and not to be in touch. I decided that eight o'clock was a decent hour to call, considering the level of my concern. She answered right away, her voice shaky and low.

"What the heck, Danielle?" I said. "Where are you? We're worried sick about you. You never miss a staff meeting."

Pause.

"Sorry, Hayley. I've been so ill. You don't want to hear the details. I'll just leave it there."

"Did you eat something bad?" Always the first thought in the food critic's mind. Because if you eat out as often as I do, you're bound sooner or later to ingest a bad clam. But I'd had lunch with her yesterday—we all ordered the same fish tacos—and I'd never felt the slightest bit queasy. "Is the stomach flu going around?" I asked.

"I don't know anybody sick," she said. "My mother thinks it's vertigo—that thing where the crystals in your ear get discombobulated and throw off your balance."

"Doesn't that mostly happen to senior citizens?" I asked, not wanting to scare her with the next thing that popped into my mind: that she'd somehow gotten hold of the same poison that killed Caryn Druckman. Maybe in a lesser dose . . . but still . . . scary.

"Have you been to the doctor?" I asked, and then added before she could protest: "I think you should go."

"It's just a little stomach upset," she said.

"Then you would have come to work."

"How mad was Palamina?"

I hemmed. "Luckily, she was distracted by the weather."

15

*The next day, I buttered a slice of it, deli-
cious and long-deferred toast, and had it
with my coffee. As toast always will, it
seemed morning-bright, and clean of com-
plications. Women, I thought, remember
everything. Bread forgives us all.*
            —Adam Gopnick, "Bread and
                Women," *The New Yorker*,
                        November 4, 2013

By the time I reached my scooter, I realized that I was
starving. Not that a half hour training session burned
that many calories, but try telling that to my gut. I
would take a spin over to Grant Monsarrat's kitchen
and kill two birds with one stone: ask him what he'd
seen at the zombie parade and hope to grab something
to eat that would tide me over until lunch and possibly
beef up my takeout piece.

I parked the bike and approached the restaurant,

which looked deserted and mostly dark. No surprise, as they were known more for late-night action than breakfast. Though I thought I remembered their hours as eight a.m. to two a.m.—someone should be minding the stove. I tried the front door first, but it was locked. So I went around back, past the ripe-smelling Dumpsters and stacks of recyclable cardboard waiting on wooden pallets. The lights in the high windows of the kitchen were on and the door was propped open. Outside, two slightly dusty calico kittens lapped milk from a foil pie pan. The smell of bacon frying wafted from the kitchen and caused my stomach to growl.

"Hello!" I called, poking my head inside the door. Shelves loaded with cans of tomatoes and beans and sweetened condensed milk and sacks of rice and flour and sugar lined the short hallway. "Anybody home?"

Half a minute later, Grant appeared—the chef I'd seen cooking in the Beach Eats truck, his hair pulled back in a man-bun, eyes early-morning red, and a fresh apron tied around his narrow waist. "Help you?" he asked, looking behind me and to either side. "Bring your truck around back. I don't like to drag the stuff through the restaurant."

"Oh, I'm not here for a delivery," I said. "I'm Hayley Snow. I'm the food critic for *Key Zest* magazine."

His nose wrinkled and he shook his head—disgusted. "I'm in no shape to provide you a meal right now. We're shorthanded and struggling to get our prep done for the day. Come back later when we open, and I'll make you anything you'd like."

I tossed off a laugh. "I know better than to ask for special treatment. Never fair to surprise the chef off hours and expect a decent meal. That's not why I came." I paused, wondering how to explain. Why would he care what happened to a stranger? How to put this so he wouldn't slam the door in my face? Direct was always best. "I need a tiny minute of your time to ask some questions about the zombie parade and the woman who died there. You were working the Beach Eats truck—am I right?"

His lips pinched shoelace thin. "Yes. But if you're asking about what happened to her, I didn't know the woman. Didn't see anything. There's nothing I can add. You know this is Fantasy Fest week, right? We're expecting to do two hundred covers tonight. That's twice our usual traffic. I'd like to help, but I don't know anything and, like I said, I'm slammed." He started to back away. One of the kittens ran over and wound between his legs. He scooped it up and kissed its head.

"I'm surprised that you have time to work here and in the food truck both," I said, trying a sympathetic smile as he put the cat back down. "But everyone on this island has to grind harder than we ever think is possible while the crowds are here, right?"

"A friend owns Beach Eats," he said. "I help him out in a pinch once in a while for big events."

My stomach growled loud enough that both of us could hear. I patted my midriff and grinned. "Sorry," I said. "Your bacon got to me. I was so hoping to include this place in my killer takeout roundup, but the text is due to my editor this afternoon. There was a mix-up with my order the other day, so I didn't get to try your food."

He wiped a hand over his forehead, shifted from

one foot to another. "Staffing this kitchen is a beast sometimes. I'm sorry we messed up the other day. I could make you a bacon, egg, and cheese on a hard roll. Tell you about some of our takeout dishes. That's the best I can do."

"I would love that," I said. "I would be so grateful."

He scooted the kitten back outside, then held the door open and directed me to a stool by the stainless steel counter in the middle of the room. "My sous-chef called in sick this morning. I'm afraid he's got the Duval Street flu. Do you know Kat, aka Catfish?" He grinned and pointed to a woman wearing a white coat and a long dark braid who was chopping vegetables near the sink.

"Yes, I think we met the other day when there was a little mix-up with the takeout."

"Apologies for that," Kat said with a warm smile. "It's so hard to get decent help on this island." She wiped her hands on her apron and bustled across the kitchen to shake my hand.

"She's our hostess with the mostest, and my front of the house manager, but she helps out in the kitchen too, thank god," said Grant. "That's what I love about this place—there is always someone willing to pitch in when I need it. Although to be honest, usually it's Kat. She doesn't have culinary training, but you know what she does have?"

I shook my head. "Her grandmother's recipe stash?"

They both laughed.

"No," he said. "She's super loyal. She understands my vision and she wants to help me achieve it."

"You deserve it, knucklehead," she said, chuckling again.

Grant scrubbed his hands at a small sink in the corner of the kitchen and then took his place at the stove located on the central island. I slid onto the stool across from him and began to ask him about the menu, the touches that made their burger special (blue cheese, bacon, and a homemade sweet red pepper relish), the double frying process they used for potatoes, their patented tweaks in the Key West Cobb salad, substituting shrimp and mango for the usual chicken and avocado. As he talked, he cracked an egg onto the sizzling griddle, flipped it over once the edges crisped, and swaddled it with a thick slice of orange cheese. Then he loaded the whole thing onto a toasted roll, along with five strips of perfectly crunchy bacon.

"We believe that bacon goes with everything," he said. "And cheese, too, everywhere we can think of. Sweet dreams are made of cheese, you know?" He sliced the sandwich in half and put it in front of me. "Coffee?"

"Heaven," I said. "With a splash of milk? Thanks." I bit into the sandwich, savoring the slightly runny yolk, the melted cheese, the perfectly crisped bacon. Then I remembered I should have taken a photo. I put the breakfast roll back down and rearranged it so my teeth marks didn't show, then snapped a few pix.

"So you own this place?" I asked.

"He will in a couple of weeks," said Kat proudly. "It's in the works. We were just thinking about names."

"You don't want to stick with Paradise Pub?" I

asked. "You'd have the name recognition factor. This restaurant has been around awhile, right? I've heard the locals like it." I blushed, realizing I was reminding them that even though I liked to consider myself a local, I'd never set foot in their place.

"Yeah, it's been around," said Grant. "But I'm not sure we want that kind of recognition. The former owner didn't care a spit about cleanliness or trying out new recipes or anything. He wanted us to just serve the same slop every day."

"What names are in the running?" I asked, wiping up a bit of melted cheese on my plate with the last nugget of hard roll. A shame to let any of it go uneaten.

"I think it should have his name in it," said Kat. "All the famous chefs do that. Like *Grant's You That* or *Grant's Grub* or *Grant's Reef* or *Grant's Gruel*. Or how's this: *Granted!* with an exclamation point at the end."

"The famous chefs are full of sh—" He stopped and looked at me. "Hot air. That's why they have to keep their names in the limelight. In case someone should forget how important they are." He laughed, the skin around his eyes crinkling as he relaxed.

"Maybe something that highlights your food," said Kat. "Say, *Cheese Wiz* or *Mustard's Last Stand*."

"The Daily Rind!" I added, pointing at the pile of bacon on the counter.

Grant groaned.

"What were you considering?" I asked.

"Something a little nautical, maybe, or Key West-y at least. *Conch'd Out? Squealin' Keel? Bar None? Salty Crock?*"

"I like all of those," I said. "A little bit funky, which

I think is what you're going for." He nodded. "So the other day, at Beach Eats, what were you serving?" I asked.

"Zombie everything," he said, smiling grimly. "Death stalks a cupcake with spooky green hands poking out of the icing, killer cookies with skulls painted on them, stuff like that."

"And were you serving only to the royal court?" I asked.

"What sense would that make?" asked Kat, who was now banging pots and pans into the sink full of sudsy water. "The idea is to make money so we can get paid." She laughed and wiped her forehead with a soapy hand. "Sorry, but I get annoyed when everyone thinks we should give our food away."

Grant glanced over at her, then back at me. "Why do you ask?"

"One of the theories the police are considering about Caryn Druckman is that she was poisoned," I said with way more authority than I had any right.

"You can't think we poisoned her?" said Grant, his voice vibrating with outrage. "And then you have the nerve to come here and beg for breakfast?"

I held both hands up. "Slow down, I'm certainly not accusing anyone of anything. It's just that my friend Danielle is on the hot seat and I don't know where to turn to try to help her. My thought was you might have seen something that didn't look right. Or maybe we'll think of something together."

Kat came across the kitchen to stand next to the chef. She put her hand on his arm, patting the golden hairs that shone above his tan. "As Grant said, we were serving sweet treats and lemonade, like that," she said. "Our stuff was geared more to the younger set. There were other booths serving beer and wine—lots of booze goes down the hatch this week. And the cart with hot dogs—remember?" She glanced up at him and crooked a smile. "They were boiled, not grilled, and not one decent condiment to disguise them other than that hideous yellow mustard. And even worse, no-brand ketchup."

She stuck her tongue out, and then wiped her hands on her apron. "Ugh. The thing is, if any of the food was poisoned, how in the world could there be only one victim? Surely she wasn't the only person in that big crowd to eat whatever it was she ate."

Sensing a stray bit of cheese, I patted my cheek with a napkin. "Yes, exactly. That's what makes figuring it out so hard. What if Mrs. Druckman was terribly allergic to something, but all the other people who didn't have allergies were fine?"

"Nice to meet you," said Kat. "I need to get the stuff put away in the pantry before the crowds get here." She waved and disappeared into a big closet on the far side of the room.

"We always worry about peanuts," said Grant, who appeared to have recovered from my possible accusation. Or at least he was pretending. "We avoid them like the plague even though I have a killer recipe for Asian peanut sauce."

I nodded, remembering how livid Chef Edel Waugh had been when someone replaced the olive oil in her kitchen with peanut last December. On her bistro menu, they'd made a big deal of insisting they used no tree nuts in their food. A customer's anaphylactic shock could have cost her a fortune in money and reputation. "If you remember anything, give me a buzz, okay?" I gave him one of my *Key Zest* business cards and thanked him again for breakfast.

Outside in the parking lot, the stray kittens had finished the milk and were grooming each other. I paused for a minute, watching the little cats circle each other and finally curl into a fuzzy ball of black, orange, and white fur.

Could a man who fed stray cats kill someone? Of course it depended on the stakes. How much of his skin was in the game. And what was the game? I shook my head. Why was I even thinking about this? What sense did it make to accuse him—even in the privacy of my own mind—when there were plenty of other food trucks at the event, not to mention ten thousand zombies. Besides, he was a nice man, serious about his restaurant, who worked two jobs to make it happen. And made a killer breakfast. I was pricking the wrong soufflé. I puffed out some air and got on my scooter, pondering what to do next.

Considering the humidity and the fact that I'd exercised in my street clothes, I desperately needed a shower. Everything on me, down to the pores of my skin, now reeked of sweat and bacon. But I also needed to get to *Key Zest* and polish the final edits on my takeout article. And track down Christy Haussler, the face painter. And find Seymour, Danielle's king. And by the way, find out what the heck was actually going on with Danielle.

16

Do not allow watching food to replace making food.

—Alton Brown

First stop, I decided, would be Duval Street and chatting with Christy. Then the office. Then home for a shower before chasing down Seymour. I drove a few blocks south on Caroline Street and parked in front of the Coffee Plantation. As I approached Duval, I had to remind myself that it was barely nine a.m. This four-block section of the street had been designated by the city as the "fantasy zone." In a nutshell, this meant that so-called costumes that would not be acceptable anywhere else could be trotted out here. I would not try to tackle the question of why a person would want to wear them in public.

Keeping my eyes averted from the more daring ensembles, I hurried along the sidewalk to find the painters. A woman resembling the description that Jennifer had given me was working in a booth between Caroline and Charles Streets. The booths were set back from the sidewalk and about two feet above street level. Jennifer's friend, a stocky woman with short hair and a pleasant smile, faced out toward Duval with her paints spread out on a tray, while her customer faced in. The woman being painted wore an athletic bra top and shorts. Still revealing for ordinary social circles, but modest in fantasy zone terms.

"Good morning, are you Christy?" I called. "I'm Hayley; Jennifer mentioned me to you yesterday?"

She laughed, a lovely silver tinkle. "I wondered if you'd been scared away. Come on up. How can I help?"

I made my way closer and took a seat on a folding chair that had been squeezed into her booth. My legs were almost touching those of her customer. I paused, once again wondering how much to say and how to explain my own involvement. I pulled out my phone and showed her the photo of the scene at West Martello before the parade had begun. The direct approach had insulted Grant and his sidekick Kat, but I shouldn't have that problem here.

"See the person with the zebra stripes on her face? Is that kind of painting familiar to you? It seems that the police consider her to be a person of interest in the zombie bike ride death."

Which wasn't true exactly, as Torrence had told me the zebra face was no longer a lead they were following. But honestly I didn't believe him. And I was beginning to feel desperate.

"Excuse me for a second?" Christy asked her customer. She put her paintbrush down, took my phone, and studied the photo. While she looked, I noticed a photograph on her tray that her customer must have brought, and compared it in my mind to the painting emerging on the woman's face and neck. The backdrop was a deep blue, speckled with planets and stars in silver and gold. Sweeping across the woman's chest and neck up onto her face, I recognized Orion's Belt and one of the dippers. And Pegasus, Zeus's horse, thundered across her forehead.

"This is completely lovely," I said. "One of the most beautiful paintings I've seen."

"Thank you," the woman said. "This is my fourth Fantasy Fest and I wouldn't go to anyone other than Christy."

Christy blushed and nodded her thanks and returned my phone. "To me it looks like an amateur job. Do you see? The demarcation between the white and the black is blurry, almost as if they either hurried the work or the painter's hands were shaking." She held out her own hand and looked at the fingers. "That would be a career ender, right?"

Her customer nodded.

"You're trying to figure out what happened to the woman who died while cycling." Christy rubbed her chin thoughtfully.

"Do you remember painting this woman's face?" I flicked through my photos until I found a decent one of Druckman. "Jennifer wondered if it might have been you because the transitions were so sharp." I pointed at the woman beside me. "Similar to what you're doing here."

Christy shook her head. "Nope, not mine. And

I didn't get there until almost four because I was busy here, so I missed the excitement."

"You were riding in the parade too?"

"Oh no," she said, laughing again. "There is no rest for the wicked this week. I sell ice cream most nights at Mallory Square. But if there's another event on the island that allows food vendors, I try to be there too. So I had towed my ice cream cart over to East Martello for the last couple of hours of the party. I was parked over there." She tapped the right side of the screen. "You can't quite see it in this photo. And then once the zombies took off toward Duval, I had to hustle up to Mallory Square and set up all over again."

I certainly wasn't going to say it aloud, but if Caryn Druckman ate ice cream right before she collapsed . . .

"So can you think of anyone who paints like this?" I asked.

"None of my friends off the top of my head," she said. "I'll keep my eyes open though."

Once I thanked her and admired the constellation painting again, I hustled back to my scooter and zipped over to the office. Nine o'clock. I had just enough time to tighten up my article, add a snippet about Grant's breakfast sandwich, and check in with Danielle.

Palamina had beaten me to work. For today, she'd dyed her hair a deep red, and she wore a flowing purple sash or scarf over what appeared to be a black cat body suit. I stuck my hand in her office to wave hello—a miracle that she and Wally could survive in that small space—and trotted back to my cubby.

I scratched out a tentative first line.

One thing about Key West, it's an island. A small, compact space with lots of restaurants to choose from within blocks of most domiciles. And that means the urge for takeout food is not quite so, well, urgent.

A lousy lead if I'd ever written one. But even though Palamina tended to drive me bonkers, hovering over our schedule and our work as though we hadn't a brain cell flickering among us, she had given me one tip that I used over and over: You can fix anything, but you can't fix words that haven't been written. She was a fast writer—once she'd done the research for a story and had a little time to mull it over, she poured all her ideas out on the page. Then she could hone and shape and polish.

So I scribbled my fractured impressions of the visit to Grant Monsarrat's kitchen onto the page. When I heard Wally clomp up the stairs, I saved the document and went down the hall to join them. "Morning, Wally," I said. He smiled in response, but Palamina cut him off before he could answer.

"Where's Danielle?" she asked as I took my customary seat. Nearest the door. A psychological escape valve.

"Sick," I said, trying not to look guilty. I wasn't technically lying, simply repeating what Danielle had said. Was it the truth? Doubtful.

Palamina frowned, tossed the fringed end of her purple scarf over her shoulder, and banged her fist on the desk. "Who's going to put the magazine together? Dammit. We can't wait for next week—we're surfing the Fantasy Fest wave. Next week is way too late; we'll be waterlogged trash on the beach of magazine life."

Even furious, Palamina waxed poetic.

"Let me give her a quick buzz. I'll be right back."

I leaped up and raced down to my office, punching in Danielle's number as I went.

"Palamina's having a heart attack," I said without greeting her. "Where are you?"

"Sick," she croaked.

"Really?"

"Scared sick," she said. "The police have been here again." Her voice dropped to a hoarse whisper. "How can you be dating that man? I mean, he's a hunk, for sure, but he's so mean."

Of course she meant Bransford. My first instinct was to defend him, until I remembered that he was probably entertaining his ex this week. "I think that nightmare's over. I'll tell you more when I see you. What did he do?"

"The worst was when he made me drag out my zombie costume and the two of them spent twenty minutes going over it."

"Looking for what?" I asked, trying to imagine what kind of evidence might have rubbed off onto the killer from the victim.

"You think they told me anything? And then they took it with them."

"I'll see if I can find out what they're looking for, but for now, get out of your bunny slippers and nightgown and get your butt in here. Thirty minutes, got it?" I trotted back into Palamina's office.

"She got mixed up on the time—she'll be here in half an hour. She's taken so much cough syrup that I think her brains are addled."

I didn't look at Wally, because he knew me—he'd be able to tell that I was lying. I caromed back to my office to do a little more work while we waited for Danielle. First, I texted Torrence to ask why the cops were bothering Danielle. Then I flicked through the messages on my phone and realized that I had not returned the call from Danielle's aunt. And given how the cops had visited Danielle again, and how weird she was acting, and what Victoria witnessed between Danielle and Caryn Druckman at the Coronation Ball, it felt important to call her back.

I punched redial to return her call. "Marion, it's Hayley. So sorry I didn't get back to you yesterday. I've been running from one thing to the next."

"Not a problem," she said, her voice pressured. "It's just that we're all worried about Danielle. I know she would never hurt a flea and her mother knows it and I think you do too, but I'm not so sure the police feel the same way."

I channeled my psychologist friend, Eric—I missed his calming influence, but he was busy distributing extra therapy hours necessitated by the zaniness of the Fantasy Fest week. So instead of blurting out questions and suspicions and observations in my usual haphazard way, I said: "Uh-huh?"

"She was in over her head in this competition," said Danielle's aunt. "She never imagined it would turn out so cutthroat. I've been around the block a few times, so when there's a competition, I always expect a few people to turn sour."

"You were ready to stick up for her if she needed you."

"Of course," she said. "We're family. And not just One Human Family, but blood." One Human Family is the motto of the City of Key West, designed to remind us of our tolerance and acceptance of all kinds of people.

"Did she end up needing you?" This trying to let the other person talk without interruption in order to let the real story emerge, as Eric did in his therapy practice every day, was turning out to be harder than I'd expected.

"She did," said her aunt with a curt laugh. "I gave that unpleasant woman a piece of my mind. And told her she'd have me to answer to if she didn't back off." She was silent for a moment. "I know you're dating that detective. I was just thinking, if it comes up, you could mention to him that we Kamens stick together. I hope you don't misunderstand me. I would never have hurt her, but I wasn't going to sit on the sidelines and watch her badger my niece. You get what I mean. Don't you?"

"Uh-huh." I was about to tell her that even if I saw Bransford this week, the chances of our discussing her intentions toward the dead woman were minuscule, when I heard Danielle come into the office. Then came Wally's whistle, calling the meeting to order. "Gotta go," I said, and hung up quickly.

Danielle looked worse than I'd ever seen her. Blond

hair uncombed and greasy, bags gray like ashes under her eyes, and worst of all, a pair of faded, stained, aqua-colored sweatpants that I wouldn't have worn in my own bedroom. Not that I was looking my best either at this very moment, but Danielle prided herself on her grooming. Adorable outfits, perfect makeup, and not a hair out of place—she'd gotten only more meticulous running for queen. She was blathering apologies to Palamina about her tardiness as I came into her office.

"Are you feeling any better?" I asked as I took a seat, wiggling my eyebrows as a signal to slow down. I put both hands on my upper chest and demonstrated taking a huge breath, my shoulders rising and then releasing along with the air I'd taken in.

Danielle took a shallow breath that I doubted would help one bit. "Not really. A little. I'll survive. We have a lot to do today, right?"

"Correct." Palamina drummed long purple fingernails on her desk. "I've written my piece on the press conference, though they didn't give us much to work with. And done a follow-up call with Lieutenant Torrence." She glanced at me. "I don't know how you get anything out of him. With me, he was closed up like a sick oyster."

I bit my lip to keep from snickering out loud. He would not appreciate that description, though he'd probably admit he hated getting grilled about police matters by outsider journalists desperate for headlines. "Lots of chocolate," I said. "That's the best way to grease his skids."

Wally winked behind her back. "Next time, maybe

put Hayley on it. She's been massaging her relationship with the PD since she arrived on the island. It's like everything around here. You're not considered 'local' until you've been here a couple of decades."

"Massaging?" I grimaced. "That's an unfortunate description. How about *refining* or *improving* or *developing*? Sheesh." I took my own shallow breath. "On the food front, I should have the takeout piece ready later today. Chef Grant made me an amazing breakfast sandwich this morning, and I have the section on Garbo's Grill ready to roll. And I finished the zombie bike ride piece yesterday. It's short because of the tragedy, okay? It didn't seem right that that story should make a big splash right now."

Palamina nodded, looked at the list on her iPad and then back at me. "And you're attending and reporting on the pet masquerade this evening. Can you get that to me before nine-ish?"

"Um, sure." I'd forgotten all about that, but I knew my mother would be happy to attend, and probably Sam too.

"Wally's finishing up with our advertisers, so that's under control. Danielle, I'd like to have you work on the layout today so we can make sure it's good to go in the morning."

"I'll do that, no problem," said Danielle. "And I'm so sorry about being late." Her eyes were glassy and her lips quivered like tomato aspic.

Palamina's eyes narrowed and she stared Danielle down. "Speaking of the press conference, I heard a few rumors that you might be a suspect. Do I need to point out how crucial it is that you keep the rest of us apprised? We can't afford a conflict of interest if we're reporting on the story. Not even a whiff."

"Look," I said, "if Danielle was a serious suspect, she wouldn't be here. She'd be in the county jail. And your concern would be a moot point."

Wally nodded. "And who is going to put the e-zine together if we send Danielle home? I completely trust that she'll let us know what we need to know." He put his hand on Danielle's shoulder and stared back at Palamina.

"Okay. That's all I've got for now," said Palamina after a minute of silence.

"Come on back to my office," I said to Danielle. "I'll show you what I have for photos so you have a general idea for the layout." Which she didn't need—she could lay out a magazine issue in her sleep, but I was afraid she'd melt down in the front office if I didn't do an intervention.

She trailed me down the hallway and burst into tears once I'd shut my door behind us. "What in the world did Bransford think was on your costume?" I hissed.

"Honest to gosh, they think I killed that woman," she sniffled. "If I had any idea that this stupid contest would end up getting me involved in a murder case, I never would have signed up. No matter how much money I raised for AIDS Help."

"Did he actually say you are a suspect? Because like I said to Palamina, if they really had any decent evidence, you wouldn't be sitting here looking like yesterday's leftovers. You'd be wearing an orange jumpsuit." I felt as though I needed to be definite and stern with her or she'd reel out of orbit and never come back. I handed her a tissue. She wiped her eyes and tucked her hair behind her ears.

"They keep making me go over the story, as if I'll tell the truth the second, third, fourth, fifth time through. I told him everything I knew the first time around. Druckman was unpleasant to the point of cruel, but it never occurred to me to hurt her. And besides, I won that silly contest. Wouldn't it make more sense to knock her off if I'd been desperate for the crown, but she'd won, and I could then step in and take over?" Danielle sat up and straightened her shoulders. "And besides that, how the heck was I going to kill the woman when I was at the front of the bike parade? What, did I poison her and spill the substance on my outfit? Are they stupid?"

"Not so much stupid. Dogged," I said. "That's more like it. And you could have given her some kind of long-acting poison and then moved on past her."

Suddenly she focused on me, looking me up and down as if noticing my appearance for the first time. "It's like it's casual Friday around here. Or sloppy Friday, anyway. Except for the big boss."

I laughed. "We both look like something the garbage men left behind. Next stop for me is the houseboat to take a shower."

"What am I going to do about this murder suspect business?" she asked, her face getting pink and her lower lip quivering. "You can say everything you want about how their questions are standard procedure, but you didn't see the look in your boyfriend's eyes when they put my stuff in the evidence bag. He thinks I did it. And I really, really need your help." Tears welled up in her eyes and threatened to spill over.

I grabbed her by the shoulders. "Look, first of all, you should talk to a lawyer. Call Eric; he can tell you who to use. And then you've got to pull yourself together and set up the magazine. Go on about your business as usual. I'll get my article to you ASAP. And then I'm going to talk to Seymour and see if he noticed anything the day of the bike ride." A sudden thought struck me. "Aren't you supposed to reign over the pet masquerade contest tonight?"

Now the tears gushed down her cheeks. "I don't think I can handle any more publicity," she said. "If Palamina's heard rumors—and, trust me, no one tells *her* anything—imagine what's really circulating around town."

I squeezed her shoulders again. "You can do this. Think sticks and stones. Get your work done, and then go home and get beautiful. I'll meet you at the Casa Marina at five. My mother wanted to go anyway. We'll figure it out, okay?"

She didn't say anything.

"Okay?" I asked again. "It will look a lot worse if you don't show up."

17

We say grace and then we Instagram and then we eat.
          —Overheard in a cupcake shop
                  in Adelaide, Australia

As I parked my scooter in the Tarpon Pier lot, a gust of wind blew up, nearly knocking it over. I set the kickstand, glancing at the sky. Except for the super-humidity, it looked like a perfect day. Blue sky, light breeze, with only the occasional gust. On the far eastern horizon I did spot a small mass of gray clouds.

Hearing the unexpected roar of a big boat engine up our finger, I broke into a trot. As I reached our houseboat, I saw where the noise was coming from. The Renharts' boat was now connected to a small tug, smaller than the size of their home. The lines securing the houseboat had been untied from the dock. As the tug backed away, churning the water behind it and spewing clouds of black diesel, their houseboat pulled out of its slip.

Mrs. Renhart was out on the deck in a lawn chair clutching the elderly black cat. Dinkels, I thought was its name. Schnootie the schnauzer ran back and forth across the deck barking like a maniac. Jack, the long-haired gray cat, peered out of the galley window, probably wondering what the heck he'd gotten into.

"We'll see you next week, after the storm passes through," Mrs. Renhart yelled over the noise of the engine and the schnauzer. "I think he's overreacting, but Mr. Renhart insisted." She buried her face in the cat's fur. "Be safe," she called out.

"We will!" I hollered back. "See you in a couple of days, I hope."

The engine revved up louder, and she shouted something else that I couldn't make out clearly, but it sounded like *Instagram*. I pulled out my phone and took a photo of the boat, then posted this to my Insta-gram account, adding the tags #goodneighbors and #roadtrip and #KeyWest in the text box. And then I tagged her account. Whether Mr. Renhart was right or wrong about the storm, the sight of their boat steam-ing toward the cut that would release them from the safe confines of the Garrison Bight to the Gulf of Mex-ico freaked me out. What if the big one was really coming?

Connie emerged from the cabin of their boat with baby Clare perched in a carrier on her back. Clare gurgled and smiled. "Say hi to Auntie Hayley," Connie said in a singsong voice and waggled the baby's hand into a wave. "She's the one who gave you those sweet

Babar books, signed by the author himself. And you can touch the pages when you turn twenty-one. Wearing gloves."

I burst out laughing. "They aren't that valuable. Maybe if they had been signed by the original de Brunhoff. Can you believe that the Renharts have bolted out of town?"

Connie's face fell. "I was just coming down to tell you. We're leaving too."

Then I noticed that all her gorgeous tropical plants—including the mini lime tree and an old fig she was desperately protective of—had been moved off their deck.

"Ray thinks I'm crazy," she said. Then shrugged. "It's just nothing's the same with a baby. I can't bear the thought of taking a risk that might put her in danger. So we've rented a condo in Orlando for a couple of days. We'll see Disney. I've never been to Harry Potter World in Universal Studios. And this way, when Clare agitates to visit Mickey Mouse because all the other kids are going, I can tell her she's already been. And I'll have pictures to prove it."

She looked as if she was going to cry, so I pulled her into a hug. "I understand; life feels different with a baby to protect."

"Ray's going to tie some extra lines on the boat and we're packing up some things—mostly hers." She patted Clare's plump little arm. "And we'll call you along the way. The condo has two bedrooms," she added. "You'd be welcome."

"Hmmm, two cats, Miss Gloria, my mother, Sam, and me, all in one bedroom? I think we'll take our

chances. But keep me posted and I'll do the same." I
hugged her again and kissed the baby's forehead, then
returned to my home.

Inside our boat, Miss Gloria had the Weather Channel running, the volume jacked up high. "Too many
variables still exist for us to be able to accurately predict how strong Tropical Storm Margaret may get or
whether it will become a hurricane," said the weatherman. "Florida residents and visitors should continue
to monitor local news for further instructions, ensure
disaster supply kits are fully stocked, and prepare to
evacuate in the event that the intensity of the storm
increases."

"You've been through a lot more storm scares than
I have," I said. "Do you think it's time to clear out?"

"Mr. Renhart is no sailor, I know that much," she
said with a laugh. "I wouldn't judge by his choices."

"Wonder why he paid for a tug?" I said. "Surely his
houseboat has a motor."

"It might take him a year to get to Fort Myers that
way. A tug's a lot more powerful. I just hope he had
the sense to hire someone who knows what he's doing.
Supposing they get out to sea and the storm changes
direction and, instead of coming here, it bears down
on them right where they're headed? There would be
not so much as a splinter of that houseboat left over.
And to take his wife and those poor animals on the
boat while it's towed? And all the money he's spending? I think he's crazy. Completely bonkers. We're right
as rain right here."

I nodded, feeling somewhat reassured, and fired up

my computer. First I checked my messages and my social media feeds. Mrs. Renhart's houseboat already had seven likes on Instagram. I thought she would be pleased with that early response.

I polished the opening of my takeout article, added Grant's breakfast sandwich, and decided the whole thing looked a little thin. I called my mother. "You guys are going to the pet masquerade affair tonight, right? Might you want to try out the Polish food place on White Street? I need another venue for my takeout piece. I don't know what they're serving at the pet event, but in case it's only dog biscuits, we'd be fortified."

My mother laughed like mad and went to ask Sam. "We could both use a lighthearted night," she said when back on the phone. "Sam says I'm driving him to drink, trying cakes. Chef Martha from Louie's says we can bring in whatever we want. But Sam says you make a better cake than anything we've tasted so far, and he's beginning to think—again—that I'm subli-mating my fears about getting married."

"Are you?" I asked. And then before she could an-swer, I added: "And I know this is where I should be silent and let you talk, but if you let this guy get away, you'll be sorry for the rest of your life. And so will I."

My mother heaved a great big sigh. "I know you're right, honey. I've only got a few mini jitters."

We made a plan to meet at the Pierogi Polish Market on White Street at four o'clock, and I went inside to take a shower. Still no message or call from Bransford. When would I find a man as nice and straightforward as my mother's Sam? I hoped I wasn't headed for a series of bad choices that were still related to emotional baggage that I thought I'd shed after first Chad and then Wally dumped me.

Once I was dressed and ready, I had a quick snack of a tiny sliver of strawberry cake and sat down to make a list of what I'd learned about the murder. Maybe if I got organized, I could figure out whether there were things I'd overlooked. Danielle clearly wasn't capable of doing this by herself. I divided this into two sections, What I Knew and What I Didn't Know.

—WIK. Caryn Druckman was an unpleasant, pushy woman who desperately wanted to win the position of Fantasy Fest Queen. WIDK. But why did it matter quite so much? Why was she willing to get into public fisticuffs with Danielle?

—WIK. The person painted with amateur zebra stripes was somehow of interest to the police. Or had been earlier. Which led me to the next point . . .

—WIDK. If Druckman had been murdered by poison, was it something she ate or drank at the zombie party? If so, how did the poisoner manage to target only her? And was it possible that Danielle was meant to die? And why did Danielle's relatives care quite so much about her winning the crown? And why in the world were the cops interested in her zombie costume?

I was relieved when my alarm went off, telling me it was time for supper, and pets and their owners dressed in silly costumes.

18

Chefs and avid eaters scorned anything that might qualify as health food, which by the standards of the time included any vegetable cooked without bacon.

But as Freud knew, repressed urges find ways of bobbing to the surface again.
—Pete Wells, "Performing a
Healthy Twist in Tight Quarters,"
The New York Times, July 29, 2015

My mother and Sam were waiting on the wide covered porch of the two-storied home that serves as the customer service area of the delicatessen. Two enormous menus were posted on the outside wall next to the sash windows of the old house.

"I'm glad you're here," Mom said. "The longer we stand in front of the menu, the more this guy wants to order." She put her arm around Sam's waist and smiled up at him, patting the slight round of his belly at the same time. So sweet together, the two of them.

After a quick consultation on their suggestions, I ordered potato cheese pierogi, another order of the dumplings stuffed with meat, and a third set with a sauerkraut filling. Then I added a side of beet salad, a kielbasa sandwich, and a last-minute addition of hunter's stew.

"You could feed the whole island with that order," Sam said, and sat on a wooden bench on the porch, the only seating available for eating "in." He winked at my mother. "See, I'm not the only person who orders big. I'll wait here and watch the world go by while you girls look around in the shop."

My mother and I went into the little market to peruse their merchandise. We drooled over colorful jars of pickles, beets, chocolate, cookies, spices, and other items identified only in Polish, and then studied the meat counter that showcased pounds and pounds of glistening sausages, pork chops, and chickens so fresh they looked as though they'd just wandered off the street. When we returned to the porch, Sam was sipping a Polish beer.

"This is kind of a relief after spending the afternoon on Duval Street," he said. "Not nearly so frenetic."

"What's new in your world?" Mom asked me.

Where should I start? "Danielle is upset because the cops came to question her again."

"The cops? Which ones?" my mother asked. "What did they want this time?"

"One of them was Bransford, and she said he was

hard on her. They ended up taking her zombie costume with them. I've never seen her show up to work looking such a mess. I told her I'd try to chat with her Fantasy Fest king, Seymour, after the event tonight. I'm sure the police have already talked with him, but maybe he'll remember something that lets her off the hook definitively. I hope." I held up crossed fingers, and she crossed hers too. "Oh, and the Renharts had their boat towed away this evening. The mister thinks the hurricane is coming through." I sighed. "And Connie and Ray are taking the baby upstate to Disney."

My mother turned a little pale. "Do you think we should clear out too?" She clasped her hands to her cheeks. "I would be sick about losing the ceremony on the beach, but we shouldn't be foolish about this either."

Sam took her hand and squeezed. "We'll do exactly what the authorities tell us to do, okay? They've had a ton of experience with storms."

I flashed her what I hoped was a reassuring smile. "Besides, Miss Gloria thinks we're okay, and she's been through a lot of hurricane seasons down here. We'll keep a close eye on things."

The young woman at the takeout window called my name and Sam and I went to retrieve the food. The luscious scent of fried onions and sauerkraut wafted from the stack of Styrofoam containers.

"Good lord," said my mother. "We really went to town this time."

We laid everything out on the built-in wooden table overlooking White Street and began to eat. I was crazy for the sauerkraut and mushroom pierogi with sour cream dipping sauce, but Sam preferred the potato and cheese filling. As we worked our way through the kielbasa and the hunter's stew, I took a few photographs and jotted notes into my phone.

When we had eaten as much as we could without being gluttonous, we returned to Sam's rental car and headed across the island to the Casa Marina resort. Mom and Sam and the rest of my family had stayed here for Connie and Ray's wedding a year and a half ago. It's a spectacular property, built by Henry Flagler in the 1920s. Once you pass through the hotel lobby, the property opens up to an enormous outdoor space, studded with fire pits, bars, swimming pools, and reflecting pools, all leading to a grand vista of the Atlantic Ocean.

Today the grounds bustled with pets and their owners, strutting in their costume creations. The outfits were definitely a tier above what I'd come to enjoy seeing at the New Year's Eve dachshund parade. On the far side of the biggest pool, a band wearing furry gray hats with pointy ears swung into "You Ain't Nothin' but a Hound Dog." We worked our way through the crowd in the direction of the beach. There were dogs dressed as royalty and cats in tutus and birds dressed as English valets and Dracula and even a few pigs. The din was intense, a cacophony of barking and cocktail party chatter, and underneath all that, the music pounding. We grabbed a plastic glass of white wine from a passing waiter and pushed toward the water. A makeshift stage had been erected perpendicular to the beach. The chairs in front of the stage were already filled, and observers had begun to crowd in on either side.

"I'm glad we ate," said my mother with a wink. "I think you were right about the snacks being mostly dog biscuits."

We wiggled through the viewers until we got a clear view of the stage. Sam spotted Danielle and the rest of the royal court seated at a table just off to the side of the steps leading up to the stage. A thin man wearing a crocheted dog hat complete with snout and floppy ears approached the microphone.

"Welcome to our annual masquerade contest," he said. "We are delighted that you came out to support us and this most worthy cause, AIDS Help. From what I saw walking around earlier, I can see that the judging tonight will be very challenging indeed. But I believe our distinguished and lovely panel is up to the task. With no further ado, I bring you this year's king and queen of Fantasy Fest, Mr. Seymour Fox and Miss Danielle Kamen."

Danielle and Seymour swished up onto the stage as the crowd cheered. She looked stunning in her purple gown with the gold sash draped across her chest and a sparkling tiara in her hair. As we got closer, I noticed that under a layer of makeup her color was still pale, like one of the porcelain dolls that I had loved as a child. Though how many other girls had forced their dolls into playing chef and waiter?

Danielle waved and smiled and maybe someone who didn't know her would have thought she was having a blast.

"Isn't that the girl who poisoned her rival?" said the

woman in front of us to her companion. "I can't believe they didn't fire her on the spot. They should not have a murderer representing our town."

My mother clamped her hand on the woman's shoulder. "She did no such thing. You should have some facts before you start making that kind of accusation. Where I come from that's called slander."

"Well, excuse me for living," said the scolded woman. She grabbed her boyfriend's arm and dragged him away from our group.

Back onstage, the MC announced: "And we are also happy to introduce their Royal Courtiers, Miss Kitty Palmer and Mr. John-Bryan Hopkins."

The MC's lips quivered for a moment and I wondered if he was going to mention the death and obvious absence of Caryn Druckman. I desperately hoped that he wouldn't. Once the runners-up took their bows, all the royalty trooped back down the stairs to the judges' table and sat facing the stage.

"We have five categories tonight," said the MC. "Overall creativity, best canine, best feline, best other, and best owner/pet look-alike. Now, may the contest begin!"

The band ratcheted up their volume to an earsplitting level and people and their pets began to stream across the stage.

"That's precious," said my mother as a woman dressed as a flowerpot trotted by carrying her midsize mutt, who was dressed as a butterfly.

"I like the gold diggers." Sam snickered, pointing out three women wearing tight gold sheaths and gold-sprayed hard hats as they posed at the edge of the stage in front of the judges, towing small dogs with coins and dollar bills attached to their fur.

"It's a guy thing," I told my mother. "Don't pay any attention to him. He's just feeling some last-minute oats. Let him have enough line and he'll hit the end and jerk back." I pantomimed a choking movement.

Sam elbowed me in the ribs. "I thought we were pals."

The pets continued to troop across the stage: Chihuahuas dressed as peacocks, multiple versions of lionfish and lobsters and snorkelers and mermaids, a few pet-person zombie combinations probably left over from the bike parade. And near the end, a white cat shaved except for his lion's ruff and puffy tail, both dyed pink, a goat spray-painted red wearing devil horns, and a small pig with green wings. The final entry was a well-built man, naked to the waist, wearing a string mop on his head and another strung around his waist. He strutted across the stage accompanied by a Puli dog with a long white corded coat, who honest to gosh looked like a moving mop as he trotted.

"He's got winner written all over him," said Sam.

"And the dog's not bad either," said my mother with a giggle.

The audience nearest the judges' stand began to rustle and murmur, and a man shouted: "Someone call nine-one-one. We have a lady who's ill."

Two blue-uniformed policemen waded into the crowd, pushing the looky-loos back and calling for calm. Based on the expression on my mother's face, the same terrible thought struck us both at the same time.

"What if it's Danielle?" I said. "We need to help her."

We squirmed through the crowd toward the royal table. Danielle had appeared ashen when I'd seen her across the lawn, but now she looked pale as Snow White. Her bearded king, Seymour, hovered helplessly nearby, playing the role of the biggest dwarf. The police got busy pushing the crowd back. Dogs shrieked their disapproval, cats yowled; I even heard the nay of the dyed-red goat. All I could think of was Caryn Druckman; how she'd collapsed in the zombie bike ride and ended up dead. My mother took my hand and squeezed so hard that I knew she was thinking the same thing.

When we got ten feet from the judges' table, I saw the twins, Danielle's mother and aunt, trying to get closer, their faces sick with concern.

"Let her through! Let her through!" I hollered, shoving some of the spectators to make a path. "This is her mother!"

Enough of the gawking people moved aside so that Mrs. Kamen could rush through. Paramedics arrived, one bombarding Danielle about her symptoms and the other interviewing people nearby about what they had noticed before she collapsed.

Seymour watched in horror with the rest of us as they loaded Danielle onto a stretcher and rattled her across the manicured grounds, off through the main hotel lobby toward the waiting ambulance. I came up beside him and patted his shoulder.

"I'm Hayley," I said. "You may not remember because it's been so crazy this week, but we met at the coronation party. I work with Danielle at *Key Zest*."

"I remember," he said with an instant smile. But his eyes look glazed and I figured he would have said that to anyone who approached him. He was in automatic royal politeness mode.

"What happened here?" I asked.

"I'm not sure. She didn't look one hundred percent well when she arrived. But she said she was fine, just a little tired. We are all kind of worn-out from the last couple of months. And upset about what happened on the bike ride." Now he met my gaze. "It was serious already but now this is totally scary."

"I'd love to talk with you soon," I said. "Can I call you in the morning?" He nodded and read off his cell phone number so I could punch the information into mine.

The organizers of the pet masquerade scrambled to settle the remaining judges back at their table and quiet the bystanders so they could announce the winners. Meanwhile, Sam and my mother and I slipped through the crowd and out through the lobby of the big hotel. We half walked, half trotted to the place near the bocce courts where Sam had parked the car. None of us said anything, but I suspected we all had the same worry on our minds: Had Danielle been the victim of Druckman's killer? It seemed absurd to think that two people could have been poisoned in big crowds—the logistics were mind-boggling. But I couldn't get that thought out of my head.

19

> *My salades composées were thickets of
> yearning, drifts of leaves and flowers,
> sprigs of herbs and tiny carrots that
> looked like they had been blown there by
> some mighty force of nature. I was fueled
> by sublimated rage, the outsider with
> something to prove, taking the ingredients
> I was handed and making sure they tran-
> scended their limits.*
>
> —John Birdsall,
> "America, Your Food Is So Gay,"
> *Lucky Peach*, May 16, 2015

"I'm going to assume they've taken her to the ER at
the Lower Keys Medical Center?" Sam said.

"That's my bet," I said.

He started the car and roared up Flagler to reach
Route A1A, then over the Cow Key Bridge and onto

Stock Island. Minutes later, we were parked in the big lot that adjoins the back of the golf course. We rushed into the ER. I have visited here a number of times in the past, both for my own unfortunate injuries and for friends and family. But I'd never seen this many tutus and painted faces in the waiting room. Some of the stricken appeared to be intoxicated, others were slightly bloodied. I imagined that the more serious cases had probably already been triaged.

My mother reached the information desk first.

"We are here for Danielle Kamen," she said. "She was brought in after an incident at the pet masquerade event. She was a judge. And she's this year's Fantasy Fest Queen. She's beautiful and blond and she had on a purple gown and a tiara. She'd be hard to miss." She glanced around the room. "Though you have quite a few unusual getups tonight." She flashed an encouraging grin at the woman manning the desk. "Has she been admitted? May we see her? We're her dear friends; my daughter is like a sister to her."

The clerk had launched into her speech about patient privacy, when I saw Danielle's aunt across the room. I touched my mother's arm and pointed, and we abandoned the gatekeeping clerk and sprinted over to the hallway leading to curtained cubicles, the first line of defense in the ER. Aunt Marion disappeared into the third cubicle, and we squeezed in behind her. Danielle was lying pallid against the white hospital sheets, an IV snaking into the delicate skin on top of her hand and an oxygen tube in her nose. Her mom sat on the far side of her bed, a hand placed protectively on her shoulder. On the plus side, her eyes were open and she was definitely breathing. Even so, my mother was unable to suppress a gasp of dismay.

"What in the world happened?" I asked. "We saw you go down like a sack of turnips right in front of the stage."

Danielle blinked slowly, her eyes now brimming with tears. "I don't know what happened," she said in a whisper. "I wasn't feeling great to begin with, but I wasn't about to shirk my duties after all those people worked so hard to get me elected."

My mother took a step closer and put her hand on Danielle's temple. "Honey, first you have to take care of yourself or you're of no use to anyone." She looked across the hospital bed for confirmation from Danielle's mother and aunt.

Honestly, to me it appeared that their agreement with this statement was begrudging. But my stubborn mother held her silence until they both nodded.

"I don't know what's wrong with me," said Danielle. "One second I was enjoying the dogs in costumes and then suddenly I felt so woozy and my head started to spin. And I thought I might throw up."

"We suspect it's vertigo," said Danielle's aunt. "It runs in the family—our inner ears are overly delicate."

"Had you eaten anything unusual?" I asked Danielle.

"She's hardly eaten anything at all in the last two days," said her mother. "I have a feeling she's just dehydrated." She patted her daughter's untethered hand. "For that matter, it could be a stomach virus. All these people crowding into town, you know they bring thousands of crazy germs along with them. And here we locals sit like jelly in a petri dish, ready to take them in and let them multiply."

"The doctors have ordered all the tests they can think of," said Danielle's aunt. "They aren't going to send her out into the world if she's had a heart attack or stroke."

Danielle looked alarmed. "I'm a little young for that, don't you think? I think it's just stress."

"Miss Druckman's death has been a terrible shock for all of you. And I can see how feeling sick would make you worry about your own health." Sam patted her feet, swathed in a white blanket. "You said the cops were back to talk with you again earlier?"

Danielle took a quick peek at my face. "I'm not trying to be mean about this, Hayley, but that Bransford . . ."

"Go ahead," I told her, bracing to hear about something terrible that he'd done. I hated feeling somehow responsible for his harsh public presentation.

"He keeps saying things like *We have plenty of evidence that you hated her. And I'm not saying there isn't good reason for you to have these feelings. But now she's dead. And you had excellent access to her throughout the zombie party at East Martello. We have photos and witnesses that corroborate this. Help us understand what happened.*"

By the time she'd finished parroting his words, she was bawling and the machines attached to her were beeping so loudly that a nurse came running.

"What are all you people doing here?" she demanded, and made shooing motions until we backed out of the cubicle.

Once Danielle's mother had promised to call us with updates and we'd exited the ER, feeling worried and frazzled, I asked Sam to drop me off at the Polish deli, where I'd left my scooter. "I'm going to nip up to Sunset and check in with Lorenzo," I told them.

"What I don't understand," said my mother as I scrambled out of the backseat, "is what's going on between Danielle and her mother. There's something strange about her presentation—did you notice? Once Danielle's out of the woods, I think we should visit them again."

"Tomorrow." I kissed her on the cheek, blew another kiss to Sam, and then hopped onto my scooter and fastened the helmet.

The ride from White Street to Mallory Square took twice as long as usual. The streets were clogged with visitors who seemed to have come to the island equipped with a death wish. I leaned on my horn more times in that short trip than I had since I bought the bike. The air felt oppressive, sticky, and hot, and waves of heat radiated up from the streets. Maybe the visitors had fried their brains.

I parked near the Custom House Museum and forged through the sunset viewers, many of whom were heading north to Duval Street. The sun had set, but there was still enough light to see the remains of the nightly party. From the looks of the folks buzzing his T-shirt display, Dominique the cat man must have just wrapped up a successful performance. I walked in front of the Westin and over the short bridge near the aquarium. Just after the bridge, food vendors lined each side of the walkway.

I stopped first to chat with Christy Haussler. Her face lit up when she saw me. "How about a coconut ice on the house? Have you ever done a review of Mallory Square snacks?"

"Great idea," I said. "And I'd love one. Though we had an enormous dinner at the Polish deli. But we didn't have dessert, and my stomach is letting me know." I patted my midsection, which let out an audible growl. "And I also had a big breakfast at the Paradise Pub, cooked personally by the chef/owner. But a little sugar can't hurt, right?"

She grinned and handed over the ice cream. "Did you ever find that painted face you were looking for? And how is your friend?"

"The answers are no and not that well." I told her how Danielle had taken ill at the pet masquerade party.

"That reminds me, I was thinking about your questions about what I noticed before the zombie bike ride," Christy said. "I remembered that Beach Eats was serving some kind of fancy cocktail for the royals. I'm guessing the police already talked to them. Seymour Fox is the owner of the food truck. And Paradise Pub, though I've heard he sold it."

"To Grant," I said. "I should go back and talk to him again."

She looked puzzled.

"Grant Monsarrat. He's the new owner of the pub, right? He was working at the food truck too."

Christy dished up ice cream for the customer behind me, then returned to our conversation. "I could be wrong, but I don't think Grant bought it. I could swear it was a woman."

"I'm sure it's him," I said. "I talked with him and his girlfriend this morning. She's already redecorating the front of the house, and they seem to have put a lot of money into the kitchen. The front of the house still looks a little shopworn, but I'm thrilled they're starting with a clean kitchen."

"Terrific," she said. "I love to try new places."

The people behind me in line had begun to grumble about how I was blocking the cart. "I'll talk to you later," I said. "Have a great night."

I wandered past the man who plays guitar, and sings badly, and then sends his dog around to pick up tips and put them in a bucket. Not my idea of a skilled performer. A little farther along the pier, I waited for Lorenzo to finish up with his customer, a large woman in an orange shirt with a dachshund tucked under her arm. Sniffling into a Kleenex, she thanked him loudly and levered herself out of the chair.

I held up a finger to the woman a few feet away who seemed poised to take her place. "I just need to speak with him for a moment; I won't take up much time." I flashed her a quick smile. "I'm not asking for a reading, promise."

"How are things?" he asked as I slid into his customer chair. "Did they find out who killed that woman?"

I shook my head. "And they keep circling around my poor friend like vultures on carrion. And then she collapsed at the pet masquerade earlier this evening. I left her in the ER."

He frowned. "An attempt on her life?"

"Oh lordy, I sure hope not. How would someone

think they could get away with trying to kill people so publicly?"

"People are strange," he said, looking very sad. "I was going to call you in the morning anyway. I'm leaving the island tomorrow, taking Lola and heading north to Fort Myers."

Lola was his white kitten. I'd gotten very fond of her last spring when he'd left her with us for safekeeping. I felt a lurch in my gut. "Are you sensing that something is going to happen that the rest of us don't know about?"

He smiled. "Not unless you count sensing my mother nagging. She's so worried about the path of the storm—she's worked herself into hysterics. And you know this is not my favorite time of year on this island anyway." He leaned in to whisper. "Most of these folks don't really want to hear what's in their future. Too scary. The rest of them wouldn't recognize their unconscious if it hit them on the head. They are too busy medicating themselves with alcohol and who knows what else."

He took my hand and squeezed. "Never mind the tarot cards in this case—pay attention to the weather reports. If the authorities tell you to leave, just do it. I stayed through one hurricane and it ripped the roof right off our house. The rain was pouring in, gushing down the dining room walls. I had no choice but to go up on a ladder and try to jury-rig some kind of cover to replace the roof. I ask you, do I look like the kind of man who's experienced in home repair?" We both giggled.

I felt distraught at the idea of him leaving, but on

the other hand, he looked at wits' end. He was drenched in sweat, his hair curling like an old-fashioned permanent wave. And the people around us pulsed with a frenetic energy that could make the calmest person anxious. Which I imagined was even harder to take for a man so tuned in to the people he met. He absorbed a lot of anxiety from strangers, without much opportunity to discharge it.

"Keep me posted, okay?" I begged him.

When I finally reached home half an hour later, Miss Gloria was sweating on the back deck, eating ice cream out of the carton with Mrs. Dubisson, her best friend from down the finger, and our cats. She had two small bowls laid out on the ground, and our felines had finished licking the bottoms of the bowls and were now licking the cream off their whiskers.

"Ahoy there, matey," Miss Gloria called out. "Permission to come aboard is granted!" Both of the women chuckled with a heartiness that made me suspect that they had had a teeny tiny tipple to go along with their dessert.

"I should get going," said Mrs. Dubisson. "I've got a cutthroat mah-jongg match in the morning, and it doesn't pay to be fuzzy-headed." She blew us both a kiss and trundled off toward her boat.

"How was the masquerade party?" asked Miss Gloria after she'd returned from putting the ice cream away.

Obviously she hadn't heard the latest—which was unusual, because her mah-jongg friends tended to text one another with island news that had barely broken.

"We left before the end," I said, "after Danielle collapsed." Then I filled her in on the events at the Casa Marina, our visit to the emergency room, and my conversations with Christy and Lorenzo. "He's leaving town in the morning," I said. "Do you still think it's smart to stay? Where do you stand on that?"

"Standing firm against the onslaught of awesome offspring," she said with an impish grin. "Let's go look at the weather and see if there's anything new."

We each grabbed a cat and retreated to our tiny living room, where a small air conditioner was laboring to cool the space. She looked at me a little sheepishly. "I hoped you wouldn't mind. I know you like to save the environment, but I doubted we could sleep in this oppressive heat."

"Absolutely!"

We flipped on the local news and watched a piece on the zaniness of Duval Street, then an interview with the winner of the pet masquerade contest (the mop man with his Puli). Finally the microphone was turned over to the weather forecaster. She showed a graph that looked as though a dozen children with different colored crayons had been at work, and admitted that the path of this storm, dubbed Margaret, had been unusually difficult to track.

"How should we prepare for the possibility of a hurricane making landfall in Key West?" asked the anchor.

"We have asked our director of emergency management to speak to exactly that question," said the forecaster.

The weathered but friendly face of a curly-haired

woman with light blue eyes came on the screen. "Thank you for asking me to talk with your viewers today. There are some commonsense facts you should think through ahead of time. If a storm is headed in your direction, you need to know where you're going if you're not planning to stay at a shelter, especially for a category three storm or higher," she said. "Best to have several options in mind, depending on the predicted path of the storm. Which of course can change more than once, depending on atmospheric and ocean conditions." She gestured at the colored lines displayed behind her.

"Check to be sure you have cash, extra medication, water, batteries, canned food, and also food and water for your pets. By all means, enjoy the blue skies and fishing and diving and parades today, but keep in mind that it could all change tomorrow. If the storm ends up heading toward the island directly, all bets are off and we'll be calling for a full evacuation."

"That right there is a bunch of maybes and what-ifs. They are just trying to cover their patooties," Miss Gloria said.

20

From my fellow bakers, those yeasty intel-lectuals, I learned about industry and cohesion and the moral obligation to be cheerful.
  —James Parker, "Bookends," *The New York Times*, November 9, 2014

I woke up the next morning feeling unaccountably gloomy. But after I lounged in bed a few extra minutes, stroking Evinrude, listening to the slosh of water under the boat, and thinking about the events of the last few days, I realized the feelings were not surprising at all. I was worried sick about Danielle. She had texted last night to report her release from the hospital, saying she'd call me in the morning. I glanced at my bedside clock. Six thirty a.m. was too early to bother her.

The storm worried me too. Lying in bed, I could tell that the chop in our bight felt heavier than it had yesterday. Connie and Ray and the baby had split for parts north. Lorenzo was leaving this morning, and the Renharts were gone. Was the whole island sinking? I reminded myself that the police and other emergency personnel did not want thousands of people to stay in Key West if it was in the storm's bull's-eye. They would tell us when it was really time to go. I rolled out of my bunk and laid out a plan.

First stop, *Key Zest*, where I'd finally finish the takeout article while the Polish food was fresh in my mind. Second stop, Seymour's house. I was certain he'd remember more about the recent incidents when he wasn't in the chokehold of Danielle's distress. Third stop, Grant's restaurant, Paradise Pub, where I'd press harder about what he and Catfish had seen at the zombie party.

I'd worry less if I kept myself busy. And maybe even resolve some of the questions that bothered me. The Bransford business involving the reappearance of his ex-wife? I could not fix that. I couldn't even talk it over with him while our island was in chaos. So I'd have to push it to the back of my mind for now.

I made myself scrambled eggs whipped up with shredded cheddar and put a cottage oat biscuit in the toaster oven while the coffee brewed. Something told me this could be a long day, topped off by the tutu party tonight. Though with Connie and Ray and Danielle out of commission, my enthusiasm for another Fantasy Fest adventure was waning.

After breakfast, I zipped down the island to *Key Zest*. The streets were pleasantly clean and clear of zany party-goers, though the scent of beer lingered on. And the sun was already broiling and the air thick with humidity and utterly still. It felt steamy and heavy, as though we were on the verge of getting swallowed by something big. I vaulted upstairs to our office, hoping for some peaceful time to work alone.

Palamina's light was on, and I heard the clack of her special wrist-saving keyboard. So much for time alone. I considered for a moment pretending I didn't notice her and sneaking down the hall to my space. But she'd know I'd ignored her. She was like a bird, sleeping with half a brain active and one eye open.

"Good morning," I called out in a chirpy voice, keeping my head down and hoping that she wouldn't stop me.

"Hayley? Do you have a minute?"

I mustered a smile and turned back into her office. "Sure. What's up?"

She pushed a pair of rhinestone-studded cat-eye reading glasses onto her head. "What in the world is going on with Danielle? I thought we'd cleared the air and made it obvious that we needed her here."

I felt like hissing, like when the bad guy makes his first appearance in a movie, but I swallowed hard and said: "She was taken to the emergency room last night. She fell ill at the party at the Casa Marina."

Palamina frowned, the skin between her brows furrowing. I thought again how she'd regret that habit ten years from now. Or so my mother would have said.

"When she signed on for this queen business, I was not informed that it meant she'd essentially quit working. During one of the busiest periods in Key West.

Right when people are depending on us for smart reading, she bails out. I've texted her and left her several e-mails and heard nothing."

A spike of rage shot through me. "Look," I said. "No one is reading our pearls of wisdom this week. No one. They are either out on the streets partying or they are inside watching the Weather Channel."

I should have stopped there, but I didn't. I couldn't.

"When you took over from Ava, we were all thrilled. You seemed to love our mission and, well"—I tapped my chest with one hand—"us. I was excited about your ideas for expanding the e-zine's mission." I stood up straighter and hugged my arms over my chest, trying to slow down and breathe. "Instead, you pick at us, criticize every idea we come up with and every piece we turn in. You hang over us like an osprey watching a school of bluefish."

Her lips quirked as if she wanted to interrupt, but I kept talking.

"What's going to happen here"—I rapped her desk hard with my knuckles—"is that we'll all quit. I'd hate to do that, because our audience is building and I think we're all getting better at both writing and marketing. And I love my job." I stopped to suck in some air so I wouldn't cry.

"Are you tendering your resignation, Hayley?" she asked just as Wally came into the room.

"What's this about? Don't tell me you're leaving?" He looked genuinely stricken.

"Not yet," I said. "But I'll be looking soon if things keep going in this direction." I turned back to glare at Palamina. "The heart of this magazine is your people.

Us. We are the local voices that both draw in long-time residents and appeal to visitors. Readers don't want opinions from people who swoop in for the weekend and act like they've discovered the place—they want ours. They want to hear from insiders, not outsiders."

I dialed my voice volume down a little, realizing I was almost shouting. "Now I'm going to finish up my takeout article. I sent the face-painting bit over yesterday. And after that I'm taking the day off to think things over."

I stormed down the hall to my nook as Wally began to lecture Palamina.

"I don't understand what's wrong with you," he began. "You're going to end up writing the magazine by yourself. We hardly pay them enough to take abuse. And they're both amazing at what they do. I never thought I'd wish for the good old days when I was at the beck and call of Ava Faulkner. . . ."

Ordinarily I would've been grateful for Wally's support, but this time I was so mad and so sure I was right that I wouldn't have minded standing alone. And really, wasn't he partly responsible for what was happening? Weren't they supposed to be running the show together? Why didn't he rein her in when she got out of control?

I shut the door firmly, verging on a slam. Not wanting to hear what she would tell Wally in response to his tirade—that Danielle was a flake and I an impetuous and immature hothead. I tried to calm myself, using the four-part yoga breathing that had kept Connie sane during her labor and delivery. Everything I'd said, I meant. But what employee manual would advise that it was a good idea to shriek at your boss?

When the breathing didn't do much, I scrabbled through the mess on my desk until I came up with the notes from my last reading from Lorenzo. I'd drawn the Three of Swords, the Six of Wands, and the Hanged Man, reversed. The scribbles I could make out talked about broken contracts and how I wasn't feeling much reward. That I might have to make a sacrifice, let something go, or give something up. Whoop-de-do. That could be applied to about every area of my life right now. He had advised me to ride the turbulence out. And as always, even if I hadn't drawn the high priestess card—the guardian of the unconscious and the mystery of life—I should listen to my intuition and let that guide me.

So I texted Danielle.

Come in if you can. Palamina's pretty close to the edge of stroking out this morning.

My phone rang with a local number I didn't recognize. "Hello?"

"Hayley, it's Mary, Danielle's mother? So sorry to bother you, but I'm very worried."

"Is she okay?" I asked. "Did the doctors find something new?"

No," she said, "she's physically fine and, so far, no sign of poisons or other toxic substances in the drug screen. So why did this happen? That's what's got me so concerned. She's a young woman, healthy and lean. She doesn't have high cholesterol or high blood pressure or any of that. It doesn't make any sense that she collapsed for no reason."

"Do you think it could be a reaction to stress?" I asked.

"But what does that mean? Last night the doctors did an EKG—they said her heart is fine. All her vital signs were OK."

"An anxiety attack? Sometimes if someone gets anxious enough, they feel like they're having a heart attack. And the more worried they get, the more the symptoms mimic the physical effects."

She ignored what I thought had been a reasonable hypothesis, and lowered her voice, as if someone was listening. "I think someone was out to kill my daughter in the first place. But they poisoned that Druckman woman by mistake."

I hated to hear her put this into words, because deep down, I had a niggling worry about the same thing. Emotions had run so high during this event and the month leading up to it. Did Danielle have enemies that I couldn't have imagined? Did she have dark secrets that she hadn't let us know about? She always seemed so open and pure and innocent. But how reasonable was it that a killer would try to poison two people in two different public, very busy venues? Not at all reasonable. In my experience, murderers chose quiet places and definitive methods. But I would hear Danielle's mother out, because maybe talking things over would calm her down.

I gave a heavy sigh. "Okay, you tell me. Who would want her dead?"

Danielle's mother began to weep. "I don't know!

I don't know! If only I hadn't encouraged her to run for queen."

Her sobs escalated to the point that she started to choke.

"Slow down," I said. "Take a deep, deep breath." I mimicked breathing in and out, in and out. "Is Danielle doing okay this morning? Do you think she'd like some company?"

"I texted her earlier. She is exhausted and resting. I don't even know where to start to figure this out. How do you find a murderer among ten thousand tipsy people dressed as zombies?"

Danielle's mom took a shuddering breath. She was a hot, hysterical mess, let's face it. If anyone was going to make sense of all this—to figure out whether Danielle had really been a target, it had to be me.

"How about this—I'll pay a visit to Seymour. He was right beside her during both of those events. I'm certain the cops have talked with him, but sometimes talking with a civilian is less threatening, you know? Maybe that will jog loose a memory about something he saw but doesn't remember."

"I would be so grateful," she said. "And let me know about anything you learn? I'm just sick about this. How could someone want to harm my beautiful girl?"

She began to cry again. I said what I could think of to calm her down and signed off. Danielle could sometimes be a nervous Nellie, and now I was beginning to see that it ran in her blood.

21

This wine is too good for toast-drinking,
my dear. You don't want to mix emotions
up with a wine like that.
                        —Ernest Hemingway,
                            The Sun Also Rises

I Googled Seymour's address and headed off to his Old Town apartment, located near the El Siboney Restaurant. My mouth began to water as I thought of their menu. Authentic Cuban food might be just the comfort I needed after this difficult start to the morning. And then either I could add a short review of that restaurant to my takeout piece or, better still, quit shaping that one and start a new feature for next week. Though lord only knew if I'd even have a job after the altercation with Palamina.

As I approached Seymour's block, the smells of onions and cumin wafted from the restaurant next door to his home, exactly as I had imagined on the way over.

I wondered if this bothered him after he'd lived here awhile—if he was always hungry or slightly sick to his stomach. Connie and I had lived above an Italian restaurant during our senior year in college, convenient for takeout during long nights of studying. New Jersey Italian food was the ultimate comfort, but we did wonder as we left town whether we'd ever crave a meatball hoagie again. Not to worry. I was over that after a month away from the neighborhood.

I debated calling Seymour once I had parked outside his place to make sure he was home and would receive me. But I decided it might work better to simply appear.

His apartment was on the top floor of an adorable eyebrow home that had fallen into disrepair, reached by a set of rickety wooden stairs on the side of the house. The gingerbread trim around the eaves of the porch had been cut into hearts and wine bottles that mimicked a bar on upper Duval Street, formerly a speakeasy and a brothel. But this trim badly needed scraping and painting, and the weeds were growing tall in the yard. I stepped gingerly onto the small porch at the top of the stairs, testing for rotten boards, and knocked.

Seymour answered the door wearing knee-length white corduroy shorts adorned with palm trees and a T-shirt from the Green Parrot bar. The apartment smelled of coffee and bacon.

"I'm Hayley Snow," I said. "Danielle's friend and coworker? I'm so sorry to surprise you like this, but I was in the neighborhood and wondered if you could chat a few minutes?"

"Sure," he said after a pause. "Come on in. Excuse the mess."

His living room was as neat and welcoming as the outside of the home had been off-putting. Not a whisper of a mess here—the only thing out of place was his Fantasy Fest king's crown, perched on an end table so a beam of sunlight hit it and caused the faux jewels to sparkle. He gestured for me to take a seat on a flowered sofa draped with a cerulean blue fuzzy afghan. An enormous yellow tiger cat was tucked into one corner of the couch. As I sat, he lifted his head and greeted me with a silent meow. I glanced at Seymour and we both laughed.

"Meet Chucky Cheese," Seymour said. "I was just finishing breakfast. Can I get you something?" He pointed to a plate on the counter. There was a smear of egg yolk and a tiny bit of fat from a strip of bacon on his plate, nothing more.

"I'd love a cup of coffee with a splash of milk if you have it."

He padded across the worn wooden floor to pull a white mug from the cupboard and fill it with coffee. Then he splashed a dollop of half-and-half into the steaming brew and set it in front of me on a soapstone coaster. "I assume you came to talk about Danielle. Have you seen her this morning? Last night was terrible. I barely slept, thinking about all that's happened this week."

"So scary," I agreed. "And you were so close to both of the mishaps. I imagine you must be feeling shell-shocked." I paused a moment, took a sip of coffee, and waited for him to nod. "I was thinking that if we talked about what happened to Caryn Druckman, it might help us figure out what happened last night."

With some prompting, Seymour described the events of the zombie parade from his perspective. "They told us to get there early that afternoon so we could spend a couple of hours mingling with the crowd and doing some interviews with bloggers and such. The days have started to bleed together a little bit," he said, running his fingers through his reddish beard. "But I think that was the day they served us painkillers and cupcakes."

When I did a double take, he added: "I mean Painkiller the drink, not the drug. I don't drink, so I chose the nonalcoholic version—it's not that easy to stay upright on a bicycle while wearing a costume anyway. Never mind adding in booze." He picked up the crown sitting on the table near him, fingered one of the rubies, and then absentmindedly put it on.

"Tell me what you're thinking," I said, hoping he was remembering the details of the day. "The Painkiller is some kind of fruit punch, right?"

"Coconut and pineapple, maybe some other things too. Always rum, and maybe nutmeg? They're called Painkillers because they're usually very strong." He grinned. "You feel no pain after you've had one."

"Where did the drinks come from?"

He shook his head, the faux jewels in his crown glinting in the sunlight. His cat hopped up onto the back of the sofa and slapped a paw at a reflected sparkle. "The police asked me the same question. We were so busy talking with the sponsors and the folks from the local TV station and getting our pictures taken with all these amazing zombies, I couldn't have said where anything started. Someone dressed as a zombie had little cups on their tray."

"So it wasn't your Beach Eats truck?"

His jaw tightened and I thought I heard the click of grinding molars. "I don't control their menu, but they know I'm not a fan of alcoholic beverages."

"Did Miss Druckman seem sick right away, before you even got onto your bikes?"

"If she was feeling poorly, she didn't mention it to me. I could very easily believe she died of alcohol poisoning—that woman could drink most people under the table."

"But did she look sick right after you had the snacks? I mean did you notice a change in her color or her demeanor?"

"I understand what you're getting at, but honestly, she wasn't the kind of person that it was easy to get close to. She would never have asked me for help." He shook his head, frowning. "We never bonded over the last few months. In fact, I tried to keep my distance from her after a while—including getting away from her physically."

"She was mean to Danielle, I know that much," I said. "According to her family, anyway. Was she negative in general?"

He stroked the big cat and took a minute to think. "I wouldn't have said she was a bad person, but she was very focused on what she wanted. And so she didn't hesitate to step on toes along the way."

"Is that what happened at the Coronation Ball?"

The cat hopped down from the back of the sofa and

began to knead his paws in Seymour's lap. "Miss Druckman was bitterly disappointed at the results. Which I can sort of understand. We'd spent the past three months campaigning and begging people for contributions and setting up all kinds of events, and then to lose in the last moments of the contest . . . even though we all objectively understood that it wasn't about us winning or losing, it was about raising money for AIDS Help." He removed the crown and held it in his hands, studying it as though it was a foreign object. "But she loved the fuss, so I get that it might have felt harsh to her, as though someone had swept in and stolen her prize."

"So was she only hard on Danielle after she'd won? Or were they butting heads all along?"

He shrugged and looked away. I hated to press him, because his face was beginning to redden and I could smell his perspiration. But the relationship between these two women seemed as though it might be the life-or-death crux of the matter.

"I'm sorry to be a bulldog about this, but I'm worried about Danielle's safety. Would you say there was tension between them right from the beginning, back in August when the planning for the campaigns began? How did Danielle behave toward Miss Druckman?"

"Their chemistry was flat," he said. "Except for the catfight at The Bull and Whistle. However, sparks were evident all along between Druckman and Danielle's family."

Which I hated to hear, though it didn't surprise me. The idea that Danielle's mother or aunt could be mixed up in any of these troubles made me sick to my stomach. "Sparks?"

"They simply didn't like each other, that's all."

"Any conflict between you and the other king candidates?"

He laughed. "I had it easy, because the only other person foolish enough to run for king was an outsider from the get-go."

"John-Bryan Hopkins?" I asked. "In what way was he an outsider?"

"He doesn't live in Key West—he comes from Alabama. But he visits all the time and knows a lot of people. And he's a social media genius, so I suppose he figured he could lean on those skills." Seymour put the crown back on the end table. "He loved the parties and he's an amazing dancer, and he wanted to raise money for the charity; that's it. It might be worth talking to him, though, since he was in the middle of everything. Winning didn't seem personal to him, so he might have noticed some interactions that I missed."

Which made me wonder whether the contest was personal to Seymour, but I couldn't make myself ask it. "When is your next official royal responsibility? I'm wondering if the organizers will cancel?"

"Nothing official until the locals parade on Friday night," he said. "And then the big parade on Saturday. As far as canceling, I doubt it. Though the weather may get us before the organizers do." He crooked a grin and pointed to his laptop, open on the kitchen counter. From this distance, I could see the many-colored lines of the storm's models and, overlaid on that, the cone of uncertainty, with Key West in its center. "They issued a hurricane watch for the county this morning."

"Are you planning to leave town?" I asked, realizing how silly it was that I was polling people about proper behavior in the approach of a possible hurricane. But I couldn't seem to help myself.

"Not unless the authorities absolutely say we should. I've stayed on this island through some pretty good blows. This time I have obligations, but also, driving off the Keys at a snail's pace with a howling cat in the car is no picnic either. And the Green Parrot will stay open until the bitter end." He plucked at his shirt. "I've got a lot of shifts to make up because of all the Fantasy Fest meetings and events and so on."

"You're not involved in Paradise Pub anymore," I said, fishing for facts.

"I hope not," he said, his expression freezing into a polite smile. "I got talked into investing years ago, and it's been nothing but a headache."

I thanked him for the coffee and returned downstairs to my scooter. Since I was close, I drove to the cemetery to see if I could catch Miss Gloria between tours. She had become the most requested guide since beginning the gig last winter. Everyone loved her sunny personality and chipper commentary, laced alternately with respect and humor. I popped my head into the sexton's office, where Jane, the cemetery historian, told me Miss G had left for Houseboat Row because business was slow.

"Visitors are cither recovering from last night's parties or getting ready for this evening," she said. "They don't have time to absorb the peculiarities of the past."

I left the office, wondering what to do next. Maybe walking among the dead and their markers would help me think through what Seymour had told me. When a murder has been committed, I can't help wondering what desperate feelings incited the crime. Drugs and psychosis aside, how in the world does an ordinary person take the life of someone else? What twisted path must their reasoning take to justify killing?

In the case of Caryn Druckman, no clear suspect was emerging from the tangle of human emotions that seemed to surround the election of Seymour and Danielle—who liked who, and who hated who, and why in the world did the honor of the crown mean so much? And always, how well did I really know the people involved? In this case, Danielle.

I perched on a crumbling cement wall in the shade of a coconut palm, and Googled John-Bryan Hopkins. As Seymour had said, he had an active social media presence including a blog about food holidays and hundreds of thousands of Twitter followers. I sent him a direct message asking him to call me, though I didn't have much hope he'd respond.

Then I phoned my psychologist friend Eric. It always helps to mull things over with him. Plus, since Connie and Ray had left town, maybe I could persuade him and Bill to attend the tutu party with me.

I asked about the party first, really begging more than asking.

"We're clearing out of town tomorrow," he said. "We waited too long for the last storm, and then discovered that it's impossible to find a motel room that will take dogs when you're desperate. You really have to plan ahead. They say cats are even harder."

"Great," I muttered. "What about the party though? It's tonight. Can't you guys come, maybe just for an hour? One beer?"

"That's what I started to tell you," he said. "We're cooking up everything in the refrigerator in case the power goes out while we're gone. What about asking your mother and Sam to the tutu party? They like to have fun."

"Think about that," I said. "My mother at a tutu party?" Last year there were people wandering around wearing tutus and practically nothing else. I didn't know who would be most embarrassed—probably me. "But wait, you're leaving before her wedding? She'll be devastated. You're the person she's known longest in the world—aside from me, of course."

Eric and I had grown up in the same town, same neighborhood, though he was a few years ahead. And he'd used my mother as a sounding board many times when he couldn't talk to his own about private teenage boy stuff.

"I broke the news to her this morning," Eric said. "She's sad but she said she understands. How about Miss Gloria? She'd look adorable in a tutu."

I could only groan. "Really, Eric? Miss Gloria?"

He snickered. "Better idea—how about all four of you come over for dinner? Skip the tutu party altogether."

I thought about how mad I was at Palamina and how little I felt like (a) attending the party and (b) writing about it. And besides, I'd told her I was taking the day off, so I should follow through, not act like a cowed employee who didn't mean what she said. "Terrific," I said. "What can we bring?"

"I've got a coconut cake in the oven, which will use up most of our butter and cream cheese," Eric said. "So dessert and cholesterol count are covered. Do you have any tomatoes and basil left on your deck? Maybe pick up some mozzarella from the deli at Fausto's? Potluck, so whatever you have will be fine. And bring the detective if you want to."

"I don't."

22

I will bring you what you need.
　　　—said by an arrogant waiter who
　　　　　couldn't possibly know

After talking with Eric, I realized I had to see Danielle for myself. But as with Seymour, I was afraid she wouldn't agree if I called. So for the second visit in one day, I planned to drop in without phoning ahead.

Last year, Danielle had purchased a tiny apartment in the Shipyard condominium complex in the Truman Annex. Here, hundreds of small condos were crowded onto a small space near the tip of the island and most often rented to tourists. But she insisted she enjoyed the steady stream of visitors, and she liked being able to walk to town and walk to work. And almost more than anything—although you wouldn't guess this from her willowy frame—she loved her daily visits to our favorite doughnut shop on Eaton Street. This time, as I puttered toward her place, I couldn't help noticing that she'd gotten about as far from her family in New Town as she could get on this island.

Her place was located on Southard Street, which led to Duval Street if you went north, and Fort Zachary Taylor State Park if you went south. I parked my scooter in the lot behind the mass of condos, and wove along the path through the vegetation screening the pool, to her front door.

She answered my knock wearing her hair in a messy topknot and dressed in cat-themed pajamas. She looked immediately guilty. "I'm sorry I didn't answer your text," she said. "I'm just not up to dealing with Palamina right now. I simply can't. Do you want to come in?"

I followed her into a living room wallpapered in sunny yellow gingham. The white wicker couches upholstered in a tropical foliage print mirrored the scene outside.

"Want coffee?" she asked as we both sat down.

"No, thanks."

As she scuffed off her Hello Kitty slippers and tucked her feet under her bottom, I added: "I just had a cup with Seymour."

Her eyes got wide. "I didn't know you two were so friendly."

"We're not, though he's lovely. You'll enjoy spending time with him this year. If you get the chance, that is. If you can get hold of yourself and act like a normal person, not a guilty criminal."

Danielle looked shocked. One dime-sized tear squeezed out of her eye and trickled down her cheek.

"How can you say that when I collapsed last night?"

I sat forward, my elbows on my knees. "And according to your mother, who called me because she's so worried, they can't find any physical reason for what happened. Honestly, you know what it's beginning to look like?"

She looked away, twisting the hem of her pajama shirt between her fingers.

"It's beginning to look from the outside like you're tightly wound because you're worried the authorities will catch up with you."

"You're not serious." Her face paled and her lips trembled.

I sighed. "Not really, that isn't what I believe, but work with me here. It's not that much of a stretch to imagine that other people could think you killed her. That's why it's so important to figure out why Druckman hated you, if she did."

"Her feelings made no sense to me. I never did a thing to her, other than win." Now her expression grew stony.

"When did you first meet her?" I asked.

"There was an organizational meeting in early August. Anyone interested in running was supposed to attend to hear about how the contest would be conducted. And last year's king and queen came to give an idea of what to expect and jazz up the night, I suppose." She loosened her hair from the topknot and shook it out with her fingers.

"Did you have any contact with her then?"

"Not really," Danielle said. "Though we all introduced ourselves—where we came from, our jobs, and so on. She took up more airtime than anyone else, I remember that. My mother kept nudging me and my aunt and making little jokes."

"So your mom and your aunt were there from the beginning?"

Danielle nodded. "As I said, they talked me into the whole mess. I think Mom knew I'd never have gone if she didn't drag me there personally."

"Okay," I said, thinking I was learning nothing new. But remembering how Lieutenant Torrence described an interrogation: First of all, most people don't remember the details during the initial telling. And second, whether guilty or not, they hold things back. The sort of things that don't look good, or feel embarrassing, or are traumatic. So an investigator asks the same questions more than once. "Tell me again what she was like at the Coronation Ball. I don't think we'll get anywhere unless we go over things minute by minute."

Danielle groaned. "It was bad enough to live through it the first time."

I smiled in sympathy but barreled forward. "So when you attended the coronation party, did you come all dressed up?"

"You might remember that we had several costume changes. They wanted to have us dance with the Aquanettes. And your friend Randy—"

"Victoria," I corrected her automatically. "You don't call her Randy when she's in drag."

"Okay, so Victoria was as nice as she could be. And so was JB, who's an amazing dancer. I wasn't catching on to the steps right away because I was so nervous. We practiced a little bit last week, but the more anxious I got, the less I remembered." Tears welled up in her eyes and sluiced down her cheeks. "And then that horrible woman started to yell at me and correct me and suggest I drop out before I ruined the night with my clumsiness. Did she think it was all that lovely to see her great swells of flesh jiggling around?"

We both started to laugh and she clapped her hands over her mouth. "I know I could go to hell for saying rude things about a dead woman, but she brought out the worst in me."

"What else do you remember?" I asked. "Who did she spend time with that evening?"

Danielle closed her eyes, trying to bring back more details. I noticed the heavy purple circles under her eyes that made it look as though she hadn't slept in days.

"She had a little collection of snowbird ladies with her—her gang of social media maniacs. I bet they put up a thousand photos on Instagram just in those few hours. But I also got the sense she was working on a business deal."

"With whom?"

She held her head between her hands. "It may have been during the dress rehearsal. I don't know, she was talking on the phone a lot and texting someone." She shrugged.

"Maybe it was real estate? Maybe she was about to buy some property or she'd just bought it? You should ask Cory at Preferred Properties. She knows all the players in Key West—she could probably tell you." She plucked at her pajama top and smoothed her hair.

"I'll ask you what I asked Seymour. Did Miss

Druckman seem sick or out of sorts at the zombie parade pre-party? Did she have the same gang of friends with her?"

"Out of sorts, always," Danielle said. "We were mostly together as a team, doing the meet-and-greet business. Jenna Stauffer, the local TV anchor, interviewed us. And a couple of radio stations did too. She wasn't particularly generous with her remarks or happy to be there, but I can't say she looked sick."

"Keep thinking," I said. "Any little detail you remember could help. Seymour said she was quite tipsy. I guess working at the Green Parrot but not drinking himself, he could recognize a drunk when he sees one."

Danielle nodded, but then squinted. "He drinks though; I'm pretty sure of that. He carried a little silver flask and I could swear he was sipping from it." She sighed. "I guess I'd better get myself together and go into the office. Are you working today?"

I swallowed hard and grimaced. "I'm not sure I have a job at this point. I kind of told Palamina off."

"Oh, Hayley." She covered her mouth with her hand again, and I noticed her slender nails, usually perfectly French manicured, had been bitten down to the flesh. "What in the world did you say?"

I whistled out a breath. "Pretty much told her we'd all quit if she kept this up. And that would be a shame because both Key West visitors and locals want to hear our opinions, not those of imported writers."

She jumped up and began to clap. A one-woman standing ovation. "Good for you! Someone needs to stick up for us little people."

I stood up and took a bow. "It felt good at the time. Now I wonder if I worked myself out of a job. And maybe you too. Speaking of getting out, Eric and Bill are leaving the island tomorrow. Are you and your family planning to go?"

"We're Conchs," Danielle said. "We stay put until we're blown away."

23

Sam and my mother picked us up in the Tarpon Pier
parking lot after we realized that carrying food trays
on the back of the scooter would've been tricky. Especially wearing tutus. In honor of the tutu party that
we weren't attending, Miss Gloria had pulled on my
hot pink sparkly tutu over her white capri sweats, and
I wore the black number sprinkled with silver moons
and bats over my jean shorts. We brought last year's
purple tutu for my mother, and a camo-colored tutu
borrowed from Ray to lend Sam—a manly man's version, alternating layers of green and brown tulle. Connie had laughed when she handed it over, and said
that the only way Ray would get caught dead in this

item of clothing was if she could come up with a cam-
ouflage theme.

We whisked through the back streets to reach Eric
and Bill's little conch house in Bahama Village, but it
was impossible to avoid swells of partying people as
we crossed Duval Street. Most of them carried big
drink cups or cans of beer and wore tutus and other
unusual costumes, slightly less revealing than those
I'd seen in the Fantasy Zone.

We parked in front of our friends' house, and
walked around the right side through the set of double
gates that kept their Yorkshire terriers from escaping
to the street. As is so often the case with Key West
homes, the front of the house looked fairly ordinary,
but the back opened up to a glorious garden. In the
past, we'd eaten meals on the back deck overlooking
our friends' tropical oasis. But tonight was too muggy,
too close, unbearably humid. The dogs rushed through
the doorway as Bill opened the door, greeting us with
furious yipping as they circled around our ankles
sniffing the scent of cats.

"The tutus are priceless," said Bill. "Eric, you have
to see this—obviously, we haven't dressed correctly
for the occasion." He ushered us into their family
room, adjoining the kitchen. "Ignore the big mess.
We're packing away some paintings and valuables to
bring with us, in case the storm is super destructive.
But it's hard to conceive of never seeing this place
again." He looked so bummed.

"That isn't going to happen," Miss Gloria said,
reaching up on tippy-toes to kiss his cheek. "They've

only issued a hurricane watch, not a warning. And the storm is too disorganized to plot a path, really."

I exchanged a big hug with him and another with Eric, and deposited our dinner contributions on the long island that separated the kitchen from the sitting area. In addition to our platter of ripe tomatoes, mozzarella, and fresh basil, I'd stir-fried some green beans with garlic, ginger, and sesame seeds, and glazed them with a dash of sugar and a splash of soy sauce. Eric was slicing half of a beef tenderloin, which he fanned out on a pretty flowered plate with a dish of sour cream sauce in the center.

"I hope you don't mind peppery," he said to Sam. "There's a boatload of horseradish in the sauce."

"I like spicy food and spicy women," Sam answered, circling his arm around my mother's waist and tweaking her purple tulle. "If you haven't found a wedding dress yet, you look awfully cute in this." He kissed the top of her head and grinned.

"She's in deep trouble if she hasn't found a dress by now," I said. "Dress shops are severely limited on this island."

"Maybe some romantic body paint for two?" Sam asked.

Everyone laughed, and I tried not to imagine that scene in much detail.

"We're sad about missing the wedding," Eric said. "Some of the latest weather reports seem to think the storm might be moving back out to sea, so we're second-guessing ourselves, whether we should even go."

"We're pretty much committed to leaving though,"

said Bill. "We've got a reservation in Delray Beach at the Colony Hotel. We've been waiting for a chance to visit—it's a beautiful old hotel in a cute town, and they love dogs. Then we'll be able to stock up on mysteries at Murder on the Beach bookstore. And besides, after tonight there'll be nothing left in our larder. And I suspect that between Fantasy Fest and the hurricane threat, the shelves at Fausto's supermarkets have pretty much been wiped out."

"Things did look a bit thin when I stopped in this afternoon," I said.

Eric said, "And I've canceled a week's worth of therapy patients—and Bill's rescheduled all his tour guide shifts at the Truman Little White House, so we might as well make use of the vacation time." He added a bowl of potato salad and a big green salad to the bounty on the counter, and then we loaded up our plates and took seats in the family room. Bill turned up the volume on the flat-screen TV mounted against the wall.

"I don't know when there's ever been a more difficult storm to nail down," said the weatherman of the hour to the viewers. "We brought in our hurricane expert, oceanographer Dr. Jeff Chanton, to fill us in on the latest. What's the latest on Hurricane Margaret?"

"Our storm tracking planes have picked up some lateral movement, meaning it's moving slowly to the northeast, heading into the Atlantic Ocean and away from the coast of Florida," said the expert, who was dressed in a flannel shirt, wire-rimmed glasses, and a short ponytail. "Four factors help us understand when to expect a strengthening storm. Number one

is high water temperature, which we have in spades
right now." A large chart featuring Florida, Cuba, and
the water surrounding them appeared on the screen
behind him. He pointed to the red icon of the rotating
storm. "The second factor contributing to strength
would be warm moist air, which is obviously also
present."

"You said there were four factors?" asked the weatherman.

"Yes, I'll skip ahead to the fourth, which is whether
the storm is headed toward a landmass or out to the
open water. Hitting land diffuses a storm, though at
some cost to any buildings and cities and such along
its path. Crossing over water allows it to get stronger.
It's a wash currently on Margaret, because we're not
entirely sure where she's headed. Here are some of the
projected paths."

The display behind the expert showed multiple colored lines that wandered in conflicting directions—
even messier than the map we'd seen the night before.

"The third factor is vertical wind shear. High wind
shear allows the warm moist air to dissipate, while
low shear increases the strength.

"Good news for all our worried residents: We've
measured an increase in vertical winds over the past
twenty-four hours. That said, folks along the Keys and
the Eastern Seaboard should keep a close eye on our
weather trackers and make preparations in case Margaret changes course. As we've been saying all week,
this is not a storm to take lightly."

"I don't know what to make of that," said Sam as
Bill clicked the volume down.

"Nobody knows what to make of that," Miss Gloria said. "The best you can do is prepare like these guys are doing and follow your gut." Her eyes twinkled. "Mine says stay. And also, that this dinner is delicious!"

Eric got up to refill our wineglasses. "Have you heard anything new on the zombie murderer?" He looked at me as though I would have the inside scoop.

"Nobody's told me anything," I said, "but what else is new?" I explained how I had visited both Seymour and Danielle to try to flesh out who the murdered woman really was, and from there, make an educated guess about who might have wished her ill. "I hate to say this, but I don't think you can rule out Danielle's family."

"You mean the twins?" my mother asked as she set her plate on the coffee table. "I can't believe they would be involved in a murder. Certainly her mother would realize that if she committed this kind of crime, her daughter would be suspected." Mom shook her head. "I would never risk your well-being by doing something so dumb."

"What if she believed she was protecting Danielle from something worse?" I asked. "Or maybe it was her aunt, thinking she was doing the right thing."

"And twins are funny," Sam said. "I dated a twin once." He grinned at my mother, whose eyes widened in what I thought was mock astonishment. "This was well before your time. And her charms paled in comparison to yours. She was a distant planet compared to your sun."

Miss Gloria snickered. "You go, boyfriend."

"But anyway," Sam continued, "my point is that she

would've done anything for her sister. When it came right down to her or me, she chose her sister."

I realized that even though I knew Sam reasonably well and he was marrying my mother, there was a lot I didn't know about him. Things I would probably never know. People were like that, full of psychological wrinkles and shadowy corners—even the ones you'd known forever harbored secrets.

"But what's the motive here?" my mother asked. "Since when do you cause bodily harm because you want to win a contest?"

"Think 1994 figure skating debacle with Tonya Harding versus Nancy Kerrigan," said Miss Gloria. She glanced down at the small piece of fillet on her plate and then back up to Eric. "And only last year, one of the leading contestants was murdered with poisoned steak at the Crufts Dog Show."

"How many glasses of wine has she had?" Bill asked Eric as he tousled my roommate's hair.

"It's striking to me," Eric said, "that no one seems to know much about Caryn Druckman as a person, a human being. Who is mourning her versus who might be rubbing their hands with glee, in secret anyway. Have you heard anything about a funeral or memorial?" he asked.

Miss Gloria looked at me and shrugged. "Mrs. Renhart would be the one with all that dope."

I pulled my phone out of my back pocket and texted our neighbor with the question about services and arrangements. Almost as quickly, I got a return beep telling me the text was "undelivered."

"They're probably out of cell phone range," I said,

and explained how their boat had been towed off the day before.

"What's happening with your detective?" my mother asked. "Has he told you anything?"

I figured she had been popping to ask this, and probably Sam had told her to leave it alone. And so had Eric. And she'd kept it to herself as long as she could, until it finally burst through her filter from mind to mouth. In public, where I couldn't dodge it entirely as she had to know I'd prefer.

"Nothing. Nothing happening at all," I said.

"I'm sure they're all crazy busy this week—cops, firefighters, EMTs," said Eric kindly. "Even crazier than usual."

I nodded my thanks to him for putting a positive spin on Bransford's absence, even though he didn't know the story about his ex being in town. That was the mark of a good friend—don't jump to trash the boyfriend because as with any storm, the wind can change direction at any moment.

"There was one other random thing I learned earlier," I said. "Or I should say noticed, rather than learned. When I visited Seymour, Danielle's king, he told me that he doesn't drink. And so he didn't have any alcohol at the zombie bike ride. But Danielle told me that he does drink, that he carried a flask with him and she saw him drinking from it. Maybe this has nothing to do with the murder, but I found it odd."

"It could be something as simple as him falling off the wagon," Eric said, getting up to move some of our empty plates to the kitchen island. "If he's an alcoholic who's been attending meetings and all, and then he slips and takes a drink in the excitement and stress of the moment, he might very well not want to claim that slip."

"Poor guy," said Mom. "He had no idea what he was getting into when he signed on to become royalty. And if he was carrying some kind of poisoned liquid in that flask with which he planned to kill Druckman, he'd hardly be drinking it himself."

"Is there anyone else you haven't spoken with who was there and might have some insight?"

I mulled it over. "The only other person is Kitty Palmer. She's one of the tennis coaches at Bayview."

Bayview is a public park not far from the police station and Houseboat Row. Natives and snowbirds alike make heavy use both of the tennis courts, and of the pros who teach there.

"She ran against Danielle and Druckman, though my sense is that she wasn't that involved. Maybe I'll run down there tomorrow and have a chat." I clattered the plates into the sink and began to rinse them off. "And John-Bryan Hopkins, the fellow who ran against Seymour for king. He's a Twitter genius. I sent him a message but he's probably too busy to write me back."

Eric brought the coconut cake over to the coffee table—tall, fragrant, and fuzzy with coconut shavings. The dogs, who'd been snoozing on the couch between Miss Gloria and me, hopped to the floor, yapping and leaping with excitement.

"Not a chance, you guys," said Bill, pushing the animals away. "That's people food." He bowed in Eric's direction. "You've outdone yourself, my friend."

Eric grinned and plunged a carving knife into the cake. "How big of a piece do you want?"

"Enormous," said Miss Gloria, holding her arms out wide as a beach ball.

"And make mine bigger than hers," said Sam with a wink.

Eric carved big slices of the tender yellow cake, three layers filled with creamy white icing, more frosting swirled over all, and finally, a thick layer of coconut patted over the whole cake. He ran his finger over the knife and tasted, nodded his approval, then distributed the plates to us.

"I'm awfully sorry we will miss the ceremony," he said to my mother as he handed her the last slice.

"Sam and I have been talking things over," said my mother. "We're thinking about postponing the wedding until you guys and Connie and Ray are back in town. We're a little bit frozen on what to do. Should we clear out like you, or stay here and hope for the best?" Her lips trembled and her eyes got glassy.

Sam took her hand and squeezed it. "On the other hand, I don't want to wait any longer to marry this woman," he said. "Remember how long it took her to say yes?"

"Yes, we remember." I rolled my eyes. "We had to live with her while she was vacillating. It wasn't pretty. We told her she'd be crazy to take a pass on you."

"You were right, as usual," said my mother, cupping Sam's chin with her hand. "He's a peach."

"Give the weather another day," said Miss Gloria. "I think it's going to miss us. We can go ahead with the service and have the small dinner at Louie's as planned. Then we'll throw another, bigger party when everyone gets back in town. Hey, life is short. Be greedy and grab all the joy you can hold."

Caryn Druckman could have told us that.

24

Sometimes when husband call me from the kitchen and his voice is sharp as the knife he holding, Bobby look up at me and make the face, the way children do when they taste a sour green mango from the tree.

—Thrity Umrigar, *The Story Hour*

The next morning, I woke up from a deep sleep to clanking and banging. For one groggy moment, I thought the hurricane had blown through. But the boat wasn't rocking any more than yesterday and the spot on my quilt where Evinrude usually sleeps was empty and cold, meaning he'd been up for some time. He spends stormy nights draped over my neck like a fox stole.

I vaulted out of bed and trotted down the hall to the galley where Miss Gloria—Hurricane Gloria—had everything we owned out on the counter, the kitchen table, and even the floor. Tied around her waist, she wore an apron bearing the face of Randy Thompson from his stint on the *Topped Chef* TV show. And she had a checkered dishcloth tied around her head, pushing her white hair into a disheveled Mohawk.

"What in the world is going on?" I asked, hands on hips, surveying the devastation.

"Here, get a cuppa coffee. You can have the last inch, and then help me out," she said. She poured the dregs of thin liquid from the coffeemaker into my favorite pink mug and handed it to me. From the living room, the television blared, the Weather Channel of course, with news of strengthening eye walls and water temperature and wind shear trumpeting through our small living space. The national forecaster broke for the local station, announcing that an evacuation order had been put in place for visitors to the island. A determination would be made at the end of the day regarding cancellation of Saturday's Fantasy Fest parade.

"It's coming?" I asked.

"I doubt it," she said. "They are all such alarmists. But it pays to be prepared. In case we get to rocking and rolling, I thought it would be smart to put the loose stuff into the drawers and cabinets that lock. The problem is, since you moved in with all your wonderful cooking gear, the space is overwhelmed." She collapsed onto the built-in bench behind our kitchen table and swiped the checkered dishcloth over her forehead.

"But is the forecast different?" I asked, trying to figure out what was causing the worry lines etched on her face.

"Not significantly." She frowned even deeper. "But

my son Frank is having a fit. He's giving me today, and if the storm doesn't move northeast, he's making me a plane reservation. I don't want to leave"—her eyes sparkled with tears—"but it's not really fair for them to sit up in Michigan and worry themselves sick. I ought to go visit my family anyway, right?"

I felt instantly queasy at the thought of her leaving the island without me. Her confidence about surviving any storm was the reason we were all willing to stay. And down a little deeper, I felt sad that my status as the nucleus of her island family was not enough to keep her here. And then guilty to even think that.

"He's right," I said, reaching across the table to grab her hand. "If the storm isn't dying off, you should clear out. You're not a young woman."

"I'm not?" She grinned and stood up to return to work. "My darling husband thought of everything when he fitted out this boat." She pointed out the clips on the drawers that would hold them closed even in the worst turbulence. And the hooks on the pantry door, and the little railings on most of the shelves.

"But he didn't plan on your KitchenAid mixer or your Cuisinart or your collection of cookbooks or your Calphalon cookware."

"Hey, don't diss the KitchenAid. Girls my age are getting married just so they can get that mixer at their shower. As you can see"—I ran a hand lovingly over the cherry red enamel of my machine—"I wasn't willing to wait for the right guy to pop the question."

Once we had found a place for everything, I brewed a new pot of hot fresh coffee and sat at the table with a bowl of granola to read my e-mail while Miss Gloria went to shower. Buried halfway down my in-box, I found a note from Miss Gloria's son. "We are so grateful for your friendship with and caretaking of our mother."

Ha! As if I had to do anything other than rein in her zany energy from time to time. And feed her.

"We would so appreciate your support in getting her on the plane tomorrow. It was not easy to find a seat, so postponing is not an option." He had copied her itinerary and pasted it into the e-mail. So they weren't waiting until tomorrow to decide; they were planning for her to leave regardless of changes in the weather. Eight a.m. sharp.

"Will do," I answered back. Not bothering to add my sense that she'd rather go down with the ship in Key West than be alive almost anywhere else.

I began to click through the photos on the official zombie parade Web site again, hoping I'd see something new. I thought about Eric's comment the night before—how little we knew about Caryn Druckman. I mentioned this to Miss Gloria when she came out of the shower. "I'm going to try Mrs. Renhart again. Maybe they've got cell coverage wherever they landed. She would probably know about the funeral mass."

Sure enough, my text message went through, followed by a quick response. Service at St. Mary's Star of the Sea at 10 a.m. today. Hope all is well on the dock.

"I can be dressed and ready in ten minutes," Miss Gloria said.

"I didn't know you were coming," I said.

"Everything's finished here," she said, gesturing at the shipshape galley. "Mah-jongg is canceled today.

No one wants me to sit around and twiddle my thumbs. No telling what kind of trouble an old lady could find."

"You'll let me do the talking?"

"Of course," she said, her grin wide. "Don't I always?"

While I dressed quickly in black capri pants and a cap-sleeved white top and my best black-sequined sneakers, Miss Gloria donned her most subdued sweat suit—the only one not decorated with rhinestones or baby bunnies. We buzzed over Palm Avenue and down Truman to the Catholic church at the corner of Windsor Lane, an enormous white stone edifice with double towers and expansive grounds, unusually spacious for this island. The louvered doors lining both sides of the sanctuary had been thrown open to catch any passing breeze, and a handful of well-dressed people were filing in. I parked the scooter, and we removed our helmets and smoothed our hair.

"After we go to the service and solicit clues, we can light a few candles at Our Lady of Lourdes Grotto," Miss Gloria said.

I chose to ignore the comment about soliciting clues—it would only rile her up. "I didn't know you were Catholic."

"I'm not," she said. "But Sister Gabriel lobbied to have the grotto built in the 1920s to protect the island from hurricanes. Lots of island people go there to light candles and pray during the hurricane season. I try to visit every time a storm heads this way. You can believe it works or not, but we haven't had a direct hit since the grotto was constructed."

"So all that talk about how you know how to handle

a hurricane might be hot air," I said, sort of teasing.
"You've never actually lived through one?"

"We count Rita," she said. "Devastating storm
surge. And no one would say Wilma wasn't pure hurricane. And completely unpredictable at that."

She nodded gravely as we took seats in one of the
rear pews, a good way behind the other mourners,
who seemed mostly female and over fifty. The funeral
mass went by quickly, as there were few personal remarks made from the pulpit. In fact, the only family
in attendance seemed to be a cousin, introduced as
Ann Druckman. She assisted in bringing the gifts to
the altar, and later read one of the passages from the
Bible. At the end of the service, after we'd all teared
up at a lovely rendition of "On Eagle's Wings," the
priest invited visitors to a reception in the garden.

I took a small cup of juice and a cookie and wandered among the other guests. I stopped near a group
of three women that included Druckman's cousin.

"So sad about Caryn," one of the women said. "Did
she have a history of heart problems?"

"Type one diabetes and high cholesterol," Ann
Druckman answered. "As heavy as she was, she had
no business on a bike. I always teased her that the only
thing she ever exercised was her mouth. But she just
laughed. And now look what's happened. . . ."

One of the other women patted the cousin on the
shoulder. "We will miss her too. She did so much in
the service of charity in the short time she was here.
She raised a ton of money for Wesley House and the
Old Island Restoration Foundation and the Waterfront
Theater. She was tireless."

"I wonder what's going to happen to her property now that she's gone?" a silver-haired thin woman asked of Ann Druckman. "Hadn't she just purchased something new?"

"Having not seen the will, I have no idea. She did not discuss real estate with me. She knew I would not own property on this island if you gave it to me. Too risky," said Ann Druckman. "Now that I'm here, I can't really see the lure of the place either. I'd rather not be subjected to what's usually hidden under people's clothing, whether they paint their flab or not."

The women tittered.

"Most of us regulars stay away from Duval Street, especially during this festival," said the first woman. "But this week is unusual—a lot more party animals and a lot less charm. You should come back at Christmas time. All those twinkling lights on the palm trees? It's magical."

"I like my snow at Christmas, thank you very much." Druckman's cousin chuckled. "Helps with the hot flashes."

"Have they determined what actually killed Caryn?" the first woman asked in a hushed voice. "We'd heard she was poisoned. . . ."

"Nothing definitive showed up on the tox screen, according to the detective. Her blood alcohol level was super high, though that can't be the whole story. Our entire family is known to drink like fishes and it never did the rest of us any harm."

"Sometimes alcohol can interact with a medication," said the silver-haired woman. "Maybe that was the case?"

Ann Druckman scratched her scalp, thinking. "She did tell me about the high protein/low carbohydrate diet she was on for the past few months so she'd look good on the dais." She shook her head emphatically. "It's never a good idea to skip carbs. I believe that's why she sounded so cranky lately. And of course she was distraught about losing the crown to that skinny young woman who swooped out of nowhere."

Then all three women seemed to sense me hovering and listening and turned in my direction, looking a little hostile—as though I didn't belong. "You were a friend of Caryn's?" the silver-haired woman asked.

"I wouldn't say friend, but an acquaintance. Through the Fantasy Fest royalty competition. I attended a lot of the fund-raising events and admired her bulldog tenacity." I grinned and brushed the crumbs off my hands and got out of there before they could pursue my nonexistent connection with the dead woman.

After locating Miss Gloria coming out of the restroom, we headed toward the grotto, a lovely arch made of coral rock, rustic in the manner of a New England stone wall. The statue of Our Lady of Lourdes was set into the stone cave, and another statue on the ground gazed up at her. A metal stand was also located inside the stone cubby, containing candles, matches, and a few flowers. A sign on the wooden box suggested a donation of one dollar for a votive candle and three for the larger size. We each lit a tall white taper and said a silent prayer, mine for no hurricane and safety for my friends and family.

As we moved away, an older woman was finishing up her walk on the flagstones, which were laid out in front of the grotto in a big loop shaped like a rosary. I recognized her as Ann Druckman, the cousin who'd brought the gifts to the altar but had a distaste for Key West.

"Again, we're sorry for your loss," I told her. "This is Miss Gloria, my roommate. This is Caryn's cousin."

"Pleased to meet you. I'm Ann."

We chatted for a moment about the service and when Ann would be returning to Michigan—the earliest plane she could manage this afternoon.

"It must be so frustrating not to know exactly why she died," I said. "I didn't want to mention this in front of the other ladies, but I was riding near her in the zombie parade. I stopped to try to help, but I have no medical training." I held my hands open. "I wish I could have done more."

"Thank you," she said, and dabbed at her eyes with a shredded Kleenex. "What was . . . Was there anything . . . Did she say anything before they took her away?"

I put my hand to my chest and breathed deeply as the memory of that moment rushed into my mind. "Nothing I could understand. I don't think she was suffering." Isn't that what you were supposed to say to comfort a grieving relative? "I thought maybe she'd had too much to drink. Her breath had a sweet smell, and I suspected that grain alcohol punch they were passing around. Lethal stuff."

I stuttered an apology for saying too much and knowing too little.

"She was a ball of fire right up to the last moment

before she died," I added. "She brought a lot of zip to the contest this year."

"She never could stand to lose," said Cousin Ann with a tired shrug. "Go big or go home—that was her motto. I think she got that saying from the editor of a women's magazine. But it started when we were kids playing board games. If she was losing, look out— many's the time she knocked the game off the table and stormed away. I do believe that competitive fire had only gotten worse over the years. At least she's at peace now."

We nodded solemnly as she walked away.

"What did we learn?" asked Miss Gloria.

"Not much, I'm afraid. She hated to lose and she wasn't eating enough bread and cake, which caused her to be crabby."

We got onto my scooter, chuckling. This business of eschewing carbs wouldn't happen in our home. I texted Torrence to tell him the few facts I'd learned at the funeral, hoping that would motivate him to call me back and tell me what was actually happening with the case. Because it sure didn't sound as if they'd told Druckman's cousin much of anything. Now that I was thinking about the murder again, it surprised me that there'd been no police presence in the church. Which might mean the whole thing was solved. Or not. I dropped Miss Gloria off at the cemetery as she'd requested and tried to figure out what to do next.

25

*Gentlemen prefer girls who know how to
cook, whether they be blonde, brunette, or
titian.*

—Anita Loos, Foreword,
What Actors Eat—When They Eat

I considered stopping to visit my Realtor friend Cory
Held, who worked at Preferred Properties Real Estate,
which was located on the first floor of the building
housing our *Key Zest* office. Much as I wanted to find
out what deal Druckman was working on right before
she died, I wanted to avoid running into Palamina
even more. It felt weird not to be going into the office,
not to have assignments to be mulling over and rough-
ing out. I had to hope that Palamina would come to
her senses and beg me to come back to work. Unlikely,
but maybe Wally would knock some sense into her.
The odds were not in my favor.

I checked out Cory Held's Facebook page and was

pleased to see that she was holding an open house off Southard Street early this afternoon. According to the listing description, this house was a gorgeous conch home with a tiny guesthouse and dipping pool in the backyard, all on a quiet lane not so close to Duval that it would be noisy, but close enough to stumble home on foot. I supposed that in her ambitious Realtor's mind, there was some small chance that a Fantasy Fest attendee would have such a great time this week that they would be moved to buy a piece of property on the spot.

I drove over. She was propping up the OPEN HOUSE sign and draping it with strings of colored glass beads as I pulled up on my scooter.

"Hayley," she said, "don't tell me you're finally ready to get off that houseboat?"

I laughed. "On my salary? Not happening." I felt a quick clench in my stomach—maybe I had no salary at all. A neatly bearded man on a rental scooter drove up and whooped at Cory.

"John-Bryan!" she yelled and trotted over to give him a hug. Then she drew him back over to me and introduced us.

"I recognize you from the performance at the Coronation Ball," I said. "You are a fabulous dancer."

"Thanks. And I owe you a phone call," he said in a deep Southern drawl, his brown eyes large behind big black glasses. He vibrated with an energy that seemed as though it could fill a room. He reached over and folded me into a bear hug.

"Apparently you already know each other," Cory said.

"Not really," I said, and then grimaced. "I'm kind of looking into Caryn Druckman's death on behalf of my friend Danielle. That's why I messaged you," I told him. "Since you were so close to the action and yet an outsider to the politics, I wondered if you might have noticed something that other people wouldn't."

"That was so tragic," he said. "I was riding up front near Danielle and Seymour and we never knew anything had happened to Caryn until it was over."

"I wasn't so lucky," I said. "I was right ahead of her when she fell."

"Come on in, both of you, and we can chat," said Cory. She grabbed JB's arm and steered him up the walk. "And you have to see this house."

We entered a set of French doors that opened into a great room paneled in whitewashed Dade pine. The floor was constructed of wide wood boards, the honeyed color perfectly reflecting the pale peach cushions on the wicker furniture. A bamboo ceiling fan rotated slowly, causing the oversize houseplants to wave like lazy hula dancers. Cory placed a sign-up sheet for visitors on the wooden table in the vestibule next to a stack of business cards.

Then she whisked us through the first-floor rooms, which were open to the backyard with its tiny blue pool surrounded by palms and a latticework fence dotted with purple and yellow orchids, and a studio at the end of the property. "This is all wonderful, but the best is coming next," she said with a big smile.

I immediately drooled over the kitchen: a four-burner gas Wolfe stove with a copper hood, a side-by-side stainless full-sized refrigerator/freezer—not feasible on a houseboat—and a stunning coral-topped island surrounded by tall stools where I could picture Miss Gloria perching to chat as I worked. It was nothing like the fabulous professional kitchen in the Paradise Pub, but it would suit me perfectly.

"Someday," I said, sounding a little mournful. "Do you cook?" I asked John-Bryan, who was swooning over the double oven.

"He's a wonderful cook," Cory said, "famous for his honeyed smoked peaches." She winked at him. "Your smoker would fit perfectly on that deck. If you're going to spend this much time in Key West, you really need a place."

John-Bryant laughed and turned to me. "She's an amazing saleswoman and I have to say, I'm weakening." He grinned. "Now, what can I tell you about Druckman?"

"Did she seem sick to you at all over the past week? Was she a big drinker?"

He rubbed his chin as we trooped upstairs to see the bedrooms. "No to sick, but yes to drinker," he said as we admired the master bedroom with its pencil bed piled with white pillows and array of watercolors painted by local artists on the wall. "But the kind of drinker who could hold her liquor—not even show how much had gone down the hatch."

After more drooling over the gorgeous master bath—two sinks, a spa tub, and more shelves than we had in our entire boat—we headed downstairs.

"I've heard that Caryn Druckman was working on a real estate deal, or had settled one right before she died," I said to Cory. "I know you're not supposed to talk about a client's private business, but I thought since she's gone, you might have heard something unofficially." Though what did I really know, because no one official was bothering to text me back.

"What could she have been looking for? She has to own one of the nicest homes on the island already. Besides, it's a very slow time, this week," said Cory. "And now they've begun evacuating visitors. In fact, I'm probably wasting my hours here, unless I can talk this big lug into signing a contract." She squeezed JB's arm with affection. "I can't think of one property that's gone on deposit." She dug her phone out of her purse and scrolled through several screens. "Nothing on the MLS. Though that doesn't mean a deal couldn't have been done with a handshake. Though Conchs are cautious. If they were dealing with an outsider, I would think they'd go through professional channels."

"And Druckman was still an outsider, same as me," said JB. "Much as we wanted to be considered natives. And as much money as a certain person might have thrown at the situation." His eyebrows lifted above his glasses. "And all the social media in the world can't really buy you friends, though she tried her best."

"And this fellow would know," said Cory. "You have how many—like, a hundred thousand Twitter followers?"

He grinned. "Eight hundred and sixty-five thousand, but who's counting?"

After a few more minutes of chatter, I left the two of them looking through the adorable house again. I felt as if I was circling close to the answer, but not close enough to grasp it.

I decided to buzz by Grant's restaurant on the way home, thinking I would talk to him again about what he might have seen from his position behind the counter at Beach Eats during the zombie bike ride. Sometimes, when I'm trying to remember something, I set it aside for a couple of days. And out of nowhere, the missing detail floats to the top of my mind. Maybe it would work the same way with him.

I tried the front door, but in spite of the lunch hours posted on the menu outside, found it locked. I didn't imagine this was because of the storm prospects—wouldn't they have covered the windows with plywood and painted the wood with wild boasts against the hurricane? Or even more likely, they'd be throwing a hurricane party. With two drinks for the price of one, all named for storms that had brushed or hit Key West in the past: Donna's Daiquiri, Mitch's Mojito, Cleo's Cosmo, Bertha's Bloody Mary, Wilma's Last Word.

I trotted around the back of the building, but the kitchen access was locked too. The two kittens I'd seen the other day were hunkering under the Dumpster, but I didn't have the time or the means to lure them out. As I debated whether to put a call in to the SPCA and leave a message about the abandoned kitties, the back kitchen door squeaked open and Catfish emerged with a bowl of milk.

She startled and clapped a hand to her chest. "You scared me. I wasn't expecting company back here today. Everybody seems to be battening down the hatches."

"Doesn't look like you guys are planning to open either."

"Grant says maybe for bar traffic later this afternoon," she said. "We hate to cook a lot of stuff and have no one in the dining room to eat it." Her eyes welled with tears. "I hate this. There are so many ways a restaurant can fail, but I never believed a hurricane would get us."

"Maybe it's heading out to sea," I said. "Maybe it will turn out to be nothing. We said prayers at the hurricane grotto this morning." I smiled with encouragement, trying to figure out a graceful way to transition to my question. "I know I've asked about this before but hope you don't mind if we go over once more what you saw at the zombie party. I figure you and Grant had the best view from the Beach Eats truck."

"They still haven't figured out what happened to that woman?" Catfish asked. "Our police department . . ." She shook her head in disgust.

"They're busy with Fantasy Fest, I suppose." Then I explained that I'd gotten conflicting reports, what with Seymour claiming he didn't drink, but other people assuring me that he did. "Did you happen to notice him drinking out of a silver flask? I know it's unlikely that you'd remember, but I figured it was worth a try. He's this year's Fantasy Fest King."

"Honestly, I was too busy serving and cleaning up to notice much of anything. But there weren't many sober people at that party, I can assure you." She set the saucer of milk down and watched the kittens lap it up noisily. "I'm thinking we should bring them inside if the storm hits. Or would that be more frightening to the poor little guys than riding it out in familiar territory? We're all toast anyway, I'm afraid," she said, and started to cry.

"How many storms have you lived through here?"

"Twenty years' worth. Wilma was bad, but this one scares me more." She looked on the verge of full-blown hysteria. As I wondered whether to offer a hug, she wheeled around and disappeared into the kitchen.

26

Someone needs to tell these chefs their
food is no good. They need to know so
they can cut their losses and move on.
—Amy E. Reichert,
The Coincidence of Coconut Cake

On the way home, I stopped at the Bayview tennis courts on the off chance that Kitty Palmer, the third candidate for queen, was either teaching or playing. She was the last person I could think of whom I hadn't met who might have some insight into Caryn Druckman's behavior over the last months and weeks, and hence her death.

I heard the *whop, whop, whop* of a tennis ball hitting rackets before I could see the players. A tall, muscular woman with short brown hair was playing with the head pro, Paul Findlay, walloping any ball he hit over the net into the corners of his court—keeping him scrambling. He seemed relieved to take a break when

I signaled to Kitty that I hoped for a moment of her time.

She trotted across the court to the bleachers where I waited. I introduced myself and explained briefly that I was trying to help my friend Danielle, the Fantasy Fest Queen, who now appeared to be high on the police list of murder suspects. "You were right there as the relationships developed between Danielle and Druckman and also Seymour. Would you say there were sparks between any of them right away?"

She perched on the bench, took off her sunglasses, and wiped her face with a white towel. "Everyone was civil at the beginning, of course. The organizers worked hard at trying to make the competition seem fun. They wanted to psych us up so we'd spread the excitement and get lots of people to attend the events. So everything was peachy for a while." She stretched her leg out and massaged her calf. "However, in the month leading up to the coronation, the friction between Caryn Druckman and Danielle emerged. And then something was going on with Seymour. Or that's what I saw, anyway."

"What were their problems? Obviously they weren't in direct competition for a title."

"Mmm." She squinted and slid the sunglasses back on. "I couldn't say that I knew the subject—I tried to stay out of the drama, which was not easy, I can assure you. Druckman wanted to be a big wheel in this town; that's how I'd sum it up."

But what did that have to do with Danielle? "So, you'd say there was more trouble between Seymour and Druckman than Danielle and Druckman?"

Kitty laughed. "Oh, she never liked Danielle. She thought she was a local twit with beauty and no brains. And she complained a lot about Danielle's family. But the organizers kept telling her to keep her focus on the ball. That the point was raising money, not winning." She began to bounce a tennis ball on her racket and I could see she was impatient to return to her game.

"And what about John-Bryan? How did he fit in?"

"Thank goodness for him—he was in it for the fun, and if he hadn't been there to lighten up the mood, more dead bodies than the one might have turned up."

"Was there a lot of drinking among the candidates? Did you notice whether Druckman commonly drank at the events?" I asked.

"Definitely, but she was the kind of woman who could hold her liquor and you'd have no clue how much she knocked back. That's why I was so surprised to see her swerving around on her bike. I chalked it up to a lack of balance and grace, but maybe it was just plain too much to drink." She held an imaginary phone up to her ear as she got to her feet. "Give me a buzz if you think of any other questions."

I trudged back to my scooter, drenched by the humidity—and I hadn't hit one tennis ball. Had I found a motive for murdering someone? It seemed not yet. As I drove the few blocks back to the houseboat, I noticed traffic clogging Truman Avenue and heading north on Route One.

Inside our cabin, Miss Gloria had the TV blaring.

"They've finally, definitely called for an evacuation," she said. "The town has canceled the Fantasy

Fest parade. And the locals parade too, though good luck telling the locals anything. All visitors are expected to leave by ten p.m., and residents by morning."

"That would explain the traffic jam," I said, trying to sound cheerful, but failing miserably. "We'll drive you to the airport early tomorrow and then clear out ourselves. We'll take Sparky with us, if that's easier."

She nodded her thanks, looking as though she might burst into tears. I texted my mother the plan and then watched the Weather Channel for a few minutes with Miss Gloria.

"Maximum sustained winds have increased to near seventy-five miles per hour, moving Margaret from a tropical storm to a Category One hurricane on the Saffir-Simpson Hurricane Wind Scale. Additional strengthening during the next twenty-four hours is forecast." The anchor turned to the hurricane specialist. "This one is hard to predict, isn't it?"

"Absolutely. The current track is one possible path in our spaghetti model." The map showing all the colored lines appeared behind the weather people. "We are still hoping for a slight weakening as Margaret encounters high shear and dry air in the eastern Caribbean Sea. But residents and visitors in the path of the storm should evacuate promptly as directed."

Then the screen flashed to the Our Lady of Lourdes Grotto, where we'd lit a candle this morning. A reporter was standing on the church grounds, holding a microphone, his curly hair swirling.

"I'm reporting to you live from Key West, Florida, where local and state officials have pulled the trigger on the big Halloween parade and posted an evacuation notice. As you can see"—he gestured to the little cave with its flickering lights—"folks are still hopeful." In the background, a couple of teenagers waved at the camera crew. I clicked off the television.

"I guess we'd better pack a few things up," Miss Gloria said.

I filled a small suitcase with clean underwear and a few changes of clothes, and then got the cat food and litter and the carrier ready to go, and put everything by the door. Now what? I couldn't stand to spend the night watching weather reports. So I opened up my laptop and began to make notes on what we'd learned— and what we hadn't—about Caryn Druckman.

I started by reading some of the Key West Facebook groups. Leigh had been right—the locals were crabby. Unhappy about the hordes of rude tourists, the restaurants catering to tourists with New York prices for mediocre food, and out-of-towners snatching up real estate and renting it out to snowbirds so that low-to-middle-income workers had no shot at affordable living on the island.

Then I clicked over to Druckman's Instagram account, leafed through her photos, which included many, many shots of the AIDS Help royalty events, and then switched over to Facebook. A ways down into her feed, I noticed several unflattering photos posted to her timeline with rude comments about the woman, her appearance, her incessant need for attention, and the persona she had developed as the Key West maven.

Why hadn't she removed these? When I clicked on the names of the people who had posted to her timeline, phony accounts came up. It was almost as though a cyberbully had cracked the Facebook code and figured out how to harass her publicly.

Seymour was obviously lying about his drinking, but why? Did it have something to do with these taunts? Danielle's family was another possibility. Did one of them have the computer expertise to do this? If Druckman believed that they had posted all those unflattering photos, she might have blamed Danielle. And that would explain her rage, which led to the catfight on Duval Street in front of The Bull and Whistle.

I glanced at the clock on my built-in bedside table. Midnight—way too late to call Danielle again. And at this point, my focus needed to be getting some rest so I could help pilot my family to safety tomorrow.

27

She rose from the table in her white pantsuit, picked up the plate of offending toast, and slowly made her way across the dining room to the kitchen expediting station. The cooks saw her coming and scattered like roaches.
—Michael Procopio, "The Cheese Toast Incident," Food for the Thoughtless, May 20, 2014

Early the next morning, we waited in the parking lot for Sam and my mother to pick us up. The weather had deteriorated overnight and I'd barely slept as the boat rocked in the heavy chop, with Evinrude yowling his distress.

The fishermen that Miss Gloria's son had hired from the marina across the causeway struggled to tie extra lines from our home to the dock. They could barely keep their footing as the waves in the bight seethed, pounding our ramp. Evinrude and Sparky cater-wauled inside the cat carrier, expressing their outrage about the small space and the intermittent fierce gusts of wind and the general disruption to their cat lives. I sympathized completely and tried a comforting shush.

"They know something awful's happening," I said.

Miss Gloria laughed. "They don't need to be pre-scient to figure that out. The wind's got to be blowing forty miles an hour, maybe more. I don't feel right leaving you here," she said, gripping my hand with both of hers.

I felt a hitch in my breathing, but I tried to smile through it. "It's just for a little while, until the worst blows over. We can pick you up at the airport anytime you're ready to return. Your sons are right: You need to get out of here. I should have insisted you leave yesterday."

Sam pulled into the parking lot, my mother riding shotgun, looking frightened but determined. I opened the door for Miss Gloria, then handed the cat carrier and our small bags in after her. I hurried to the other side of the car and slid in, my hair swirled to a nest of unruly curls.

"Okay, we're off," said Mom in a strange singsong that betrayed her underlying anxiety.

We were all, it seemed, trying to be strong for one another.

"But where will you go after you drop me off?" Miss Gloria asked. "Honestly, I don't think you should drive in this weather."

"I'm certain that I read the new town hall has been designated as a shelter. We'll be back together in no time," said Sam in a hearty voice. "The hotel insisted all the patrons leave. I suppose they don't want to be responsible for us if the worst happens."

Bands of rain began to lash the car, and the wind kicked up strong enough that Sam had to fight to keep it in the right lane. The trunks of the palm trees lining the street bent sideways, their fronds whipping fiercely in the wind.

"It's a wonder they don't snap in half," said my mother.

"They're built to withstand the big storms. Just like me," said Miss Gloria. "I don't feel right abandoning the island."

I took her hand and held it in mine. "We promised your sons and we're not going back on that now. They're already mad that we waited this long."

Once we'd crossed the island, Sam steered the car slowly toward the airport. The sea to the right boiled, restless and gray.

My mother squawked as a wave broke over the seawall and sloshed across the sidewalk and onto the pavement. "I have to be honest—we shouldn't be out here. That ocean could wash us away in a New Jersey instant. I can't believe they are flying planes in this weather."

Sam said nothing, just gripped the steering wheel tighter and focused his attention out through the windshield. We finally turned into the drive leading to the airport and headed up the short hill to the arrivals. There were no other passengers, no taxicabs, no baggage porters poised to drag luggage into the building. One lone figure dressed in black towing an enormous designer suitcase waved us down.

"Good gravy," I said. "It's Chad Lutz." My former boyfriend, the guy who invited me to Key West on a whim two years ago and dumped me in record time.

"We'd better stop and see what he wants, darling," said my mother to Sam. He pulled to the curb. As I pushed open the door and stuck my head out, my hair whipped over my eyes.

"All the flights are canceled," he hollered above the wind, his voice terse. "No one's going anywhere."

My mother rolled down her window, strands of her auburn hair whirling out of its bun. "Do you need a ride?"

He hesitated for a moment, but when Sam popped the trunk he hoisted his suitcase in. I scooted over on the seat and put the cat carrier on my lap to make room for Chad, and introduced him around once he'd packed himself in.

"I guess we all waited too long," Mom said.

"No one really expected the storm to turn back this way," said Chad. "Though when it comes to hurricanes, you shouldn't plan on anything, I suppose. Where are you headed?"

"We were going to drive north, but now we're going to try the shelter at the town hall," Sam said. "Miss Gloria was supposed to fly out in an hour, but I guess she's going with us too." He glanced in the rearview mirror and gave her a smile. "She's an old hand at weathering storms."

"They close the shelter on the island with anything

above Category Three," Chad said grimly. "I just got a text that it's closing. They don't want people staying— it's too dangerous."

"A little late to tell us that now," I grumbled.

"I believe they've been hounding us all week," Sam said. "Some people didn't want to believe this was coming." He glanced back at us and quirked another smile.

"They wouldn't take animals at the shelter anyway," Miss Gloria said, patting Sam's shoulder. She stuck a finger through the grid on the end of the carrier and touched Sparky's nose.

"If you like, you can come back to my apartment," Chad said. "It's a former navy building, as Hayley may have mentioned. They built it so strong that even if this island is wiped flat clean, that building will still be standing."

"I'm not going anywhere without the cats," I said, clutching the carrier to my chest.

"Bring them along," Chad said.

"We don't have a litter box," Miss Gloria piped up— which was not the truth. I had to pinch myself to keep from bursting into hysterical laughter. Chad had not enjoyed Evinrude's brief tenure at his apartment, even with my meticulous attention to the litter box. What a time to test his humanity.

He grimaced, trying to smile. "Then we'll have to make do. Did you say *cats*, with an *s*? As in more than one?"

Miss Gloria snickered. "I don't think you've met my Sparky." Sparky stuck one black paw out of the other end of the carrier and swiped at Chad's arm.

We headed south on Truman and then across on Whitehead, finally reaching the Southard Street corner. The Green Parrot bar was shuttered up tight. And the Courthouse Deli's windows were covered in plywood, the sidewalk empty. Even the famous bench, which had its own Facebook page and had been the subject of thousands of photo ops, was gone.

"Wow, even Benchie evacuated," I said.

We passed the abandoned guardhouse at the entrance to the Truman Annex and took a right on Emma. Several blocks over in front of the Weatherstation Inn, two large palm trees had crashed across the road.

"I think you'll have to pull the car to the curb and leave it here," Chad said, gripping the headrest of my mother's seat and shouting to be heard over the wind. "We'll hope it's in one piece when the storm's over."

"It's a rental," Sam said. "So there's insurance. A car can be replaced. The important thing is to get these ladies into the building."

"I'll help Miss Gloria," Chad said. "You take the cats. Hayley can help her mother."

We flung the doors open and began to run. The wind was blowing hard into our faces, and without Chad's assistance, I didn't think tiny Miss Gloria would have made it. She didn't have enough bulk to fight the gusts. But minutes later, we were gathered in the garage that ran under the length of the Annex building, part of Harbor Place condominiums. The sound of the wind howling and the waves beating against the navy bight was deafening. The canvas covers on the few cars left behind flapped furiously.

"Let's keep moving," Sam said. "If it floods here, we're toast."

"The garage never has flooded before," Chad said. "But there's always a first time."

When we reached the end of the covered garage, we dashed the final fifty unsheltered yards through the driving rain to the front door of Chad's building. The windows were dark—either the electricity had been severed, or no one else had been foolish enough to wait the storm out. He unlocked the door and we tumbled inside, panting and soaking wet. Emergency lights illuminated the hallway dimly, showing the tile floor covered in an inch of water. In the distance, a smoke alarm shrieked. Both cats resumed yowling their dismay from inside the carrier, and Sam panted from their weight.

"No point in taking the elevator," Chad said as he pulled the outer door shut tight, "even if it's working. I'd be afraid we'd get stuck in the shaft."

"Been there, done that," I said, "not ever going to do that again. I'll take the kitties this time."

As we climbed the stairs to the third floor, my phone buzzed with a text message. I set the cat carrier down on the landing to take a breather and see who'd sent it. Nathan Bransford. Finally. Where r u? Hope you got the hell off this island.

I texted back, informing him that we were holing up in Chad's apartment. Where r u? I added.

Took an emergency call with Torrence. On Duval Street, but it's flooding. A tree fell on the cruiser so we'll walk back to PD.

I tried to judge how much danger they could be in. Was his text intending to say good-bye?

"Can you squeeze in two more?" I asked Chad, my heart pounding and my hands suddenly clammy. "Nate Bransford and Steve Torrence are trapped downtown."

He shrugged. "Why not? We can all go down together."

I texted Bransford back. Come on!

28

*It's a very uncomfortable feeling indeed.
When you try to eat a lump comes right
up in your throat and you can't swallow
anything, not even if it was a chocolate
caramel.*

—Lucy Maud Montgomery,
Anne of Green Gables

Once we'd staggered inside the apartment, we could
see how the storm raged outside Chad's floor-to-ceiling
living room windows. Sheets of rain sluiced across the
glass.

"I hope it's hurricane-proof glass as the condo association promised," he said.

A plastic deck chair pinwheeled across the small
deck and slammed into the window, startling us all.
Out in the harbor, waves dashed against the metal
breakwater and sloshed across the cement pier and
onto the condo property's lawn. The boat slips were

empty, the floating docks pulled out of the water and tied to the cement.

"Aren't you supposed to stay in a room with no windows?" my mother asked Chad. She had Sam's hand locked in a death grip. "Do you have an inside bedroom?"

"Both the bedrooms have floor-to-ceiling windows," I said, then wished I'd let Chad answer. An ancient wave of embarrassment washed in; why did I have to remind everyone how intimately I knew this place?

"The master bath is probably our best bet," Chad said. "The walk-in closet is smack in the middle of the apartment. Tight quarters, but hopefully not for long."

He herded everyone through the elegant living room with its granite coffee table and multiple nubby sofas, which Evinrude had enjoyed scratching, and then through the master bedroom to the bathroom. The closet at the rear of the bathroom was roomier than any closet needed to be, but still a snug fit for us. A knock on the door banged and Chad went to answer. Within minutes, my two police officer friends tumbled in and stood at the edge of the bathroom, dripping onto the limestone floor, soaking wet and wild-eyed.

"Go on in," said Chad. "I won't worry about getting the carpet wet at this point."

"Crazy out there," said Torrence. I hugged each in turn, handed them towels from Chad's stash under the sink, and explained the plan. "We figured we'd be better off in here, away from the glass."

Chad shut the outer bathroom door and came into the closet after us, carrying a Coleman lantern and a hand-crank weather radio. From a reusable cloth grocery sack, he took a six-pack of Perrier, two bags of potato chips, a bottle of Cuban rum, and two big bars of chocolate.

"All the food groups," said my mother. "Smart man."

He grinned and shut the door behind him.

"This is cozy," said Miss Gloria as she unzipped the carrier and set the cats free. Evinrude shot out and bolted across the legs and laps in his way and began to frantically claw at the door.

The lights blinked and went dark, and my cell phone made its losing-the-signal chirp. "This is not good," I said, peering at the dim screen and hoping for a glimmer of bars.

"Cell tower must have gone out," said Chad. "I'll get the radio working." We heard the whirring noise of his crank, and the battery-operated light came on along with a static-y weather report.

"Extreme weather warning: Hurricane-force winds are expected to brush Key West within the half hour. Extreme sustained winds of over one hundred thirty miles per hour are predicted. Take immediate shelter in the interior of a well-built structure. Repeat . . ."

"I never did talk to my sons to tell them the plane was canceled," said Miss Gloria in a trembling voice. "They'll be sick with worry." She sounded so sad, she nearly broke my heart.

"Use our satellite phone," said Torrence, handing it to her. "Briefly."

So Miss Gloria called her sons, who were not happy about the news that she was still on the island. "It's where I should be," she said softly. "It's my home. Your father and I stayed through thick and thin for more than twenty years. It didn't feel right to leave. And anyway, they canceled all the flights. So I'm here with Hayley and Janet and Sam and two police officers. I love you and I'll call you once the storm's gone by."

Then I called my father, who wasn't home. But I knew my stepmother would get him the right message, even if I was struggling for words. "He's so proud of you, Hayley," she added. "And I am too."

"Give Rory our love," said my mother over my shoulder.

And finally Chad put a call in to his mother, and left a mushy message—for him—when she didn't answer.

"Anyone you want to talk to?" Torrence asked Bransford, holding up the phone. He shook his head. Either he'd said his good-byes, or he didn't believe we needed to say them, or he couldn't bear to do it in public.

"Lorenzo might say that Key West had this coming," I said after a long silence except for the wind howling around the building and periodic unidentifiable bangs. I pictured the feeder bands of the storm wobbling over the condominium, wiping out swaths of the island as they went. "He says this city was born in the sign of Capricorn. Which means it's hard, and focused on money."

"How in the world does a city have an astrological sign?" asked Torrence.

"I asked Lorenzo the same thing," I said. "You look at the date when the place was founded—the time is important too. Plus, Key West is strong in Saturn. If you think about it, Saturn as a planet is cold and distant. But Lorenzo says Key West has got Leo in its moon, and that explains why our town is gregarious and entertaining. Look at all the kings and queens we have in our city. It's not just Fantasy Fest. Everybody who comes here or lives here wants to be a king and a queen of something."

"I doubt there'll be much left for them to fight over when we're finished with this storm," said Bransford. He looked as though he wanted to add more, and I could imagine what was going through his mind. He is the least woo-woo person I've ever met. And Capricorn, through and through, like Key West, only without the softening effects of Leo. All pure cold judgment, focus on the lessons of the father—at least on the surface.

"We never understand quite how thin the line is between life and death," said my mom. "I mean, we know it in the back of our minds but we don't let ourselves know it, if you get what I'm saying." Then she blinked back a few tears and sandwiched Sam's hand between hers.

The quiet was broken by the sound of the satellite phone ringing. Bransford answered. "It's your father," he said, unsmiling, and handed the handset to me.

"Just called to say I love you, Hayley," he said gruffly. I told him the same, unable to get anything else out around the lump that had risen in my throat. "Let me speak to your mother," he said.

"Yes?" Mom asked, holding the phone gingerly, like an overripe banana.

We could hear the loud clearing of my father's throat.

"Are you sure this Sam is going to treasure you?" he asked. "I know you didn't feel that way all the time in our marriage. And I'll always regret that."

"I'm sure," she said, her voice barely over a whisper. "Thank you."

"Speaking of life and death and kings and queens," I said once she'd hung up and I couldn't bear the tension one more minute, "did you guys find Caryn Druckman's killer?"

"We have leads," said Bransford. "Good ones, but nothing that could put someone behind bars. The investigation got pretty well sidelined by this storm."

"Trying to get everyone off the island and safe," said Miss Gloria. "And some of us just wouldn't cooperate."

"All this talk about the importance of money in Key West," said Sam, "don't you think that death had to be about money too?"

"Danielle did say that that woman tried her hardest to stuff the ballot box at the Coronation Ball," my mother said. "I think she was astonished that she didn't win. In the end, though, her money wasn't enough to get the job done."

"But then why did she end up dead?" I asked. "Doesn't it seem more like she might've killed someone else, rather than having been killed herself?"

"Like Danielle," said my mother, frowning. "She would have been the logical target, if Druckman wasn't already dead."

The satellite phone squawked again—Chad's mother returning his call.

"I'm okay," he said to her after her torrent of concerned words. "I'm here in the apartment with some friends."

More questions from his mom.

"Hayley Snow is here and her mom and a few others. We even have a police contingent, so if anyone needs CPR, we're all set." There was a pause while he listened to his mother, his face and neck reddening. "Okay, I'll tell her. Love you too."

He hung up the phone and turned to look at me. "She insists that I tell you that I should have married you when I had the opportunity."

"Your chance for that is long over, pal," Bransford grunted, and then reached over to put his hand on my knee.

I grinned. "Watch out for those wild displays of public affection." I blew him a kiss.

The lights in the closet flickered on again, and for a moment, the air conditioner ground to life.

"Speaking of getting married, Sam," said my mother in a soft voice, "I sure am sorry that we didn't get to our ceremony on the beach." She looked pale and tired in the overhead light, but her eyes brimmed with love.

"I could marry you right here and now," said Torrence. "You already have the license. And we've got plenty of witnesses."

Sam took my mother's hands. "Let's do it."

"Would you?" she asked Torrence.

Miss Gloria clapped her hands. "The perfect idea— a hurricane wedding. You can tell this story to your kids for years."

"I'm her only kid," I said, smiling.

Torrence nodded and suggested we all take hands. "Dearly beloved," he said, "we are gathered here in the presence of friends and God and the mighty power of nature to join this woman and this man in holy matrimony."

By the time he finished with the miniature service, and my mother and Sam had pledged to stick with each other through life's stormy and calm periods, and we'd pledged to support them, Miss Gloria and my mother and I were in tears. Then came a huge bang and a ripping noise and the lights flickered and the power went dead with finality and we were left in the dark; left with only the noise of the wind and our own ragged breathing.

29

Somebody give me a cheeseburger!
—"Living in the USA,"
Steve Miller Band

Nathan had hold of one of my hands and my mom had the other and Evinrude was pressed close to my stomach. The small space had begun to stink like fear. I was certain the roof was gone and we were next. Instead, the gusts seemed to die down a little and the banging of the door in the apartment's inner hallway slowed to a gentle tap.

Finally Bransford spoke up. "I'm going to take a look outside and see what's happening," he said.

"The rest of you stay right here," said Torrence.

But the other two men scrambled to their feet as well and followed the cops out to the living room, allowing a swath of light into the close quarters of the closet. The cats bolted out after him.

"Honest to gosh," Sam hollered back down the hall.

"I think the storm's moved away. I even see a little patch of blue."

Miss Gloria and my mother and I hurried out to the living room to have a look. The palm trees were still blowing like mad, and most of the flowers in the fancy condominium landscaping and the landscaping of the time-share next door had been ripped off the bushes. It looked like a sea of bare stalks, like a cornfield after the harvest. A single Jet Ski had been blown onto the sidewalk and slammed against the metal fence.

"We need to get back to work," said Bransford, and Torrence nodded his agreement. "I'd feel a lot better if you all would stay inside."

"How long?" Miss Gloria asked. "I can't imagine Chad wants us to move in, even as excellent company as we are." Bransford gave her his trademark glare.

"We'll try," I said with a shrug of the shoulders, not meeting the two sets of worried eyes. "We'll wait until it calms down."

"I'd hate for you to make it through the worst of the storm and then get taken out by a coconut," Bransford said.

I crossed the room and kissed him on the lips, and he gathered me in tightly and then let go. "We'll be okay," I said, gripping his biceps and looking deep into his eyes. "I'm glad you were here. Really glad."

"Hey," said Chad, once our police friends had clomped down the stairwell, "I think congratulations are in order. And I happen to have champagne in the refrigerator. It could be weeks before we'll get power back, so we might as well drink it."

"Why not?" Miss Gloria said. "We have a lot to

celebrate. We're still alive, for one, and our two dear friends tied the noose—err, knot!"

We all laughed like crazy people and Chad popped the cork and poured the sparkling liquid into his best blue wineglasses—the ones he'd preferred strongly that I not use when Evinrude and I were in residence. And then we toasted my mother and Sam and watched the wind and the whitecaps in the harbor until the champagne was gone.

"I wonder if it's safe to go out?" Sam asked.

"Honey," said my mother, "the officers suggested we stay inside."

"For the rest of our lives?" Sam asked.

Miss Gloria giggled. "Suppose we see what they're saying on the radio?"

Chad retrieved the emergency weather radio from his big closet and tuned in the local news station. A disembodied voice reported that the storm had blown off to the east and appeared to be heading east of Miami and out to sea. The whole mess had been downgraded, with winds now blowing at category one levels. We slapped our palms together in a team cheer, and laughed giddily at having escaped the worst. In a few minutes, when the blue sky started to break through the clouds in big patches, we went outside to look around.

Chad led us through the private garden that belonged to the condominium, where the sidewalks were now carpeted with pink bougainvillea petals and plastic bags and coffee cups. The whitewashed stucco walls of his building were also spattered with leaves and mulch and one unlucky seagull, and even a fish. He unlocked the gate that released us out to the world.

It was totally strange to see the slips empty along the Westin pier, which would normally be bustling with all kinds of boats. At this time of evening, there would have been Jet Skiers landing after a day of hard macho bouncing, sunset cruises getting ready to board, and good-sized fishing boats chugging in, along with the occasional yacht. I wondered how long it would be before the big cruise ships docked here again. I pushed away a needle of worry about Miss Gloria's houseboat—whether it would be habitable. Whether it would be there at all. And where we'd possibly stay if it wasn't. And what would happen to Miss Gloria if her home was gone. I could bounce back—I knew that—but, good gravy, she was eighty-one.

But wasn't the important thing that we'd survived without a scratch on us, when honestly it had looked for a while as though we were burned toast? I put one arm around my mother's waist and the other around Miss Gloria's shoulders and tried to shake off the gloom.

A few other hardy/foolish residents began to emerge as we walked down Caroline Street to look at the condition of the town. Power lines hung loose from the poles, and some of the foliage was stripped from the trees, but I swore I smelled the enticing odor of grilled seafood that had to be coming from Garbo's Grill. My stomach rumbled in response.

"Let's go in," my mother said when we reached the patio where the food truck was usually located. "I'm starving and I bet my brand-new husband is too." She beamed up at Sam.

Sure enough, the truck was open for business, the courtyard bustling. We walked to the back of the patio, which was crowded with storm survivors, some seated at metal tables, some standing in line, all telling their stories, giddy with relief at having dodged the big one. In the background, generators roared to life.

Chef Eli called out from his spot at the counter in the truck. "Folks, we've got to eat up what's going to go bad. So anyone who needs a meal is welcome to get in line. Who knows how long the electricity will be out? In the meantime, it's all for one and one for all. We have a tip jar out—if you can afford the money, you're welcome to pay. If not, dinner's on us. If anyone would like to help wait on tables or even bus, let us know. No previous experience required." A wave of laughter twittered through the crowd.

"Why don't you guys get a table," I suggested, "and one of you wait in line? I'm going to see how I can help while we're waiting." I went around to the back end of the truck and identified myself as willing.

"From food critic to busgirl? That's quite a promotion," said Eli's wife, Kenna, who was slapping condiments on burrito skins and passing them to the grill. She grinned. "Too bad your killer takeout article came out just as we're having to give everything away."

"The goodwill is bound to carry over," I said. "Food karma is a powerful thing."

She handed me a plastic bag and I began to circle the patio and pick up trash. Catfish Kohls was helping too, busy carrying trays of food out to the people waiting at the tables. My trainer, Leigh, was also on duty, ferrying supplies from the small closet at the back of the property to the truck.

"Don't think this counts as your aerobics for the day," she joked. "I'll let you know when the power's back on at WeBeFit," she added. "For now, Dan's decreed all our sessions should be canceled. Too darn hot inside the gym."

As I worked, chatting with the customers and other volunteers, a sense of camaraderie emerged. No one complained about having to wait. No one said a peep about their requested dish being sold out. One good thing about this hurricane scare: We were simply grateful that we, and our wonderful island paradise, had survived.

I took a few pictures of the scene. As a couple of service bars miraculously emerged on my phone, I posted my best picture to Instagram. I looped quickly through the feed on my account—amazing how badly I'd needed a hit of social media after only a few hours in the dark.

Then I flicked over to Druckman's feed and scrolled backward. My attention caught on a zombie bike ride photo that I hadn't noticed earlier in the week. Caryn Druckman was front and center, reaching for a pastel-colored drink in a paper cup offered by a zombie waitress who held the tray up over her shoulder and avoided jostling from the crowd in an astonishing display of acrobatic balance. The Beach Eats truck was in the background. And with a jolt, I realized that Mrs.

Renhart had not been yelling at me to take a photo and post it to Instagram as they chugged away; she'd wanted me to look at Druckman's Instagram.

The server's tray was empty. There was only one drink left in the photo, and it was being delivered directly to Druckman.

I glanced over at Catfish as she glanced at me, noticing me study the phone and then look back up at her. The sunlight broke through the leaves of the palm above us, dappling Kat's skin, reminding me of the zebra stripes. I remembered how Seymour had insisted that someone served them mixed drinks, probably a knockoff Pusser's Painkiller based on his description of tasting coconut, pineapple, and rum. And then I recalled that Catfish had insisted the truck had served no alcoholic beverages at all.

Why had she lied?

Was she protecting someone? Did she know the person who had made the drinks, one of them possibly poisoned?

Grant—that's who was in the chef's position. And then I realized that their relationship had felt way more charged than just employer/employee, the times I'd seen them together. And however Druckman had been involved, Grant had so much to lose, buying a restaurant with a reputation for iffy food and questionable hygiene.

My gaze met Kat's as the pieces of information in my mind clicked into place. She dropped the tray on the nearest metal table, vaulted over the short chain-link fence that marked the property, and began to run. I didn't think I could catch up with her, and besides,

Bransford and Torrence would kill me. So I texted them both. Grant Monsarrat is your murderer. Catfish Kohls just took off down the alley behind Garbo's Grill. Toward Smokin' Tuna. She's gone to warn him—or that's my guess.

"What's going on?" asked my mother as I rushed up to their table, dropping my garbage bag at her feet.

"I'm pretty sure I figured out who killed Caryn Druckman. And Catfish just bolted down that alley toward where he's probably hiding out." I pointed. "I'm going to try to follow her. Could you run back and grab the car and meet me over at the Paradise Pub?" I asked Sam. "Dollars to doughnuts, that's where she'll end up."

"Don't—" my mother started.

"I won't do anything foolish—we just survived a big hurricane. I'm not going to get wiped out by a crazy man. Text me when you're on the way?"

Sam took off back toward the Truman Annex, and my mother and Miss Gloria trucked behind me, hands clutching the mango hot dogs that had just been delivered. No one in her right mind would leave a mango hot dog behind.

30

"A writer's personality is revealed by her connection to food," said Olivia. "Some people are feeders and some are withholders."

—Lucy Burdette,
Death in Four Courses

In the time I decided not to try hopping the fence but rather to go around out through the usual entrance, I spotted Catfish loading onto a scooter. She revved the engine and blasted off toward Front Street. I broke into a trot, hearing my mother and Miss Gloria huffing behind me.

"Wait for Sam to pick you up!" I hollered over my shoulder. All we needed was a heart attack in the family while chasing down a possible accessory to murder. There wouldn't be a paramedic available for miles.

I turned up Greene Street and picked up the pace, heading for the Paradise Pub, which was the only place

I figured she would go—probably to warn Grant. When I was almost to the restaurant, a black-and-white cruiser with lights flashing sped by me and pulled into the back parking lot where I'd seen the kittens yesterday.

I felt sad about having gotten it wrong with the chef. I'd really liked him—and liked his food too, once he got away from the overly fried stuff. He hadn't looked or sounded like a murderer, but as Torrence had told me more than once, not all bad guys wear black patches over their eyes and have hooks instead of hands.

Two officers with guns drawn crouched on either side of the back door to Grant's kitchen. "Freeze, Key West police!" they shouted as they flung the door open. A blast of gunfire repelled them back into the parking lot. One of them spotted me and waved me furiously away from the scene. I ducked behind the Dumpster just as Miss Gloria came huffing into the lot.

"Get over here now," I yelped. I'd been scolded often enough for muddling in dangerous situations. I was even beginning to think the cops were right—leave the tough stuff for the trained professionals. When she got close enough, I grabbed her hand and reeled her in beside me.

More cops arrived in cruisers with sirens howling. Two uniformed officers and Lieutenant Torrence leaped out of the first car. I could hear an echoing siren that could have been police stationing themselves at the front door. Torrence edged over to the open door, the two uniforms following him with their guns drawn. They started into the kitchen, but fell back out at the sound of a gun firing.

He pulled a phone out of his back pocket and dialed. "Catfish? It's Lieutenant Torrence. I'd like to talk this out so no one gets hurt." He turned toward the restaurant so we could hear only snatches of intense conversation. Then Torrence backed away, a look of worry and disgust on his face. He strode over to my place behind the Dumpster. "She hung up on me. She wants to talk to a woman. I told her none of our female officers are available so she said she wants to talk to you."

"She wants to talk to me? About what?"

He looked even more disgusted. "I would never ever do this, but our hostage negotiators are tied up at the jail. A couple of the inmates escaped when the power went out." He removed his cap and ran his fingers through his hair. His radio crackled, and Bransford's voice came over the airwaves.

Torrence explained that Catfish might consider coming out and setting her hostage free, but only if she could talk to me first.

"Catfish has a hostage?" I asked. "I thought it was Grant in there—"

"What the hell?" Bransford tinny voice blasted out of Torrence's phone. "Tell me one reason why that is a good idea. Since when do we start putting our civilians in danger because a murderer requests it?"

"One of our officers was able to look in the high window on the side of the building. She's got the chef tied up with a knife to his throat," Torrence said grimly. "As well as Danielle Kamen. And she's got a gun and has proven she'll use it."

I squeaked with dismay at the thought of my friend in danger.

"She insists she'll only talk to a woman officer," Torrence continued.

"Hayley's not an officer," said Bransford, dismissing me instantly.

"Then who else have you got?" asked Torrence. "We've called around. As far as I can tell, there's not a female officer on the island right now."

There was more back and forth about where the women police were (nowhere close), where the cops with guns would be stationed, and how my safety would be assured: I was only to talk to her from the safety of my position behind the Dumpster.

"I don't like it. Hayley, how do you feel about this?" asked Bransford. His voice sounded strained and angry.

Shocked, stunned, terrified—those were the words that came to mind. And sick about Grant and especially Danielle in danger. What if I said something stupid and someone got shot? "I'll do what I need to," I said. "If it will save Danielle and Grant, I'm happy to try."

"I don't like it either," said Torrence. "But from what I saw in there, we send officers in and two people die for sure. If the SWAT team was available, of course we'd use them.

"Just be smart and ask questions in a nonthreatening way," said Torrence. "Talk to her, but don't try to be a hero. Start with some reassurance. Ask if she has what she needs in there. And whether everyone is okay. And then ask what we can do so this ends as a win-win. Don't worry about what's possible, just get her talking." He dialed the phone and handed it to me.

"Catfish? It's Hayley Snow. Are you all right in there? The lieutenant said you'd like to talk to me, and I'd love to talk to you. See if we can figure a way to get you and Grant out safely."

"Lost cause," she said. "And Danielle's going down too."

Danielle screamed, a horrible burbling sound full of desperation and fear.

"Danielle?" Miss Gloria pushed past me, darted up to the kitchen door, and disappeared inside. "You let that girl go right now. She never did anything to you," she yelled as a ring of cops circled closer with guns drawn.

"I'm going in after her," I said to no one in particular. "She needs me." I hurtled past the cops and burst into the back door.

The kitchen, which had looked so cheerful and welcoming on my last visit, had a gloomy feel this time. A pile of dirty pots and pans spilled out of the sink. The floor was sticky with something spilled, and there was a funky odor coming from the trash can.

"Catfish? Catfish, are you here? It's Hayley. Is Miss Gloria okay? Please let's talk this out so no one gets hurt."

"Are they crazy sending you in here?" she growled, her voice coming from the big pantry on the far side of the kitchen.

"I'm coming over there," I said, pressing the quaver out of my voice. "Don't shoot anyone."

I moved closer to the pantry and peeped into the opening. Catfish had the gun trained on Miss Gloria, who sat against the wall, looking small and scared. A beam of light from the high window above the shelves fell on her face. Her face looked older, worn, and wrinkled. Grant was slumped into a corner underneath the shelf containing canned goods. His arms and hands were taped behind him and he was taped at the ankles too. A large swath of silver duct tape had been slapped across his lips. His eyes were wide, frightened, and pleading.

If it was even possible, Danielle looked worse. The makeup around her eyes that she so carefully applied every morning was running down her cheeks in black and purple streaks. Her beautiful blond hair was a rat's nest, stuck to the duct tape wound around her head. It was the least of her problems, and mine too, but I had to wonder whether some of her golden curls would have to be cut off.

"Focus, Hayley," I muttered to myself.

"Why on earth did they send you in here?" Kat asked.

"Believe me—no oné sent me," I said. "They are all outside having major heart attacks. There won't be enough beds for all those guys in the coronary unit," I said, doing my best to sound cheerful and unconcerned. "How about you let these three go and then we can chat more comfortably?"

Still pointing the gun at Miss Gloria, she pulled a chef's knife off the shelf and held it at Danielle's throat. She pressed until a droplet of bright red blood popped out of the cut and ran down my friend's pale neck. Danielle began to cry again.

Time to regroup. If none of us was going to live through this experience, at least I could try to get her to admit to the murder. "I'm guessing, then, it was you who poisoned Caryn Druckman. But I don't really understand why."

"I thought you did understand how much this restaurant meant to us." Using the knife, she pointed to Grant and then to herself. "He's a brilliant chef, and you must know yourself that a chef who owns his own restaurant can write his own script when it comes to the menu. The Paradise Pub was killing his creativity. And we were earning peanuts. But with me beside him in our own place we were going to be the hottest place on the island. With the best food too."

She looked at me as if I was supposed to respond. Plain enough to see that this was not the time for a mixed review. "That breakfast he made me was amazing." I cleared my throat. "And I loved all your ideas for the classic but new takes on island fare. And your ideas for naming the place were brilliant. But what did Ms. Druckman have to do with any of that?"

Catfish scowled. "She soured the deal we had set up with the previous owner. Seymour ratfink Fox."

"Seymour?" I asked.

She nodded. "He agreed to sell to Grant. They shook hands on it. And then she ruined everything by coming in on top of us with better terms. Better in what way, you might ask?" she added. "Not better for the locals. Not better for anyone who would be eating there. What the people of Key West wanted was his cooking.

"But she wanted a platform for her stupid northern ideas of foodie trends. She couldn't stand to lose anything. And losing that dumb contest made stealing this restaurant seem more important to her." She stabbed at Grant's chest with the tip of the knife for emphasis and he squawked through the duct tape. "And she trashed our dreams. You've not seen what he's like when he isn't doing what he loves."

She turned to him again and shook her head with disgust. "Actually you're seeing it right here. He's lifeless. And our life together would be over. I could not allow that miserable bossy bitch to stand between us and our future."

"I understand that," I said. "But why are these two tied up?"

"Grant didn't get that I poisoned her to help him. That everything was going to be okay. And then your silly friend came barging in here last night with her talk about clues and how close she was to figuring things out. And how it wasn't her family who killed Druckman. And if one of us did it, we needed to confess. Obviously, I couldn't let her go."

Suddenly I heard an ear-piercing crash-bang and a light flashed and a huge black shape shattered the small window and I was crushed to the floor under the weight of an enormous officer wearing a black jumpsuit and a helmet. "Drop the gun and the knife right now or we shoot," called out another officer.

Out of the corner of my eye, I saw Catfish hit the floor, flattened by two more SWAT team members. Once they had her safely cuffed, they led her out, cut the tape off the others, and we stumbled back into the sun.

I rushed into my mother's waiting arms. "I can't decide if that's the bravest or the stupidest thing you've ever done," said my mother. But her eyes floated with tears as she stroked my hair off my face.

31

He looks at her like she's afternoon tea
and he's parched.

—Jenn McKinlay,
At the Drop of a Hat

In the parking lot, Danielle tearfully explained that her aunt had harassed Caryn Druckman by posting the unflattering photos on Instagram and Facebook. So certain that her relative had not been involved in the poisoning, she thought about what I'd told her about Beach Eats and decided that maybe the poison came from there, and figured Grant was the logical murderer. She had driven over to Paradise Pub to warn Kat that her boyfriend had poisoned his rival.

But Catfish had already tied Grant up, and she knew that Danielle would rat her out to the cops. She felt she had no choice but to tie up Danielle too.

"What was she planning to do with the two of you?" I asked.

Danielle shook her head mournfully. "She couldn't have killed Grant. She loved him so desperately. But me? Nothing good was going to come of it."

"Why didn't you call the police? Or me?"

"Remember, we were in the hurricane of the century, Hayley. You think I didn't think of that? I had no cell service. And there were certainly no cops around."

After the police car left with Catfish handcuffed in the backseat, headed for the Stock Island jail, and Grant and Danielle had been checked out medically and taken off to the station to give their official statements to the detectives, we decided it was time to face the music. Either the houseboat would be there, or it wouldn't. Miss Gloria was trying hard to put on an optimistic face, but we all knew her heart would be broken if she'd lost her home on Tarpon Pier.

It took us almost half an hour to get across the island. Many trees had been knocked down, requiring detours, and the roads were clogged with trash and live wires. Without the normal hum of electrified life, the town was eerily quiet, though some of the residents and town employees were already stacking palm leaves and detached shingles in piles by the side of the streets. Here and there we heard the noise of generators and leaf-blowers roar to life.

As we rolled up the Palm Avenue causeway in Sam's car, Miss Gloria said from the backseat beside me: "I'm going to cover my eyes. Tell me if it's okay to look."

Which was a little funny if I thought about it, because what if the houseboat was destroyed? How long would she keep her eyes covered? But I kept my smart mouth shut, realizing almost as quickly that I too was scared silly about what we might find, and ready to be heartsick for her—and me—if our home was gone. She had been so brave for so long.

As we crested the hill, my gaze searched the horizon, desperately hoping to see the same landscape of roofs and pipes and ropes that we'd left only hours earlier.

Sam slowed the car and pulled into the far end of the parking lot.

"The boat with the big smiley face on the roof is missing its porch tarp," I said, taking Miss Gloria's cool hand and rubbing it between mine. "But I see Connie and Ray's place right behind it. And oh my gosh . . ." My voice swelled with joy and my throat with tears. "Our home is there too."

Miss Gloria threw her arms around me and rested her head against my shoulder. "Oh thank god, thank god. I thought we were goners this time."

Once Sam had parked, we sprang out of the car and hurried up the finger. The two-story yellow houseboat was missing its roof, and the speedboat usually filled with trash seemed to be missing altogether. As we arrived at our place, the Renharts' boat chugged into the slip next door and banged against the pilings. Mrs. Renhart waved furiously, doing a little happy dance with the fluffy gray cat she had clutched in her arms. Then she put him down and picked up the old black cat and danced him around too. Schnootie the schnauzer leaped from one side of the deck to the other, yelping furiously.

Mr. Renhart's voice rang out over the cacophony of

sounds. "Will you shut that damn dog up? Or I swear I will take her back to the pound."

"Oh, Schnootie, rooty-tooty, you know Daddy doesn't mean that," Mrs. Renhart crooned, swooping the dog up and clutching her to her neck.

Good gravy, it felt fantastic to be home.

After checking on our boat, we caught up on the adventures of our seafaring neighbors, which boiled down to Mr. Renhart getting into a huge fight with the tugboat driver and deciding he'd turn around and come back home and take his licks like the rest of us.

"Where did you ride the storm out?" I asked.

"The lee side of Big Pine," said Mr. Renhart.

"The cats were amazing," said Mrs. Renhart. "Born sailors. Schnootie?" She looked down fondly at the gray dog, who panted at her feet. "Not so much."

"Speaking of cats," I said. "We'd better buzz down the island and retrieve ours from Chad's place."

"I'll go," said Sam.

"And Chef Martha from Louie's Backyard called," said my mother, holding up her phone. "They won't be open in time to host our reception—they have no power. But they'd love to have us pick up the food and bring it somewhere so we don't lose everything."

"Here!" said Miss Gloria. "We'll have a big party to celebrate all our good news right here on the dock. We can do what Garbo's Grill was doing—welcome anyone who needs a meal. Say five o'clock?"

A police car pulled into the lot and Bransford emerged. We watched him lope up the finger.

"Thought I'd check on you all," he said. "And

thought you'd be interested in hearing that Catfish Kohls was charged with murder. As you can imagine, Grant Monsarrat is crushed. He still hopes to pull his business out of the embers, if Seymour's willing to sell it to him. And make it friendly to both locals and tourists."

"How in the world did she kill Druckman? And why?" asked Miss Gloria.

"Seymour Fox had made a deal to sell the Paradise Pub to Grant. But Druckman started to pressure him over the last month about selling it to her instead. She offered a lot more money, cash, not extended credit as Grant Monsarrat would have required. Seymour got more and more upset and fell off the wagon along the way. Finally he withdrew the verbal contract with Grant. Apparently Catfish flipped out and put isopropyl rubbing alcohol in Caryn Druckman's punch, figuring if she was dead, Seymour would have to sell the place to Grant."

"That must have been the funny sweet smell on her breath," I said.

Bransford nodded. Though he had been talking to everyone, he was staring at me as if he had something else on his mind.

"What is it?" I asked.

"Can I have a private word?"

"Of course." I glanced at the others, gave a little shrug, and then followed him to his car.

He cleared his throat, but his voice still came out raspy. "I've told my ex not to come back. We're finished. She comes, I tell her it's over between us, she cries, she leaves. We've been finished for quite a while now; she simply can't quite accept it. I don't understand why you would think I'm still involved with her."

"Ziggy's babysitter said a woman was here visiting and you were out all night, and she thought it was your ex."

I watched him struggle to stay calm. "The dog sitter is not a credible witness—remember that, okay? Ziggy loves her and she's available at all hours, but she's dizzy as heck. I was *working*, Hayley. Fantasy Fest, re-member?"

I squirmed a little, keeping my gaze pinned on the cleft in his chin so I wouldn't risk my voice wobbling. It felt silly to have doubted him and an enormous relief to hear the truth.

"I know you'll never become Mr. Communication, but I thought you'd text, at least let me know you were okay."

He stared at me for a full minute. "A seventeen-year-old girl died yesterday morning from an overdose of tainted heroin. She was here with her friends for a week of fun. After we failed to resuscitate her, I had to call her parents with that news. I thought of calling you, but it all felt too grim, and I honestly didn't know how to say it without breaking down. And then we had to deal with her friends, who were completely hysterical. And then the evacuation."

"I'm so sorry. I'm an idiot."

"No," he said quickly. "For an outsider, this job takes some getting use to. And some wives and girl-friends never do. And it's been especially hard these last couple of years, with people attacking officers.

And a few rotten officers attacking people. And over-all bad feelings between cops and civilians. So it feels hard to ask this." He swallowed and his Adam's apple bobbed down and then up. "But I wondered . . ." He turned a deep shade of red and pulled his sunglasses back over his eyes. "I wondered if you might like to try moving in with me."

I gulped, my temples throbbing and my heart racing. Good gravy, I hadn't seen that coming. Something in his cautious heart must have gotten shaken loose by the hurricane scare. Or maybe the sadness around the dead teenager had done it. Or maybe something else that I might never know. Because he wasn't a talker.

And now he looked anything but soft and open, his arms crossed over his chest, his sunglasses mirroring a distorted image of me. I paused for a minute to put into careful words the reaction that welled up inside.

"Thank you very much for that offer. But this is my home for now," I said, looking back at the motley group of boats and neighbors and family clustered on the dock. "I'm planning to stay here until I find an-other place that feels even more like home. Experi-menting with living together doesn't feel that way to me. I've sort of tried that, you know? With some un-satisfactory results." I grimaced and grinned.

He wasn't smiling at my weak joke.

"Though I appreciate the offer." I reached out to touch his hand, but he'd taken a step back, leaving me pawing at the air. "And it's a good offer, just not quite right for me at this time."

Good lord, I was starting to sound like a rejection letter from a literary agency. "Though I'd definitely accept an invitation to go out to dinner and see where we go from there. If that's okay?

"But better still, we are going ahead with the reception, right here on the dock. All the food my mother ordered and Chef Martha prepared would go bad if we didn't eat it." I looked straight at him. "It would mean so much if you came. We're starting at five."

He nodded after a minute. "I'll try. We'll see what things look like out there." He waved in the direction of Old Town. Then a smile flickered across his face. "I liked the way they did it though."

It took me a minute to figure out what he meant. "Mom and Sam? You liked the wedding ceremony in the closet during a hurricane bit?"

He rolled his eyes. "Not the hurricane. Small guest list. No fuss. No big poufy dress and monkey suit. No ridiculous dance steps in front of a crowd. Been down that road already. With some unsatisfactory results, as you would say."

I grinned and reached over to chuck his chin. "Are you asking me something?"

"Not exactly. Someday. I might." He shuffled a step away.

I swooped in and gave him a five-star kiss and then a casual wave before he drove off, and I swiveled away to help Miss Gloria.

Let him think I was all about the minimalist wedding, as if I hadn't had dreams about all the trappings of a wedding, like forever, like every girl in America. But I could give him plenty of space. Hey, I was in no hurry either. He never would have gotten near the subject if he wasn't serious.

And if it came down to it, we'd call in the hostage negotiator to rescue us from the bare-bones ceremony and reception that he was picturing. I noticed then that Mrs. Renhart had been watching the whole thing, probably listening too, as she brought Schnootie to the little grassy strip alongside the parking lot. Both of the old cats had followed and were sniffing around the barnacle-encrusted ropes coiled at the end of the finger.

"So the new kitties did well in the storm?" I asked.

"As though they were born and raised on a boat," said Mrs. R. She stooped down to run her hand along Jack's spine and then Dinkels'. They both rumbled happily in response.

"Hope that guy pops the question soon," said my neighbor, her eyes narrowed as she watched Bransford's cruiser pull out into the Palm Avenue traffic. "You know what, Hayley? After adopting these cats, and Schnootie, marrying Mr. Renhart was the best decision I ever made. I hope you're as lucky in love as I've been."

"Wonderful," I said. "Amazing," I added, trying to stifle a look of disbelief, as she trundled off home, a cat under each arm and Schnootie trotting behind.

My cell phone rang and Palamina's number came up on the screen. I considered refusing to answer, but decided I should face the worst and get it over with.

"Hayley, I called to apologize about my behavior lately. I've done some thinking and decided you're right. I haven't been treating you and the others with the respect you deserve. I got freaked-out about being head of this magazine by myself. In New York, I never had to make a decision without a dozen people pawing through the work and editing it to within an inch of its life. I was a little cog in a big machine. And the more I thought about this responsibility, the tighter I got. And I took that out on you people.

"But while the storm was raging, I realized I'm not by myself. First of all Wally's my copilot."

I swallowed the *Duh* that rose up in my throat.

"And second, you and Danielle are in this with us. And you're great at your jobs and I need to trust you. I'm sorry about how I've acted. If there's anything I can do for you, I'd like you to have a relaxing few days off."

It took me a moment to process what she'd said. "Apology accepted," I said.

"But I mean it about some time off. What can I take off your plate?"

I mentally ran through my list of pitch ideas, which was running a little thin because of the chaos over the last few days. "The only piece I've really started is something on Robert the doll. I've got the notes and photos, but I haven't shaped it yet."

"Send them on. I'd be happy to do that for you."

"You'd better go over to the museum and talk with him first. He's been known to haunt people who don't ask his permission."

Her laugh came quickly, high, and shrill. "Don't be ridiculous, Hayley. He's a stuffed doll. Spooky looking for sure, but he doesn't have any power. Not over me or anyone else. Unless you give it to him, the way you do with that Lorenzo character."

So she wasn't completely reformed—she couldn't resist a zinger. For a moment, I considered arguing with her further, insisting that she consider all the damage Robert had done to blustering visitors in the past.

On the other hand, if Robert put a curse on her, we could write him a note and beg for forgiveness. Tell him she wasn't a local. Like all of us Key West immigrants, she was still learning the ropes of living on the island.

On the other, other hand, maybe she and Robert made a perfect match.

Recipes

Key West Boiled Dinner

This recipe is based on one I saw in Epicurious
.com, but it's been tweaked to suit Hayley, who
serves it to her mother and her mother's fiancé
their first night on the island. It's super simple to
do the preparations ahead. Then cook at the last
minute when your company arrives—and look
like a domestic goddess.

Serves six

1 lemon, quartered
4 garlic cloves, peeled but left whole
2–3 bay leaves
5 tablespoons Creole seasoning (like Tony Chachere's)
½ to 1 pound multicolored fingerling potatoes
1½ pounds large Key West pink shrimp (or other fresh
    local shrimp if possible) in shell
1 package sausage of your choice, cut into 2–3 inch
    lengths
1 package frozen corn on the cob, or fresh if it's in season

Bring a gallon of water to boil in a big pot. Squeeze the
lemon into this, and then add the lemon quarters,
the garlic, the bay leaves, and the Creole seasoning.

Simmer the seasonings together for a few minutes.

Meanwhile, wash the potatoes and rinse the shrimp. Add the potatoes to the water, simmer until almost soft. (About 10 minutes, depending on the size.) Add the sausage and corn, simmer a few minutes. Finally, add the shrimp, simmer until they turn quite pink— another 2–3 minutes.

Dump the whole pot into a colander, drain, and serve the ingredients on a large platter.

Serve cocktail sauce (⅔ ketchup to ⅓ horseradish) and Dijon mustard on the side, along with a green salad.

Everyone takes as much as they want and peels their own shrimp as they go, until you are left with . . . nothing but shells and cobs!

Strawberry Cake with Strawberry Frosting

Hayley makes this to celebrate Sam and her mother's engagement and upcoming wedding. It's a sheet cake, so it serves a crowd. But it's stunning, especially if you make it during strawberry season.

Ingredients for the strawberry cake
1 cup butter, softened
2 cups sugar
2 large eggs
2 teaspoons fresh lemon juice
1 teaspoon vanilla extract
2½ cups cake flour
¼ teaspoon table salt
½ teaspoon baking soda
1 cup buttermilk (or 1 cup milk, with 1 tablespoon cider vinegar added)
⅔ cup chopped fresh strawberries

Butter well a 9 x 13 inch pan, and heat oven to 350°F.

Using an electric mixer or food processor, beat the butter with the sugar until light and fluffy. Beat the eggs in one at a time. Beat in the lemon juice and vanilla extract. Combine the flour, salt, and baking soda in a small bowl. Add ⅓ of the dry ingredients to the butter mixture, alternating with adding ⅓ of the buttermilk. (I used a cup of milk with one tablespoon of cider vinegar instead of buttermilk.)

Pulse in the chopped strawberries until they are small pieces and the batter begins to look pink.

Scrape the batter into the prepared pan and bake for about 40 minutes until a toothpick stuck in the center comes out dry. Cool the cake on a wire rack.

Ingredients for the strawberry icing
4 ounces cream cheese, softened
½ cup chopped strawberries
½ teaspoon vanilla
⅓ cup sugar
1 cup heavy cream

Beat the cream cheese with the strawberries until mostly smooth. Add the vanilla and half the sugar; beat those in. Whip the cream with the remaining sugar until thick. Fold the whipped cream into the cream cheese/strawberry mixture. Spread the icing on the cooled cake and refrigerate until serving. Decorate with strawberries if desired.

Hayley Snow's Shrimp Salad

One of the great joys of writing the Key West mysteries is imagining what the characters would really do, and that includes considering what they would really eat. They are characters in a book, but they honestly begin to feel like real people. I can picture Hayley Snow and Miss Gloria on their houseboat wondering what to have for dinner. And then I can imagine them remembering that—oh joy!—there are shrimp left over from the night before.

Then Hayley goes to work. She looks in the fridge again and finds celery and onions and capers. And Miss Gloria goes out to the back deck and picks some fresh dill and a few beautiful ripe tomatoes. And then they whip up a quick but delicious shrimp salad served over greens and sliced tomatoes, with maybe a delicious leek biscuit on the side. Can't you just see it? And that night my husband might say, Where did this recipe come from? And I say . . . Hayley made it, of course. . . .

Serves two, generously

½ pound Key West or Stonington pink shrimp
1 small mild onion, diced
1 stalk celery, diced
1 tablespoon capers

1 tablespoon chopped fresh dill
1 tablespoon mayonnaise

Boil the shrimp until just pink. Drain, then shell and clean out the veins. Cut these into bite-size pieces. Add the onion, celery, capers, and dill, then mix the mayonnaise in. Serve over crisp salad greens or a sliced tomato

Mango Hot Dog

One of the best food trucks in Key West serves a mango hot dog that is to die for. Garbo's Grill adds sliced mangoes, sliced jalapeños, and some kind of supersecret sauce for which I did not have the recipe.

So I wandered off into my own version of grilled hot dogs with a spicy mango relish. My guests, to be honest, looked at this askance when it first came to the table. But every single eater was a convert by the end of dinner.

Enough relish for six hot dogs

1 ripe mango, diced
1 jalapeño, seeded and minced
1 small red onion, minced
½ teaspoon sugar
A couple of squeezes of lemon
Good quality hot dogs (I used all-beef, no-nitrate dogs
    from Niman Ranch. My hub doesn't usually like
    natural hot dogs, but these were good!)
Good buns to match

Combine all the ingredients, mango to lemon.

Serve the salsa on grilled hot dogs, on toasted buns, with good mustard.

Hayley Snow reviews this hot dog, eaten at Garbo's Grill, in this book. She loves it as much as I did!

Eric's Coconut Cake (Almost)

My friend Eric (the model for the psychologist character in the Key West mysteries) is famous for his coconut cake. And I've been looking for a recipe for coconut cake for forever, so I begged for his. Of course, never able to quite leave a recipe alone, I did change things up a little from what he sent me. I used less of the cream of coconut and one block of cream cheese in the icing instead of two. Oh, and unsweetened coconut instead of sweetened. It was delicious, if I say so myself. I think I will try this as a sheet cake next time I have to take something to a party. . . .

Serves ten to twelve

Ingredients for the Coconut Cake
1¼ cups all-purpose flour
1¾ cups cake flour
1 tablespoon baking powder
2 cups sugar
¾ teaspoon salt
1½ sticks unsalted butter, softened but still cool
2–3 ounces Coco Lopez from an 8-ounce can (save the rest for icing)
4 eggs, room temperature
1 cup milk
1 teaspoon vanilla extract
½ teaspoon almond extract

Heat oven to 350°F. Prepare two 9-inch cake pans by buttering them well, lining with parchment, and then buttering the parchment too.

Mix all the dry cake ingredients in the bowl of an electric mixer or stand mixer at slow speed. Add cool cubes of butter, a few at a time, along with the Coco Lopez, and continue beating on low for about 1–2 minutes. Beat the eggs in one at a time, mixing well but minimally after each.

Mix the milk with the extracts.

Add ½ cup of milk mixture to flour mixture and beat until combined. Add remaining ½ cup of milk mixture and beat for about 1 minute.

Pour batter evenly into the two prepared cake pans.

Bake until toothpick inserted in the center comes out clean and cake springs back when touched, in the neighborhood of 25 minutes. (Watch this because you don't want to overcook.)

Cool the pans for ten minutes, and then remove the cakes, one to a plate and the other to waxed paper, and allow them to cool to room temperature.

Ingredients for the coconut icing
1 8-ounce block cream cheese
1 stick unsalted butter
Coco Lopez—the rest of the can
1 teaspoon vanilla
About 1½ cups confectioner's sugar
6 ounces unsweetened flaked coconut

Beat everything together except for the coconut. Then taste to see if it's sweet enough for your audience. Ice the top of the first layer, and then sprinkle with coconut. Add the second layer, ice the whole cake, and sprinkle the coconut all over, patting as needed.

And then watch your people swoon. . . .

Knockoff Painkiller Cocktail

This is one of our favorite ways to celebrate after a day on the water, but you can drink it on land as well!

Serves one

4 ounces pineapple coconut juice (Knudsen, for me)
2 ounces orange juice
1 to 2 ounces Pusser's or other dark rum
Sprinkling of fresh nutmeg

Combine the liquids in a cocktail shaker filled with ice. Stir well, and then pour into a glass filled with ice and garnish with a sprinkle of nutmeg. This is definitely tasty enough to serve without the rum too, if you prefer. . . .

ALSO AVAILABLE
FROM NATIONAL BESTSELLING AUTHOR

Lucy Burdette

Fatal Reservations
A Key West Food Critic Mystery

Hayley Snow looks forward to reviewing For Goodness' Sake, a
new floating restaurant that promises a fresh take on Japanese
delicacies like flambéed grouper with locally sourced seaweed.
But nearby land-based restaurateurs would rather see their
buoyant competition sink.

Sent to a City Commission meeting to cover the controversy,
Hayley witnesses another uproar. The fight for Mallory Square
has renewed old rivalries between Hayley's Tarot-card reading
friend Lorenzo and a flaming-fork-juggling nemesis, Bart
Frontgate—but things take a deadly turn when Bart is found
murdered. If Lorenzo could read his own cards, he might draw
The Hanged Man. He can only hope that Hayley draws Justice
as she tries to clear him of murder…

Available wherever books are sold or at
penguin.com

OM017⁹

ALSO AVAILABLE
FROM NATIONAL BESTSELLING AUTHOR

Lucy Burdette

Murder with Ganache
A Key West Food Critic Mystery

For better or worse, Hayley has agreed to bake over 200 cupcakes for her friend Connie's wedding while still meeting her writing deadlines. The last thing she needs is family drama. But her parents come barreling down on the island like a category three hurricane and on their first night in town her stepbrother, Rory, disappears into the spring break party scene.

When Hayley hears that two teenagers have stolen a jet ski, she goes in search of Rory. She finds him, barely conscious, but his female companion isn't so lucky. Now Hayley has to assemble the sprinkles of clues to clear her stepbrother's name—before someone else gets iced.

"I can't wait for the next entry in this charming series!"
—*New York Times* bestselling author
Diane Mott Davidson

Available wherever books are sold or at
penguin.com

OM0143